JACK AND THE FIRE EATER

A NOVEL

KORY M. SHRUM

This book is a work of fiction. Any references to historical events, real people, or real places have been used fictitiously. Other names, characters, places, and incidents are the product of the author's imagination. Any resemblance to actual persons, living or dead, business establishments, events, or locales is entirely coincidental.

No part of this book shall be reproduced or transmitted in any form or by any means without prior written permission of the publisher. Although every precaution has been taken in preparation of the book, the publisher and the author assume no responsibility for errors or omissions. Neither is any liability assumed for damages resulting from the use of information contained in this book or its misuse.

TIMBERLANE
PRESS

JACK AND THE FIRE EATER

AN EXCLUSIVE OFFER FOR YOU

Connecting with my readers is the best part of my job as a writer. One way that I like to connect is by sending 2–3 newsletters a month with a subscribers-only giveaway, free stories from your favorite series, and personal updates (read: pictures of my dog).

When you first sign up for the mailing list, I send you at least three free stories right away. If free stories and exclusive giveaways sound like something you're interested in, please look for the special offer in the back of this book.

Happy reading,

Kory M. Shrum

For Charley,
the goodest boy

CHAPTER 1

May I be so bold as to admit I only half live on the nights I do not see you? And in the days, when we are always apart, I wonder where you might be and with whom. Who is so lucky to see your face in the sunlight?

— FROM A LETTER ADDRESSED TO
LORD SILVER

Jack tore through his room, tossing boots and breeches. His pillows and clothes. But no matter where he looked, be it under the bed or in his wardrobe, he couldn't find the silver piece.

He checked the time. If he did not hurry, he was going to be late.

He lifted his frock coat from the floor and checked the pockets.

His probing fingernails scraped the edge of something and stopped.

There.

He pulled out the coin and held it up to the light. One

side glinted with a rearing cobra, the other the mischievous smile of a cat.

"Finally. You little bastard."

He admired the coin for a moment, enjoying the way the light played over its etchings. It was no bigger than four centimeters across, but it had a surprising heft.

With a flourish of his hand, the coin disappeared as if into thin air.

In a way, it had done just that.

One look at his room gave Jack pause. It was a wreck, but he had no time to tidy it now.

Instead, he grabbed another, cleaner frock off the back of the plum-colored chaise and closed the door behind him.

He hadn't made it halfway down the stairs before he caught sight of his mother in the foyer. She wore one of her afternoon dresses, her brunette waves pinned up off her neck, revealing a long tan throat. The bare skin drew attention to the pearl earrings she wore.

He'd gifted her the earrings for her last birthday and was glad to see that she favored them.

"Good evening, Mother."

"Good evening, dearest. Your father wants to see you in his study."

"Can't," Jack replied, arriving at the door. Unfortunately, the footman handing her the mail was blocking his exit. "Tell him I'm going out."

A hand went to the lace of her collar. "He said it's important."

"Can't you just—"

"He *insists*. If you don't go see him, he might put you under house arrest again."

The last time Jack had been placed under house arrest, it had been the longest, dullest, most excruciating three weeks of his life. This was especially true after his father had caught Lord Pickerington's youngest son climbing over the balcony's stone ledge.

Naked.

Before the young man lost his grip altogether and fell into his mother's fuchsia shrubs, his bare arse in full view of the morning's breakfast party.

After this, his father had the garden patrolled, and Jack's windows watched day and night, for weeks.

Under such restrictions, it was a wonder how Jack had managed to keep his skin on his body.

Of course, his father had delivered far worse punishments than house arrest.

His mother placed a hand on his arm. "I'm sure it won't take long. He's quite busy. And your father always gets to the point quickly, doesn't he?"

"The point of a blade?" Jack wondered aloud. Because once, after accepting such a summons to his father's study, the conversation had ended with a knife pressed to his throat.

True, Jack had been a little drunk and *more* than a little insolent, but still, he'd thought the conversation had escalated rather absurdly.

"That was only once," his mother said.

"It only takes once."

"He loves you," she said, and brushed the black curls off his forehead. Her hands smelled of lilac. "He just has a hard time showing it."

Jack said nothing to this.

Her soft brown eyes searched his face. Then she pulled back her hand. "Where are you going in such a hurry anyway?"

And that settled it. He would no sooner tell his mother

where he was heading than step into a pit of vipers. Besides, even if he was twenty minutes late, that might be considered fashionable, as if he couldn't quite be bothered to show up.

Let Lord Silver wonder where I am.

Such nonchalance would hide the desperate eagerness consuming him from the inside out.

"To the baron's study, of course." He kissed her cheek and sprinted off for the adjacent corridor before she could ask any more questions.

His footsteps rang through the hall. At a large wooden door, he stopped, raised his fist to knock. Before he could, a voice called out.

"Come in."

Jack twisted the gold handle and stepped into his father's study.

It was darker on this side of the house. Less cheerful than his rooms upstairs.

His father's pale face was pinched in concentration as he regarded several papers spread over the desktop. The ruby stone bearing the family's crest glinted on his finger as he lifted a page and turned it over.

Behind him, bookcases with dusty, unopened volumes stretched from floor to ceiling.

As if he even reads, Jack thought bitterly. As a child, Jack had loved to read, but every time he'd found some corner in which to curl up, his father would ruin it.

Go riding. Go hunting. Feed the dogs. For the Lord's sake, do anything but lie around like that.

"Jacinth, please take a seat," his father said without looking up.

Of course it was *Jacinth* and not Jack. His father never used his pet name. His mother, his sister, Nanny, all of his friends—even the staff—*everyone* called him Jack.

But to his father, the Baron Siran, he was always Jacinth.

Jack sank into the plush armchair, crossing one knee over the other and clasping it with his hands. His father continued to read the papers with great interest.

As the large standing clock ticked, its pendulum marking each passing moment, Jack's patience thinned.

Finally, he said, "If this is a bad time, Father, I could—"

"No." He looked up from the page, letting it fall flat against the desktop. He laced his fingers on top of it. "This is urgent."

I could hardly tell.

"What's happened?" Jack asked.

"You're engaged. I offer my congratulations."

Something tightened in Jack's chest, his vest squeezing like a belt across his ribs.

"I'm what?" Jack wondered if he'd heard him correctly. He'd had quite a bit to drink the night before and very little sleep. "What did you say?"

His father's blue eyes finally met his. "You're engaged. Congratulations."

A tight, panicked little laugh escaped Jack. "And to *whom* might I be engaged?"

Because while he had certainly had more than a few lovers, he could not recall making any such promises. In fact, he was barely twenty-two and thought marriage was a deplorable and sad state of affairs in which two people who barely got on formed a political or financial alliance in order to elevate one another.

No. Even if he *had* been drunk, he would never have made such a stupid offer.

Unless...

"Oh dear God," he began, a hand on his vest. "Did I—"

He couldn't bring himself to say *sire someone*. But that was certainly what he was thinking. He'd gone and made some young lady pregnant, and now her family was demanding satisfaction.

At this point, his father took pity on him. "You're engaged to Lady Clara Nightingale, daughter of Count Nightingale."

"No." Jack frowned, his hand falling to his knee again. "No, I'm fairly certain I haven't met her. I couldn't have—"

"I've arranged this," his father added.

"You've *what*?" Jack's voice cracked. Both of his feet hit the floor.

"I've arranged this marriage for you. It's a very good match. She's beautiful. She's well connected and very accomplished. She's been bred very well. All of her family have an excellent pedigree."

Pedigree.

"Forgive me, but are we talking about a lady or a horse?"

"Jacinth."

"I don't want to get married."

"You don't have to love her."

"You're such a romantic."

His father's expression darkened. "I don't think you understand the gravity of your situation."

"Oh, I understand marriage is very grave indeed," Jack said. "A grave *mistake*. It's made no one *I've* ever met happy."

His father's jaw clenched, color filling his cheeks.

Now I've done it. I'll be lucky if I even make it to the inn tonight.

Jack's eyes flicked to the clock, and seeing how quickly time was slipping away from him, he decided to keep his mouth shut going forward. Whatever his father wanted to say, he would say it.

If it came to blows, as it sometimes did, he would let his father have those as well.

His father twisted the sigil ring on his pinky finger. Never a good sign.

"You sleep in my house. You eat my food. You spend *my* money. And what do I get for it? A respectable son? No. An honorable son who makes me proud? Not by half. You barely completed apprenticeship beneath the viscount—"

Oh, if only you knew how often I was beneath him. A delicious memory shivered through Jack's mind.

"—and your understanding of business is so dismal I would sooner leave my accounts to your sister than let you touch them."

"You should. She'll triple your fortunes."

"She's a woman."

"She's brilliant," Jack said, his insides churning. It was certainly going to come to blows again if this man insulted Selina. "She's smarter than all of us."

"She hoards trash in her room and spends all her time sneaking about. I'll be lucky if I can find a blacksmith to take her. You, at least, have my looks and my name. Fortunately, that was enough for the count. What I ever did to be saddled with such children, heaven knows."

"She may get on with the blacksmith," Jack said. *She'll have stolen all his tools by the end of the week.* "Perhaps he has a sister. You can sell us off as a pair."

"Jacinth, you *will* marry Lady Clara as soon as humanly possible, and then you'll be out of this house."

"A silver lining."

"As soon as you're wed, I'll send you to our estate in Terrytown."

"Terrytown! That *shithole!*"

"Don't be dramatic. It will be your barony one day. The people should know you."

"There is nothing there."

"Your wife will be there. And your work."

"What work?"

"The work I give you."

"We have half a dozen houses in town," Jack said. "Why can't I live in any one of those?"

At least then I wouldn't have to give up the one thing I care about.

"*Gifting* you a country estate, thousands of acres, and a vineyard is more generosity than you deserve from me. Until you prove to me you can act like a man, you will remain in Terrytown. Run the vineyard. Build rapport with our people. Make an heir or three while you're at it."

"Father, *please.* Be reasonable. You can't possibly expect me to—"

"I do expect it!" His father stood and slammed his palms into the top of his desk. His voice was so loud that it made Jack's ears ring.

"You will do this or I will banish you from this house without a cent to your name. I won't have you under my roof a moment longer. If it were only the drinking, the partying, the lovers, I could bear it. You are still young. You have a careless streak. Fine. But the utter humiliation of a *conjurer* under *my* roof—"

Jack's breath hitched. "A conjurer? What makes you think I can do magic?"

How could he know? How could he? The only ones who knew were his friends and his sister, Selina. None of them would betray him.

"Is that what this whole marriage thing is about?" Jack

asked. He tried to seem casual, almost relieved. He put on his best this-is-just-a-big-misunderstanding smile. "If that's all it is then you're mistaken."

"I saw you!" his father hissed. His face turned red with the effort. "I saw you with my own eyes. In the street behind Everdeen's the day before last."

The street behind Everdeen's?

The very thought of the stuffy little bookshop with its cramped shelves brought the smell of dusty linen and aged paper to mind. It was Selina who had sent him. Father never let her buy books or browse. When she needed something, she sent Jack to go and fetch it for her. He always did.

But it wasn't secretly supplying his sister with books that was the offense.

No, it was what had happened after. On the street outside.

A little girl had been sitting on the muddy corner with a bloody knee. Jack asked her what had happened, and she told him a woeful tale about an older boy who pushed her down and took the basket of flowers she'd been trying to sell.

Jack did two bits of magic to cheer her up.

With the first wave of his hand, he threw a glamour over her knee. It erased the wound as if it had never been there at all.

Then, with another little flourish of his wrist, he'd produced a coin for her. Enough to buy ten bushels of flowers if she wanted to.

With a smile, she'd run down the cobblestone streets away from him, laughing.

"If you saw me, then you must've been coming out of Simone's brothel," Jack said coolly. "That's the only reason you ever visit that part of town."

His father ignored this.

"Magic will not be tolerated in this house. Those...those *lowlifes* spend all their time making ridiculous little lights and cheap displays for petty amusements while the rest of us are left with the hard work of living. Who built this great city? These large houses?"

Not you, Jack thought bitterly. *You've never lifted so much as a rock with those hands.*

"Men who actually work. Men who live in the *real* world, and not some fruitless fantasy. I will not watch you waste your life and your talents. Do you have any idea how much I've invested in you? *Any* at all? And look how you spend your time. You should be in the warehouses with me or bent over our accounting books. Now I've come to find out it's because you're in those *dens* doing God knows what. Tell me no one has seen your face."

"Better a brothel than a den, is it? I've not yet been, but give me your schedule, Father, so we don't visit on the same day."

Lord Siran came around the desk and slapped him.

The ring split open his cheek. He felt the blood well up in the cut.

"Tell me no one has seen you!" The baron shook Jack with both hands. "Tell me you haven't been so stupid as to let anyone know what you are."

What you are.

Slowly, Jack said, "No one has seen my face. We all wear masks."

Lord Siran released him. "You won't go again. I cannot take the chance—" He grimaced, took a breath, and then said, "Rumors are dangerous. No one can know."

What you are.

Jack understood, the way everyone in town understood, that the ability to do magic wasn't something to be proud of.

Many believed it meant demon blood was in the veins, that someone down the line had made a pact and that evil was now showing itself through abnormal offspring. Others believed that the conjurers themselves must've made a deal with a demon for the magic they possessed.

"Your friends. Albert and the others. Are they the same as you?"

"No," Jack said, perhaps too quickly.

"They're lazy and unskilled for no reason at all then. A shame."

Magic sparked along Jack's skin. He wanted to strike out, hurt him.

Don't, his mind begged. *Don't give him any ammunition. You'll only make this worse.*

"But they know about you?"

"Yes." Jack saw no point in lying about this.

His father returned to his seat, composing himself. After a long pause, he said, "You will get married. You will sort yourself out in Terrytown or I will make you as miserable as I possibly can."

You already do.

"The Lady Clara will be here for tea tomorrow. You will take tea with your mother. Dress well. Do not be drunk and do not disappoint me. If you do, you'll find your room and accounts emptied and not so much as a trunk of trousers to your name. Do I make myself clear?"

"Yes, sir," Jack breathed.

"Good." His father looked completely at ease now. If not for the sting of his cheek, Jack could've been fooled into thinking he'd never been struck at all. "You're dismissed."

Without a word, Jack rose from his seat and hurried for the door, his jaw working furiously. The heat and blood pounding in his temples were nearly unbearable.

No sooner had he stepped into the hallway than he was practically running for the front door.

His mother was still in the foyer, trying to look as if the vase of orchids really needed her attention. She'd been lingering, hoping to catch him. He knew this at first glance, and a pang of betrayal ran through him.

"Did you know?" he asked, without slowing his stride.

Her face pinched. "Know what? Your face!"

"Madeleine!" his father called behind him. "Come here for a moment."

He knew by her expression that she hadn't known about the engagement. She was about to find out, the same as him. The bitterness ebbed. He still had his mother then. At least one ally in all of this.

Terrytown. Leaving behind the city he loved. His friends.

Lord Silver.

Tears pricked his eyes as Jack stepped through the large doors that the footmen held open for him.

The whinny of horses and churning of wagon wheels rose to greet him. While the back of the house had lush private grounds, the front of Ansley Hall connected almost directly with the street and all its traffic.

The air was cooling, dampening the sting of his cheek. He was surprised to see that his stallion, Starlight, had already been brought around. The groom, Mr. Darby, held the reins.

"Your ride, young master."

"How did you know?" Jack asked, grateful for a friendly face.

"Your mother said you were going out." Darby offered Jack the reins, and it reminded Jack of when he was a small boy learning to ride. The way Darby had boosted him up onto the horses because he'd still been too small to lift himself.

"Thank you," Jack said, and slipped his boot into the stirrup and threw one leg over the horse.

"Be careful this evening, my lord. It looks like rain." With a little bow, Darby excused himself, walking down the footpath that led to the stables behind the house.

For a moment Jack could only look at Ansley Hall, its stone façade quite close to the street, serving as a barrier against the bustling road.

His heart clenched then as he pulled the reins and turned away.

Dark clouds sparked on the orange horizon above the inn. There, a flash of blue, then green.

They've started without me.

He kicked his horse into a run and barreled onward into the storm.

CHAPTER 2

My dear Peacock, we both know that you are in no short supply of company. Do you think I have not eyes? That I have not seen you leave on the arm of many a lord or lady? Do you believe I cannot peer into any of the inn's dark corners and see you there? Perhaps it is because I wear this mask. As numerous as the shadows may be, I assure you it does not hinder my sight.

— FROM A LETTER ADDRESSED TO
THE PEACOCK

There was an empty hitching post outside Oxley Inn. Jack dismounted and tied Starlight loosely. The horse was the most obedient he'd ever known. Should he wander off for some amusement, the beast would come if Jack so much as whistled.

"Stay out of trouble." Jack gently patted Starlight's throat.

The horse took it with flapping, eager lips and flicked his tail.

Jack left him in the shadow of the inn and went to the door.

But before he entered, he pulled a half mask from his coat.

It was blue with the eyes of a peacock covering its surface and gold trimming its edges.

Jack affixed it to his face before pushing open the door.

The smell of roasting meat and potatoes, beer and wine rose up to meet him. The raucous swell of chattering tourists and piano music raced along the walls.

The bartender, Oxley himself, caught Jack's eye and nodded toward the small wooden door to the right of the bar.

Go on down, that nod said. Jack thanked him with a nod of his own.

As he weaved his way through the tables, snatches of conversation floated up.

"Four pigs and three sheep. A good day f'me. I don't have to head back to my village until tomorrow. After I finish m'drink here, I'll be spendin' the night at—"

"No, *eighty* yards of silk, not eighteen. *Eighty*, I tell you! The lady must have ten daughters!"

"We're quite close to Devil's Field, ain't we?"

"Aye," said another. "But I came to sell me pots, not me soul!"

A chorus of nervous laughter was cut as he closed the door behind him. He waited in the pitch black until, one by one, the candle flames ignited.

The sconces lining the wall illuminated a curving staircase. He descended slowly, careful to watch his step.

At the foot of the stairs a man held up a hand, blocking his path. He was more brick wall than man. Candlelight danced across the right side of his face, making his eyes look ink black.

Jack didn't know his name, and his face was hidden by a black sack from which two eyeholes had been cut. But Jack didn't need to know him. He was muscle meant to stop any tourists or tradesmen visiting the city from wandering into something they shouldn't. Simple as that.

"The party is upstairs only," the man said in a low, gruff voice, taking in Jack's clothes and face. "Go on back and enjoy your drink, young man."

"I didn't come for that party," Jack said plainly. With a flick of his wrist, he produced a silver piece from thin air.

It floated there, twirling in the candlelight showing first the cobra face then the smiling cat.

The man watched it, his face unreadable.

"Satisfied?" Jack asked.

Only then did the man move aside and let him pass. "Go on then."

"Thank you." Jack waved his hand and the coin disappeared again.

Behind the guard was a long dark corridor. No candlelight or sconces lit the way this time. Only the bright doorway at its end gave Jack any idea of the direction in which he should go. But as he approached and heard the familiar whoops and cheers, his heart lifted with anticipation.

The sight always thrilled him.

Lanterns floated in the air, moving of their own volition. They hovered above throngs of cheerful people. There were those who clustered along the wall, laughing and drinking, but most of the spectators formed a ring, encircling the center of the room.

"Oy!"

"Over here!"

"Jack!"

Jack followed the sound until he saw the crop of frantic hands waving, trying to catch his eye.

It was his friends. All were there: Albert, Phineas, Silas, and Baz. They had laid claim to a high table by the wall which allowed them a good view of the ring but the luxury of a seat should they wish it. A lantern floated above their heads, dodging their hands as they waved.

Jack lifted a hand in greeting.

He made his apologies as he pushed his way through the crowd. The stench of beer and body odor as well as the hint of sulfur assailed him. Not to mention the unbearable heat of so many bodies pressed in together. Finally, the throng broke open and he was there at the table.

He unbuttoned his cloak and threw it over one of the stools, undoing his shirt at the collar.

Hands clasped his shoulders, patting him, shaking him.

"We thought you were bailing on us," said Albert. His bronze face was hidden behind a phoenix's mask of curling flames. It made his hazel eyes brighter. He slid a large pint of beer across the table. The foam sloshed over the side of the glass and wet Jack's hands.

"What kept you?" Silas pushed at the half mask on his face. It didn't sit well over his glasses.

The mask itself was black with red trim, and it seemed to make his very blue eyes seem even bluer. Even with the mask, the worry was evident.

"What happened to your face?" Phineas asked.

Each gaze fell to the cut on his cheek.

"It's bruising," Albert said darkly. He leaned closer to Jack's mask and lifted its edge to see the part of the mark hidden by the mask. He hissed. "Who hit you?"

"Did you have a hard time shaking someone from your bed? Or were you a little rough last night?" Baz asked, his laughter shaking his words. His dark eyes sparked playfully. His mask had a long, exaggerated nose. The color of it was a purple so dark it looked black in the lamplight. "Was it little Lord Pickerington again?"

"That was *one* time," Jack said. "And no."

"Well, who was it?" Phineas asked. He ran a hand through his blond curls, tussling them. He loved to do that, Jack knew. He did it out of habit, but when they were in public, in the view of so many others, he did it almost to the point of absurdity.

"Your hair is fine," Silas said, knocking Phineas's hand away. It caught the edge of his gilded cat mask and shifted. With a scowl, Phineas fixed it.

"We'll never guess." Albert snorted into his beer. "At least narrow it for us? Lord or lady? I wager a lord by the way it's already turning purple. Then again, there is many a lady with a strong hand."

Jack thought of his father's contorted face in the study. His demands and expectations.

The relief he felt to be here with his friends, to be out in the night and free of his father, ebbed. Dread sank its nails into his back.

Albert seemed to know his dark mood and tried to brighten it. "Ignore us. We're only jealous."

"Aye. If only God saw fit to gift me with a beautiful face rather than a beautiful arse." Baz pinched Jack's jaw and gave it a little shake. "An' ladies don' take kindly to gentlemen baring their arses in the streets."

"You would know," Phineas snorted. He was reaching for his curls again, but one look from Silas made his hand falter. "What did I miss?" Jack asked, looking over the heads to the center ring.

Two masked men traded unimpressive blows. The strikes were little more than flicks of light.

"Not much," Albert said.

"Oh, come on!" Baz said. "Tell 'im about the donkeys."

Albert licked foam from his lips. "The conjurers before this pair had a donkey each. One of purple light, the other blue. They kicked the hell out of each other."

"It was somethin' to see," Baz said.

"Badger gave his a little horn like a unicorn," Phineas said. "That was a nice touch."

"It still looked like a donkey," Silas said. "Nor were either of the donkeys solid enough to really hurt the other."

"Fair enough," Baz said. "It was like watching two pots of jelly have a go at one another."

"What was the wager?" Jack asked.

"Three gold," Silas said. "It went to the Badger."

The pair dueling now had conjured dragons. Small ones, true. But they soared through the air, trading blows with wild flicks of their tails and gnashing talons and teeth.

Jack watched the spectacle but saw little. His mind kept drifting back to his father's office. And when it wasn't there, it was in his mother's parlor with a cup of bitter tea.

The beer warmed in his hands.

Albert was watching Jack with a sharp look. "What has you in a bad mood?"

"I'm not in a bad mood."

"You aren't drinking. When you're sad, you'll still drink. Whatever's happened, it's worse than your usual melancholy. Are you going to tell me who hit you?"

Jack should've known straight away they would note the change in him.

"I'll tell you later," he said. "I don't want to ruin the night."

"The hell you will," said Albert, and took away the pint Jack had been lifting to his lips. "Tell us now or you'll wear this."

In truth, Jack didn't feel much like drinking tonight. His stomach was sour.

"Did somethin' happen, you know?" Baz flicked his eyebrows in the direction of Jack's lap. "You know sometimes when I get too drunk I can't get me—"

"No," Jack said. "It's nothing like that."

"You can tell us, Jack," Silas said, his hazel eyes pinching. "Whatever it is, tell us."

"The suspense is killing me," Phineas said.

All humor had left the table, and it was only four earnest faces watching him.

"Terrytown," Jack mumbled.

"What? Speak up. It's loud as a brothel on a festival night in here," Albert chided. "We can't hear you if you're going to whisper it."

"I don't know how you can visit those," Phineas said, wrinkling his nose.

"Festivals or brothels?" Baz snorted.

"Either," Silas said. "There are too many people."

Phineas only glared at Baz. "You know what I'm talking about."

Baz shrugged. "If you'd go yourself, you'd know."

"My father is sending me away to Terrytown," Jack said louder.

"Like on a holiday?" Baz asked, drinking his own beer.

"Like forever." And at that, Jack explained the situation, outlining his father's demands that he marry and make something of himself or he would be forever banished from the Lundenwick. That he was to wed Lady Clara, who he had never even met and would not meet until tomorrow's tea.

When he finished, he met their eyes, his cheeks scarlet.

"You're getting married," Phineas said. "*You?*"

"No wonder you look as if someone's died," Baz snorted.

"You exaggerate my need for company," Jack said.

Everyone laughed.

"How many this week?" Silas asked. "Lords and ladies?"

"Five," Jack said.

"It's Wednesday!" Phineas cried.

"We shouldn't tease him," Baz said. "It's not his fault. Some are born insatiable."

"Insatiable!" Albert crowed. "I don't think our boy Jack would be truly satisfied unless he had someone to ravish him each and every night for the rest of his life."

"I don't hear a problem in that," Baz said.

"It'll be months before you're married. Ladies love to plan this sort of thing. It took my older sister nearly a year to decide on all the lace and trims and what color even our hats should be," Albert said.

"I doubt he'll let it drag on for more than a month," Jack said. "He'll have me there next week if he can manage it."

"It won't be up to him," Baz laughed. "In these matters it's up to the ladies. Hopefully she'll have a grand vision."

"I wish I could get married," Phineas said with a sigh. "I want a home of my own. And someone to dine with every night."

"You dine with us every night, you arse!" cried Baz. "Who are we? Yer footmen?"

"Phineas is a romantic," Silas said, pushing at his mask again. "He wants to meet the great love of his life, settle down, and make a hundred babies."

"Not a hundred!" Phineas cried. "Only eight. Possibly ten."

"You want to kill her?" Albert said into his beer. "She'll be a lady, not a cow."

Jack's mood only darkened at the thought of children. He couldn't be a father. What if all the terrible things that came from his father's mouth came from his as well? And there was the matter of his temper.

"Jack," Silas said quietly. "It'll be all right. You may come to love her. My parents had an arranged marriage and—"

"Not mine," Phineas said, touching a curl.

"—and they love each other very much," Silas continued over the interruption. "They're the best of friends."

"Mine too," Phineas said.

"And it's gone to your head," Albert teased, slapping his hand away.

"My mum married my dad because he was old and rich," Baz said. "She only had to put up with him for a year before he was in the grave, and now she's quite happy ruling the house and spending the money."

"Do you want Jack to end up in an early grave?" Silas asked. "Was that your point?"

"All I'm sayin' is you don' know what'll happen. She could die."

Phineas gasped. "Don't say such things!"

"Look at 'im! He looks like he's going to the gallows tomorrow instead of tea. I'm just tryin' to help 'im."

"Help him how?" Phineas asked.

"I'm just sayin' that even if she's an ol' hag, there's a silver lining."

"What Baz is *trying* to say is that you will be all right. Everything will be as it should be." Albert reached out and squeezed his hand. "I dare say we'll enjoy Terrytown."

"But what about all of this?" Jack gestured at the roaring crowd. "You love this."

I love this.

Apart from time with his friends, using magic was the only time Jack felt happy.

Free.

Baz scoffed. "We only come to watch you, mate!"

"Watching you beat the boots off half the lads here is the fun part," Albert agreed. "If you're gone, we'll be just as happy in Terrytown. They have a tavern or two, don't they?"

"Yes," Jack said. "But the wine from our vineyard is better. What about the duels?"

Albert licked the beer foam from his lips. "You'll just have to knock us around. Maybe we'll actually learn something. None of us here can do half of what you can."

"Ah, I'd love to learn how to conjure that tiger you made in your fight against Bell," Baz moaned. "It was bloody beautiful."

"And you have that huge library at the estate," Silas said.

"Leave it to you to get hard for the books!" Baz nudged Silas. Then to Jack, "I'll be there for the country girls! There might be less of 'em, but they're as sweet as lambs."

"Really?" Phineas asked, straightening a little. "I do find city girls to be a little...sharp."

"I don't mind a sharp tongue m'self," Baz said. "Probably used to it from me mum."

Albert squeezed Jack's hand again. "Listen. You'll marry this—"

"Lovely lady," Phineas interjected.

"Lovely lady, and then take her out to Terrytown. I'd say give it a month, maybe two."

"She'll need time to properly fall in love with you," Phineas said.

"Aye. Will be easy enough," Baz said. "Just look at her through those big lashes of yours."

"If we arrive too soon, she might feel infringed upon," Silas said.

"We don't want the lady of the house to be jealous of us," Albert agreed. "We want to make a good impression."

"Aye. You'll just have to keep yourself busy until we arrive. Shouldn't be too difficult," Baz said with a wink.

"We'll be there before you know it," Albert said.

"How long will you stay?" Jack asked, and hated the desperation in his voice.

Albert put a hand on his head. "As long as it takes. It'll be fine, Jack. Better than fine. You're going to enjoy yourself. New wives are desperate to please their husbands."

Baz snorted into his beer. "I'm not sure about that."

Silas elbowed him hard.

"Aye," Baz retracted. "They're very agreeable."

"As if any of us would know," bemoaned Phineas.

The love Jack felt for his friends swelled then, and he remembered all the times they had rallied around him. The time he fell from his horse and broke his arm and the boys altered all their games so he could play with only one. And when he'd taken to bed with a bad cold. For weeks at his house, in his room, they'd entertained him with their stories and antics while he lay in bed. Silas had read stories. Albert and Baz made jokes. Phineas had been in charge of the tea and treats.

Jack looked from one face to another and brightened.

"You'd really do that for me? Come to Terrytown and everything?"

"Would we? Do you hear this?" Baz rolled his eyes. "Where 'as this boy been?"

"I wouldn't mind getting out of the city for a while," Silas said. "It's so noisy here. I can hardly think properly."

"I'm very excited to meet the country girls." Phineas ran a hand down the front of his vest. "I bet they love animals. A country wife would let me have at least six dogs, don't you think?"

Baz snorted, blowing foam off the top of his drink.

"To Jack and a happy marriage!" Albert was the first to raise his glass. Baz clinked his next, followed by Silas and Phineas.

Slowly, with a shy smile, Jack lifted his glass and touched it to the others. His heart was infinitely lighter.

"There now," Albert said, and ruffled his hair. "No more tears. Go to tea in your best suit tomorrow, a big smile on your face, and be the charming lad we all know you to be."

"Pretend you're wooing a princess," Phineas said. "My mum said ladies love to be treated as such."

"Give her flowers," Albert said.

"I'd write poetry," Silas said, pushing his mask again.

"'E hasn't met her!" Baz laughed. "What could 'e possibly say in a poem?"

The idea of Jack writing poetry for any reason at all—let alone to woo a lady he hadn't met—made him burst into laughter.

His friends, glad to see him smile at last, jumped in with both feet. The table was consumed with it. Their humor had begun to die down when Baz suddenly drove an elbow into Jack's ribs.

"Jack, look."

Lord Silver.

Jack's eyes found him in the crowd instantly even though he was a few inches shorter than most of the men in the room.

There was a grace to the way Lord Silver moved that many lacked. Jack suspected the man had taken fencing lessons from a young age, or perhaps some other fighting art that had developed in him that feline grace.

His ornate mask was silver and fastened at the back of his head, in a nest of thick dark blond hair. It was a full mask, with only the eye holes.

Because of the fine clothes he wore and the beautiful mask, everyone assumed he was a lord from a great family. Hence the name Lord Silver was born. Jack couldn't remember who had used it first, but now it was used even by those not in Jack's party.

Silver-gray eyes caught Jack's, and his breath hitched.

As was the case every time he met Silver's eyes, electricity skittered along Jack's skin.

"Look at that face," Albert said. "I can't tell if our boy Jack wants to lie with Lord Silver or kill him."

"I suspect it depends on the hour and 'ow much our lad 'as had to drink," Baz said.

"Or whether or not he's lost the match," Silas added.

It was true, Jack and Lord Silver sparred every night in which the two of them were both in attendance. And while Jack found other opponents to be easily defeated, dueling with Lord Silver was a challenge.

With Silver, he had to *work* to win, often coming up with tricks and displays that he hadn't planned. Even then, Jack didn't always manage it.

Before Silver came, Jack's duels were fun and sometimes exciting, but far from magnificent. Yet in the two years since Lord Silver had begun visiting the inn, Jack's magical abilities had grown exponentially. He learned just by watching the man in action. Every flourish, every trick. It gave Jack more ideas and ambitions than he'd had when learning largely on his own.

That was the truth that Jack only admitted to himself. Despite his frustrations, irritations, and downright displeasure at being bested from time to time, Jack knew he would be miserable if Silver stopped coming.

That became more true when the letters began.

Jack had been the first to write. He'd lost a bet to Baz and had been forced to compose a simple line.

I admit that you are more talented than I and more handsome than I.

Jack had loathed doing it, but that, according to Baz, had been the point.

They'd been in a tavern, more than a little drunk, and had used paper from the back of Silas's journal.

The next night Jack had magicked it into Silver's pocket just before a duel, too embarrassed to hand it to him directly.

He'd hoped that would be the end of it. Surely Silver would be bewildered to receive such nonsensical drivel without explanation, and it would earn him no reply.

Only it hadn't been the end.

Silver wrote back to him, magicking the letter into Jack's pocket just as he had done.

The letters began as boasts and brags on the behalf of both parties, each claiming their own superiority. But before long, harmless challenges folded into flirtation, the declarations growing bolder and more sincere as time went on.

It had gone on for nearly two years, trading letters every night.

Tonight, Silver owed him a letter.

Baz nudged him roughly. "Go on then. Have a go at 'im and you'll feel loads better."

"It's what we came to see," Albert said.

Before Jack could protest, a spark of golden fire sprang through the crowd and struck Lord Silver in the chest.

Silver turned from the man he was speaking to and looked down at the gold sparks dancing across his chest. Then he lifted his gaze and met Jack's eye.

The gold flame was a direct challenge to a duel.

Though Albert had sent it, not Jack, it didn't matter.

Lord Silver gave him a sharp nod, an acceptance to the fight. Jack rose from the table but hesitated.

"Go on," Albert said, laughing. "You can thank me later."

"Once you've rolled out of Lord Silver's bed," Baz added. Laughter circled the table again.

"Do you think they'll keep the masks on or take them off?" Phineas asked innocently.

When color rose in Jack's cheeks at the thought, his friends only laughed harder, the sound of it echoing in his ears even after he stepped into the ring.

CHAPTER 3

Are you the jealous type, my dear Silver? You need not be.
I bide my time in the arms of others only because you
continue to refuse me. When will you end my suffering?
And dare I say, yours?

— FROM A LETTER ADDRESSED TO
LORD SILVER

The crowd parted easily for Jack. They seemed as eager to watch the match as his friends did. Jack squeezed between the wooden beams marking the perimeter of the ring and stepped into the middle of the dirty pit.

The ground was hard-packed soil pounded into a floor-like surface by a thousand relentless boot heels.

It couldn't be more than five meters from one end to the other and about half of that at its widest point. It was more the people encircling them than the wooden border that created the sense of a pit. They pressed in as close as the weathered rails would let them.

Already hands exchanged notes and placed wagers as to how the match would turn out. A young man with an orange mask placed a large bet on Lord Silver, and Jack deflated a little.

I'll show you, you bastard.

Jack took the far end of the ring, positioning himself opposite the other young man, whose hand rested on one hip in a perfect pose of bored arrogance.

This one tries to drive me mad.

Jack waited for the letter, expecting it to turn up in a pocket, or on the inside of his shirt, over his heart, the place Silver had favored as of late.

But nothing came.

"What's your wager, Lord Silver?" Jack called out, removing his hands from his pockets.

"I have nothing on my person tonight," the voice behind the mask said. It was muffled, almost too hard to hear over the roar of the crowd. "But then again, I won't be losing to you."

Nothing on his person? Was that a veiled apology for the missing letter?

Perhaps he had not time.

Still, Silver had never missed a letter before. Jack's heart twisted at the very idea.

"Turn out your pockets," said the referee, a small man with wispy white hair standing at the edge of the ring.

"I have nothing—" Silver protested.

"You know the rules, my lord," the referee pressed. "A wager for every match. Turn out your pockets or forfeit the match."

Jack held up his money pouch. He handed it over to the referee without question.

"There's about ten gold in there," Jack said. "That's my wager."

Silver turned out his pockets but there was no money pouch. In fact, there was only one thing that tumbled into his gloved hand.

The cube glinted in the light, sparking gold. There were etched carvings on each side, but Jack couldn't see them through the poor light cast by the floating lamps or the room's shifting shadows.

Silver looked ready to forfeit, his posture still haughty, when his head turned ever so slightly to the right. Jack threw a look over that shoulder and saw only a sea of faces.

Who are you looking at? he wondered.

"Fine," Silver acquiesced. And placed the cube in the referee's outstretched hand. "This is my wager."

Then it was only the two of them on opposite sides of the ring while the crowd cheered.

Baz made crude gestures with his hips. Albert shoved him.

"First draw," the referee called. "One...two..."

A green spark caught Jack in the cheek. It stung like a mosquito's prick.

Jack's own spark had veered right and struck a young man on the edge of the circle. He laughed, knocking the embers from his shoulders. He shifted his mask back into place and retightened the strap at the back of his head.

"First draw to Lord Silver," the referee called.

"Lucky shot," Jack mumbled.

Silver brought himself up to his full height. One hand went behind his back, reminding Jack again of the fencing position.

A light grew in the center of his palm. First a golden yellow that folded into green.

What leapt forth from the palm was a dragon, soaring up into the air.

It opened its mouth and screeched, a flood of red and orange sparks spilling out onto the spectators' heads.

"We already saw dragons!" someone complained.

"A small warm-up," Silver declared.

The dragon was no small feat. Not because it flew and spit fire, but because of its solidity. It wasn't a thin phantom creation like what most of the conjurers crafted for their duels. It looked real enough to touch.

Even the scales sliding along its rough body caught and reflected the light as real reptilian skin would.

The dragon did a lazy, extravagant turn overhead, clearly for the pleasure of the crowd.

Then it swerved abruptly and shot forward with surprising speed, its mouth opening. It was headed straight for Jack.

A second longer and it would have slammed into him.

More out of reflex than any conscious thought, Jack brought forth his magic, pulling it from somewhere inside his gut. A yellow light formed at his solar plexus and poured from his hands, filling the ring.

He saw the great serpent in his mind before it sprang forth fully formed.

Half his own height, it opened its great maw in a silent hiss.

The dragon tried to slow itself, throwing its weight into its back legs, but it was too late. It slid into the mouth of Jack's great snake and disappeared.

Now it was the golden serpent with green eyes who

took its turn around the circle, basking in the delight of the spectators' approval.

Then it pressed its belly to the ground and shot toward Silver.

Silver produced a sword of red light, the edge of his magic wavering like a flame. The serpent fanned its hood in challenge. It struck, and Silver swung, hitting the creature across the throat. But as it began to fold, Jack changed its shape.

Now it was a bat.

Another strike and it reformed as a griffin.

Then it became an osprey, talons out.

When Lord Silver's sword cut this down too, it erupted into a murder of crows that swirled, pecked, and snapped at Silver's masked face.

The crowd clapped, but already Jack felt their restlessness.

His magic was good, but not impressive. They'd seen too many animal fights this evening.

While it was exciting to see brightly colored creatures fight in a vicious clash of claws and teeth, Jack thought he could do better with a direct attack.

Silver cast a whirlwind of white flames to spring up from the dirt and swallow up Jack's crows. They cawed miserably as they were cycloned around and around until they existed no more.

Then the cyclone spun forward and struck Jack with such speed that it felt like a blow to his chest.

Jack opened his hand and loosed a spray of water. It crashed as an iridescent blue wave onto the floor and struck Silver, pulling him nearly off his feet and slamming his back against the wooden railing.

The young man leapt across the pit with another

flaming sword, this one solid enough to disturb the wind around Jack's face as Silver thrust it toward him.

"Yield," Silver cried out.

Jack laughed. "Never."

The sword cut him then, drawing real blood from the hand that rose up to knock away the blade.

He's serious, Jack thought. *He truly means to hurt me.*

"*Yield*," the young man hissed.

And for the first time, Jack saw the fear in those silver eyes.

"No," Jack said, all his good humor gone.

Flames erupted from Jack's hands, and he slung it across the pit like whips. It struck Silver, knocking him away. As his back hit the railing for a second time, a cry ripped from his throat.

Jack shook the fire from his hands. He had not meant to do that.

Silver's fervor had brought out his own aggression, but Jack wouldn't lose control of himself. He'd vowed never to do that.

If he did, he'd be no better than his father.

What happened? Why is he so upset? Why does he attack me so violently? Why hasn't he given me a damned letter?

Jack had been foolish enough to give his name in the last letter. Had Silver discovered who he really was and not liked it? Was that what offended him?

When Silver rose, there was fury in his eyes.

I'd better strike first.

Before Silver could recover, Jack cast his magic across the ring. It pummeled Silver with wave after wave of flame.

It tore through the man's clothes. It scorched his billowing white shirt and blacked his vest. It even ate away at his boots, exposing the flesh beneath. His feet were lifted from the ground, held inches above the packed earth.

The mask began to melt from the chin up, exposing the curl of the jaw then the lips.

What beautiful full lips you have, Silver. Jack devoured the delicious bud of a rosy mouth with his eyes.

"So real," someone murmured. "I can feel the heat."

Jack had put no real heat in it, of course. He did not want to hurt Silver. He wanted only to expose him. The heat the crowd claimed to feel was only part of the illusion.

"Nothing like it," said another. "Incredible."

Lord Silver's right cheek sprang into view, and his hand shot to his face in horror, his mouth opening in a terrified O of surprise.

"No," he said, his teeth bared.

Jack leaned into his magic.

Let's see who you truly are.

The mask melted more, crossing the plane of Silver's cheeks until—

"I yield!" cried Silver.

Jack retracted his magic and Silver fell, his feet reconnecting with the dirt.

"To the Peacock," the referee called. "Our winner."

The crowd erupted in applause, his own friends jumping up and down in Jack's periphery. Only a few loud and displeased boos cut through the merriment, those who had lost the most money, no doubt.

Jack crossed the ring and grabbed the cube from the referee.

Then a hand was on his arm, squeezing. It was not a threat, but urgency was clear.

"Don't," Silver said quietly into his ear.

He still held his face, cupping the cheek as if it was wounded, or perhaps only to shield it from view.

"Please don't take it."

"Have I offended you?" Jack whispered. "You fought me as if you meant it."

Silver's eyes shimmered. Was he crying behind his mask?

"And where is my letter?"

"I couldn't," Silver whispered.

Couldn't what? Write?

Here was the terrible truth. The real reason he'd taken his father's news so poorly. Jack did not want to be sent away because he felt, after nearly two years, that he was finally getting somewhere with Silver.

Silver's last letter had been so honest, so kind. And now Jack was being sent away.

What would happen to them? Why was Silver so upset?

Jack's heart clenched. "What's the matter?"

"Don't take the cube. Don't."

The stupid cube.

Jack leaned against the wooden railing. "What will you give me for it then?"

He didn't pretend to hide his gaze as it traced the man's exposed neck and jaw.

Silver all but ignored this flirtation. "I'm serious, Jack. You'll be sorry if you take it."

Jack.

Jack admitted, if only to himself, that he liked hearing Lord Silver say his name.

If he knows my name, then he read my last letter.

Then why had he not written?

"I beg you. Give it back."

Jack wanted to reach out and touch the exposed skin. It looked soft and inviting.

He let his hand fall.

"Let's save the begging for the bedroom, Lord Silver."

Jack didn't miss the way the man's body shifted forward, toward him, imperceptibly.

But to strike me or kiss me?

Jack wasn't so sure.

"If you want it, come and find me." Jack tossed the cube up into the air once and caught it. "I'll be waiting for you."

CHAPTER 4

I suppose there are worse things than to be a wife. Though I'd rather not trade one master for another. What I wouldn't give for the day I, at last, own myself?

— FROM THE DIARY OF LADY CLARA
NIGHTINGALE

"Jack!" someone called. "Good 'eavens! What in the world 'appened 'ere?"

Jack squinted against the merciless sunlight cutting across his face. He sat up, trying to see where he was and who was calling him.

His bedroom he recognized. And it was Nanny who stood at the foot of his bed, her hands on her rotund hips and her mouth open in surprise.

"This room."

He came up onto his elbows and surveyed the situation for himself. *This room*, despite the cheerful morning light, was as destroyed as when he'd left it last night before heading out for the duel.

"Forgive me, Nanny," Jack said. "I'll clean it properly once I've breakfasted."

"What were you looking for?" she said. "Your sanity?"

He buried his face in his pillow.

"No, sir," she said. "Your mother wants to dine with you and it's nearly ten. You won't make 'er wait a minute longer. Up with you."

"Tell her I'm not hungry," he said.

"And break 'er 'eart. I'd rather cut me own throat in Devil's Field."

"Don't be gruesome," he mumbled into the fabric.

"Don't be lazy. Get up and dress yourself."

Lazy. The word stung. Jack heard it in his father's accusing tone.

"You think me lazy?"

She snorted, lifting his belt from the floor and placing it over the back of a chair. "All young men of a certain station are lazy. Up with you, I said."

She grabbed one of his arms and heaved him hard to the right, dragging Jack from the bed to the floor.

"I'll put a bowl of hot water and a rag 'ere for you. Freshen up. Though I don't know what good it'll do ya. You look like 'ell."

"Thank you, Nanny," Jack said from the floor.

As soon as the door clicked shut, he sat up, rubbing the back of his head. Using the side of his mattress, he pulled himself to standing and stripped off his nightshirt.

He had clean trousers on when Nanny came back into the room with a bowl and rag balanced between her gnarled fingers.

She set it on the dresser in front of the gilded mirror. The gray hair beneath her bonnet caught a few stray sunbeams as she met his gaze in the mirror. "Have you a clean shirt?"

"No, ma'am."

Nanny sighed. "All right, let's see what we've got 'ere."

She opened several drawers before finding a white shirt to her satisfaction. She handed it over. While Jack pulled it on, she tried to force a comb through his dark curls.

Then she found a red vest and a dining jacket.

"There you go," she said as he was patting his face dry. "Good enough. Now. Get down there. Heavens. What's this?"

Jack turned and saw that she'd lifted the cube from the bedside table.

In the morning light it looked more gold than ever. On one side, the side Nanny traced with her finger, an ornate door was carved into its face. And the handle, an inviting circle, looked as if it wanted only to be pressed open.

"I'll take that," Jack said, pulling the cube out of her hands.

She shook her head as if waking from a dream. "Where did you get it?"

"I won it in a card game," he said. "At the inn last night."

She arched her brows. "At least you don't lose your money. It's more than your father can say. Not that I would speak ill of a man in his own house."

"It's only me, Nanny. I won't tell."

She cupped his cheek. "Go on now. I'll not say it again. It's a shame to keep your mam waiting. She's got enough to be tending to."

Jack waited until he was in the hallway before he lifted the cube to his face.

It hadn't been a dream. After he'd put Starlight in the

stables, he'd stumbled to bed more than a little drunk. His friends had each bought him a round to celebrate the defeat of Lord Silver, and Jack admitted—if only to himself—that he'd lingered at the inn longer than he'd wanted, in hopes that Lord Silver might approach him.

He'd hoped he'd take him up on his brazen offer.

He would've settled for a letter.

But no matter how he searched the crowd all night, he never caught sight of the gentleman.

What has changed?

Jack had over two hundred letters hidden behind the false panel in the back of his wardrobe, each signed by Lord Silver's own hand.

It was his turn. I'm sure of it. He's never missed a letter before.

Was it because I gave him my name? Did it frighten him off?

Jack held the cube up to the light once more, and a shiver ran through him.

"I wish I understood," Jack said to the cube before, with a flourish of his hand, he made it disappear.

His mother was seated at the small round table by the window. It was only large enough to hold four, an intimate family party. A cream-colored teapot painted with delicate pink flowers was in her hands as she filled her cup with a dark aromatic tea.

Jack bent and kissed her cheek.

"Morning, Mother." He pulled out his seat and sat down across from her. "How are you today?"

"Well enough," she said. "How are you?"

"I've been better," he admitted, placing a thin slice of toast on his plate and reaching for the jam.

"Would it be the hangover or your impending marriage that ails you?"

"Both. Though one is a more permanent condition than the other."

She sipped her tea then said, "I hear good things about the lady."

"Then why are you looking at me like I'm a horse that's soon to be shot?"

Her furrowed brow didn't smooth itself out. "Because I hate seeing that mark on your face."

She reached across the table and pressed a cold finger to his cut cheek. "We will need to cover it for today's visit. She'll think you are a violent drunk."

"We could always just tell her Father beats me."

Her head lowered and the teacup was returned to the saucer. "Forgive me, Jack."

"Don't. You need not say anything." He'd gone and made her feel guilty. He didn't want to do that. "It's no matter. I barely felt anything at all."

Jack forced cheerfulness for her sake.

"I want to ask you something and I hope you will be honest with me," she said quietly. She lifted her eyes from her teacup and met his gaze. "Your father said he saw you do magic."

Jack's heart skipped a beat.

"Is it true?" she asked. "Can you do magic?"

If I say yes and you reject me— His heart clenched.

His mother threw a look over her shoulder at the doors, then at the surrounding windows. Once she seemed satisfied that they were alone, her fingers released the handle of her teacup. She placed her hand palm up on the table.

Jack thought she meant for him to take it. But before he could, a blue light formed in its center. This chrysalis broke open to reveal a beautiful butterfly, its wings opening and closing.

Then she closed her hand and the butterfly was gone.

"You?" he marveled.

A shy smile tugged at her lips. "Since I was a little girl."

"Why did you never tell me?"

Her smile faltered. "For the same reason you never told me, I suspect."

"I didn't even know ladies could do magic."

"Of course we can." His mother touched the lace at her collar. "I suppose your gatherings aren't open to ladies."

Jack shrugged. "I don't think any of the gentlemen would mind if ladies attended, but you aren't allowed to be alone with us, are you? Isn't that the height of impropriety?"

A butterfly. And a very beautiful one, clearly defined.

"I'm sorry I didn't tell you," Jack said quietly, still holding his uneaten toast.

"I'm sorry I was the sort of mother you couldn't tell," was her reply.

He wanted to rebuff this. Wanted to argue that her kindness, her love, and support were the only reason he was still here in this life, this house. He'd never been afraid to leave his father or his wealth behind. He'd been only afraid to leave her.

"That's not why I'd kept it a secret."

The door swung open and his sister marched into the dining room. The swish of her skirts dampened his words, and his mother gave his hand a sharp squeeze.

Not now, that squeeze said. Jack let the conversation drop. But his mind burned with curiosity. He wanted to learn everything he could about his mother's magic. Where had she learned it? What could she do with it? Had her parents been able to do magic too? Was it as reviled and rejected then as it was today?

Selina fell into the dining room chair with an air of irritation.

"What has you in a foul mood?" Jack asked her, pushing the plate of toast in her direction.

Her dark brown eyes rolled up to meet his. "The very idea that I had to stop *working* to come down and eat. And *Father*—"

She said his name like a curse.

"Don't speak ill of those who aren't here," their mother warned. "Everyone should have a chance to defend themselves."

"Is that so?" Selina arched a brow. "Then defend yourself now. Why did you insist I wear this hideous dress to breakfast?"

"You look pretty. Is it so terrible for a mother to want to breakfast with her children?" their mother said over the rim of her teacup.

"At least it's only you. If Father were here, I would've refused. The bastard."

"Selina!" their mother cried.

"If I had the strength to carry him myself, I'd dump him in Devil's Field."

"*Selina.*"

To Jack she said, "Brother, do you think you could help me carry him?"

Jack snorted. "Not with this headache. Can it wait until the sun goes down?"

"We could use a horse," she said, the knife firmly in her grip. She made a gruesome chopping motion with her hand.

"The demons would probably throw him back, for all he is worth."

Their mother covered her face. "These children! Lord help me."

"I think we have enough lords in this house." Selina slathered jam on her bread and took a bite. "Careful whom you conjure, Mother. I'd hate for our fortunes to turn for the worst."

She regarded Jack. "What happened to your face?"

Jack said nothing. If he lied, his sister would know in an instant. She might be only seventeen, but her eyes missed nothing.

"Your brother is getting married," their mother said, her cheerfulness returning.

Selina choked and reached for the teapot. "*Married?* To whom? Lord or lady?"

"Your brother is engaged to Lady Clara," their mother answered. Jack shrugged as if to say, *There it is.*

Both of Selina's brows rose. "Whatever has possessed you?"

"Father arranged it. And I hear he's got plans for you as well. A blacksmith."

Her face filled with color. "Of course he does."

"Your father has said nothing of it to me."

"Perhaps I'll have better luck with a husband. Maybe I'll actually be able to attend school then."

Selina's voice was bitter. "You gentlemen, always pretending to give us ladies the rights we deserve but none of the wealth to enact them. I expect more from you, dear brother."

"It's only ten in the morning." Jack took a drink of strong tea. "But if you want, I'll speak to the blacksmith for you."

Selina rolled her eyes and stood. "Forgive me, Mother. I

am working on something very important, and I had best finish it before this so-called husband comes to collect me."

With a slice of toast in one hand and a cup of tea in the other, Selina bent and placed a kiss on their mother's cheek.

Their mother turned. "When will I see you again?"

Selina waved her toast. "As I understand it, there are three meals in a day. And since you've forbidden Nanny from bringing a tray to my room, I must either join you or starve. A brain cannot work without nutrition."

"Tea then," her mother said. "Please do come in a better mood."

"I'll come in trousers," Selina said. "And if you love me at all, please don't dine with Father. I can't bear the sight of him at present."

"Only at present?" Jack asked. "He must've truly offended you."

"He has," she said, and with that, the dining room door swung shut.

CHAPTER 5

What I have done to earn your attentions I cannot pretend to know. How do you know, dear sir, you truly desire me? Perhaps if I remove this mask, you will not like what you see.

— FROM A LETTER ADDRESSED TO THE PEACOCK

Jack was in the stables feeding Starlight carrots and apple slices. The smell of hay had always soothed him. He was about to pick up a brush and comb out Starlight's dark hair when the footman said their guests had arrived.

"Maybe next time, my love," Jack said, and touched the animal's soft muzzle, feeling the bristles there.

He gathered that their guests must be Lady Clara and her mother, given the hour.

Nanny stopped him at the back door. "Wash yer hands and yer face. You smell like the 'orses."

"Maybe a lady prefers that."

"She'll not prefer to be kept awaitin'." Nanny shoved him toward the water closet. "Get."

Jack obeyed, finding Nanny again outside his mother's parlor door. He was still toweling his hands when Nanny slid the door open and bid him inside. At the last moment, she snatched the towel from his hands.

The three women were already sitting by the large fireplace. His mother was on the chaise, her body placed closest to its head, opposite, presumably, Lady Clara's mother.

The two guests were in an armchair each, with a small table between them. On it, his mother's favorite tea set, its lavender sugar and cream bowls sweet and inviting.

Jack bowed. "Good afternoon."

"Jacinth, sit beside me," his mother said.

Jacinth. He was to be Jacinth for this afternoon then.

"Of course."

He lifted his coat and sat down opposite Lady Clara.

And then...nothing happened.

A dreadful silence filled the room. In Jack's case, he couldn't be quite sure where to put his hands. He put them first on his legs, then his knees. Then he tried resting them in his lap, but they only lay there like dead fish.

All the while he regarded Lady Clara's face. His mother had been right, at least. She was a beautiful girl. Her hair was dark blond, and he liked how it curled around her face and full cheeks. Her eyes were dove gray and sharp.

But mostly, he loved that she wasn't hiding the fact she was also staring at him.

She gazed, unflinchingly. Slowly, a little furrow formed between her brows.

"Does my face displease you?" he asked.

"No," she said too quickly. "I mean—Well, no. I was just —Are you wearing makeup?"

"Clara!" Lady Justine cried, her face a mask of horror. "Don't be ridiculous. How could you—"

"I am," Jack said. His mother had covered his bruised cheek right after breakfast. "Does it not make me more handsome, you think?"

"Jacinth!" his mother cried. "Don't be so—"

But Clara was smiling, a small laugh escaping her. "If that be your opinion of yourself, then what could I say to make you think otherwise?"

"Would you *like* me to think otherwise?" Jack asked, finally deciding to lace his fingers together. "Perhaps a vain husband doesn't suit you."

"You say it as if there is such a thing as a humble husband. I've yet to meet a young man who doesn't think too highly of himself."

"Clara!" her mother cried again. To Jack's mother, she added, "I apologize. She isn't quite herself today. She is never this forward when at home."

Oh, I suspect she's worse at home, Jack thought.

"I don't mind a woman who speaks her mind," Jack said, leaning against the back of the chaise.

"Yes, don't worry, Lady Justine," his mother said soothingly. She reached out and refilled the woman's teacup. "My daughter is also quite outspoken. Jacinth is used to this."

"Is that so?" Clara asked with an arched brow. "You don't mind young ladies with a voice?"

"I thought you all had one. Was I mistaken?" he asked.

She looked up at him through dark lashes. She was clearly making some sort of calculation.

"I hear that you are very accomplished at singing, drawing, dancing, and the piano, Lady Clara," his mother said sweetly. "Do you like to read?"

"No—" Lady Clara said.

"Yes," Lady Justine said.

His mother ignored this contradiction. "Jacinth loves novels. Anything with adventure."

"Clara also loves novels. Anything romantic."

Clara scowled. "I read mostly books on economics and business."

"That will be useful," Jack said. "My father's plan is that we should move to Terrytown and run the vineyard there. One of us should have a head for business, and it won't be me."

"Don't speak like that. You did very well with your apprenticeship with the viscount," his mother said.

Only if everyone knew what he really taught me, Jack thought smugly, recalling the silken sheets on the viscount's bed, how they felt fisted in a hand.

His mother continued, unaware of his wandering thoughts. "And you have many other amiable traits. You will be a loving and kind husband. Very good company."

"Oh yes, I'm excellent company," Jack said, leveling Clara with his most flirtatious smile. "I've been studying for years all the ways to keep ladies entertained."

Color filled her cheeks. His mother drove an elbow into his ribs.

"Terrytown," Lady Justine murmured into her teacup. "That's so far away."

"By all means advocate on our behalf, Countess," Jack quickly said in a solemn voice. "I don't wish to leave town if I can help it."

Clara was watching his face again. Jack held her gaze, keeping his smile soft.

He was pleased to find he liked looking at her. There was something in her countenance that put him at ease. He was sure he'd never met her, and yet he felt as if they'd known each other for a long time.

"Where would you like to live, Lady Clara?" Jack asked.

She started. "You're asking me?"

"Has no one asked your opinion before? What terrible friends you must have." Jack offered her the little tray of cakes. She waved him away. "Or perhaps you do not have a preference for either the country or town."

She considered him as if he were a dancing pony. A marvel.

"Well, I—"

Just then someone screamed, "You *can't* be serious!"

"How dare you speak to—"

"I *won't* do it. I'd sooner have you throw my corpse on Devil's Field than—"

"What on Earth," Lady Justine began, placing a gloved hand to her throat.

"Perhaps I should step out and see what's the matter," Jack's mother said tightly. Her embarrassment was clear on her face as she gathered her skirts and rose from the chaise.

"I'll come with you, Lady Madeleine," Lady Justine said, rising from her seat as well. "I can lend a hand if you need, and I'm sure these two would like a moment to speak alone."

"Very well."

With a swish of skirts, they departed the room, and Jack and Clara found themselves alone.

"She's a gossip," Lady Clara said plainly, setting down her tea. "She only wants to know what's happening."

"This is a good house for her then," Jack replied. "Much to ascertain from these walls."

Silence swelled between them again.

When Jack couldn't bear it a moment longer, he said, "Do you really not read?"

"Of course I read. Just not romantic drivel."

Jack rose and went to the bookcases lining the walls. "My father thinks Mother's parlor is only full of romance novels and books on sewing. What he calls *lady things*."

His fingers traced the spines.

"But my sister also hides her books here. Somewhere there is—Ah, here it is."

Lady Clara gathered her skirts and came to him. She held out a gloved hand to accept the large volume he offered.

"*Jinks and Hammersmith's Complete Compendium of Finance and Economics*."

She barely glanced at the cover before offering it back. "I've already read it."

"Not this volume you haven't," he said. He opened the cover and turned the first few pages. "You see, this was Mr. Hammersmith's personal copy. All of these annotations here in the margin were his own."

Now Clara's mouth was open, her eyes bright. "How did you get this?"

"I went to Everdeen's and paid for it."

"For your apprenticeship?"

"No, my sister wanted it. I'm always fetching books for her. Her interests are varied. I believe she wanted this one to help her with her money clock."

"What's a money clock?" Clara asked, greedily flipping from page to page, her gaze barely lifting to meet his.

Jack didn't mind. He was proud to have pleased her.

"If I recall correctly, it predicts which commodities will cycle in and out of fashion. She has many such inventions. It's a shame they'll never see the light of day. She's brilliant."

Her countenance fell. She snapped the book shut.

"Jacinth," she said quietly. "Don't you hate it?"

"You're much prettier than I hoped you'd be. If I must be exiled to the country, I can think of worse company."

"Be serious."

"I'm almost never serious. I'm afraid you'll have to find a way to live with that. I'm too melancholic to waste a *single* moment being serious."

"We're pawns," she said, exasperated. She shoved the book back onto the shelf. "My father uses me. He moves me around. His expectations—"

"Ah, yes. Fatherly expectations are rather burdensome, aren't they?"

"I can't tell if you're joking or not with that tone. How do you bear it?"

"I drink too much. I lose myself in pleasurable company as often as possible. When neither will suffice, I find other distractions."

I reread Lord Silver's letters and dream of unmasking him in my arms.

Lady Clara saw something in his face then. Her eyes rounded with concern.

"I just want..." Her voice fell away.

Jack leaned his weight against the bookcase.

"What is it you want?" he asked in a low voice.

She pulled back.

"You can't tell me? I suppose that's fair. We've yet to establish any real trust. Perhaps I should go first. I want to live in town, as you know. I want to spend my days riding my horse and reading my books and my evenings drinking with my bosom buds, Albert, Phineas, Silas, and Baz. Good lads, all. You'll like them. Not one is unkind."

"Jacinth."

"Then each night, I want to fall into a pair of beautiful arms. Yours are quite lovely, but if you do not feel the same, I can find others."

I would do nearly anything for Silver's.

She pulled back. "You're very forward."

"Yes, well, this might be the only chance we have to speak plainly before we're married, and I should think that you'd like to know what you're getting."

Her cheeks were red but she held his gaze. "And while you are riding and drinking and doing as you please, what is a lady to do with her days?"

"Whatever she wants."

"*Whatever* she wants? You jest. Surely you want her to run your house. Govern your children. Plan parties and maneuver the politics of high society."

He shrugged. "If it suits her."

"If it doesn't suit her, what will she do with herself then. Read?"

She gestured spitefully at the shelves.

"She could."

"Ride horses?"

"Sure. She can ride with me."

"Fight?"

He arched a brow. "With fists or swords?"

"Swords. Both. Whatever suits."

"That should be entertaining. Will you fight me?"

"Would you allow it?" she asked, scandalized.

"Why not? I cannot hit you, as my mother raised me better. But I will be your practice partner if you like."

"A husband sparring with his wife. Unheard of."

Jack crossed his arms. "Who is to see what we do in our own home? I suppose there is always the danger of servants talking." In an imitation of a maid's high voice, Jack added,

"You'll never believe it! Lord and Lady Siran take swords to each other's throats every night after dinner." Then he dropped into a deep voice, an imitation of a footman. "A strange sort of foreplay, isn't it?"

Lady Clara laughed despite herself, her nose wrinkling.

"What else am I allowed?" she asked at last.

"What else do you like?"

Clara brought herself up to her full height then, and Jack saw they were quite close in stature. He had only a few inches on her. "What if I detest dresses?"

"Do you?" he asked. "You look lovely in them."

"Sometimes."

"Then you really are like my sister."

"You haven't answered me." She lifted her chin defiantly. "Would you demand I wear only corsets and high fashion befitting a lord's wife?"

"I'll let you in on a little secret," he said, and leaned in close to her. Her lips swelled in his vision. They were pink and plush. He wanted to catch the bottom lip with his teeth. "I'm just as fond of removing a gentleman's clothes as I am a lady's."

Her hand went to her throat. A surprised little gasp escaped her. "*No.*"

"*Yes,*" he said with a devilish smile. "So wear what you like. I'll dress you as a boy and take you around. Though Terrytown is small. No doubt there will be rumors about my handsome young lover. Perhaps that will be why we fight with swords after dinner. Are you the jealous type?"

The very idea delighted him. To have her bashing around with Albert and the boys, drinking, riding, fighting. He imagined a thousand mischiefs they could get up to.

While he daydreamed, Clara took a moment to recover. Then she said, "What if your wife doesn't want children?

What if she doesn't want to be a mother? Would you force her to do what your title demands of you?"

How to tell her the truth without frightening her?

He settled on saying, "Nothing would anger my father more than denying him an heir. It'll be the perfect revenge. I suspect one of my friends, Albert, Baz, or Phineas, will have a great many children. We could simply claim one of them as the heir and leave the business of child-rearing to his parents."

This was a flippant answer to hide a darker truth. Fatherhood terrified Jack. He believed, to his very core, that he would not be a good father. That should he have a son, it would awaken in him a beast that couldn't be satisfied except by the pain and suffering of his own flesh and blood.

He searched her face.

There.

He saw it at last. A small glimmer in her eyes. Hope.

He leaned toward her, wanting to put the last of her fears at ease. "I'm sure I will not always please you, Clara. In fact, I'm certain of it. But I won't hurt you. I won't treat you the way my father treats my mother, nor would I ever abandon you. I am not perfect, not even the smallest bit. But I will do my best."

"You really mean that, don't you?" Her own weight grew heavy against the bookcase. She looked away, her gaze settling on something outside the window.

To herself she said, "I can't imagine a life without him."

Ah, she already loves someone.

He wasn't surprised. She was very beautiful and no doubt knew all the young men in town.

"I won't own you," he said. "Though should either of us take a lover, I suggest we be discreet."

Her scowl had returned. "I was speaking of my father."

"Oh." A tight laugh escaped him. "Sorry. I just figured it —well. I mean, it's natural to wonder what the conditions of our relationship will be."

"It will be marriage," she said coolly.

"You'll miss your father then?" he asked, hoping to regain some ground. "If you're very fond of hi—"

"I hate him," she whispered.

This stopped Jack. The loathing in her face was too sharp to be mistaken for anything other than what it was.

"I've dreamed of getting away from him as long as I can remember. It is simply that I cannot believe it a possibility."

"Do not all ladies leave their homes one day?"

"I wonder." She was far away now, her gaze fixed on the roses outside the large window.

"I guess spinsters are the exception to my example," he murmured, speaking only to himself.

The spell of her distant gaze broke, and she was watching him again.

"What is it?" he asked.

"Jacinth—"

"Call me Jack," he said, keeping his gaze fixed on hers. He was certain that his eye contact was too direct to be mistaken for anything but what it was. He liked her. He wanted to kiss her. He was sure it showed.

"Jack?"

"Yes. Everyone calls me Jack. It's only my father who—"

Some recognition sparked in her eyes. They grew, doubling in size.

"*Jack,*" she spat, her face twisted with something close to horror. Now his name sounded like a curse.

He frowned. "I rather like the name."

"God help me, *no.* No, no, *no.*"

Had she heard some rumor? Surely there must be at least a dozen other Jacks in Lundenwick.

"How could I be so *stupid?*" She grabbed the brim of her pretty hat and groaned. "I thought this was some sort of punishment because—Of course it's not!"

He wanted to ask if she was friends with Lady Pickerington, perhaps, Lord Pickerington's disapproving sister. That would explain a few things.

Before he could ask, the parlor door swung open and their mothers came into the room.

"I'm sorry, Clara, but we must cut our visit short today," Lady Justine said. With a fitful little wave, she called Clara over to her side.

"What's happened?" Jack asked, stepping away from the bookcase.

"Selina needs you," his mother said, twisting her gloved hands. Never a good sign. "You'll find her in her room."

"Is it the blacksmith?" Jack asked, his tone still light. He couldn't stand these grave faces. For a moment he'd been having fun. He thought he'd almost won her over, Lady Clara, and then he'd blundered somehow and upset her.

Now he wouldn't even have the chance to fix it.

"Jacinth, please hurry," his mother said, her face pinched.

"Something worse than the blacksmith then." Jack strode across the room. "Very well."

"Selina?" Lady Clara asked as he reached the door to the parlor.

Of course, Clara would not know her. Selina never called upon the other ladies in town.

"My sister," Jack said, with a little bow first to Clara, then her mother.

With a forced smile, he excused himself from the room.

CHAPTER 6

Don't be modest, my dear Silver. It doesn't become you. Where is that proud, boastful boy who stands across from me each night, chin high. If you must know, yes, I do like your haughty manner. I find myself wondering, do you wear it always? Or if perhaps, in certain moments, might I find you more tender and servile? I should like to discover the truth of this.

— FROM A LETTER ADDRESSED TO
LORD SILVER

Jack mounted the stairs, following the angry, guttural moans punctuated with a crash and the sound of glass breaking. Outside Selina's door, he took a breath and rapped on the frame.

"Sister?"

"Hang yourself!" she yelled.

He pushed the door open with the flat of his palm. "If I do that then who will carry all your books? They weigh a ton, and our footmen are ancient. Besides, I doubt the black-smith will have the money for your habits."

Selina picked a bottle of ink off her desk and threw it across the room.

The crystalline bottle struck the wallpaper, a starburst of black splattering across the green design.

Jack stood before her but said nothing. She needed a minute. Possibly several. That much was clear. She loved this room too much to destroy it. Apparently, the ink pot was the only victim. And whatever that pile of glass beside the bookcase had been in its previous life.

A beaker? Jack wondered. Perhaps some useless glass bauble.

"Is there anything else you can live without?" he asked gently.

She seemed to be considering the same. Her eyes slid over the cluttered desk and worktables, but her hands reached for nothing. Every half-finished gadget and scrap of paper was too precious.

"I could lend you a blade," Jack said.

"What would I do with a blade? Except slit his miserable throat. Or my own."

"Don't say that," he said. "I meant for the pillows. Sometimes it's very relieving to destroy a pillow."

She sank into a desk chair, her dark hair curling around her face. It had fallen from the chignon at the back of her neck.

Jack perched on the edge of the desk. "What's happened?"

"I'm being sent away," she said plainly, her jaw working.

"Not married off?"

"Father wants to make me suitable first." Her fists

opened and closed on the desk in front of her. "It's to be three years of finishing school and then marriage."

His heart clenched for her. "I'm sorry, Lina."

"First his refusal and now this. He thinks he can break me, but he's wrong." Her brown eyes blazed.

"What did he refuse?"

"I was accepted to university."

"The university? Here in town?" he asked, more than a little shocked.

"This is the first year they've *ever* admitted women, and I was to be one of five."

"That's amazing!" Jack said. He wasn't even admitted himself the first time, given his poor academic performance. "Well done."

"For all the good it does me. Because I'm a woman, I can't attend without the permission of my male guardian. Father refused."

"Oh."

"So it's off to Miss Quimby's School for Ladies. Thirty minutes from this very moment, I'll be in a carriage bound for Edgewood."

Edgewood wasn't much better than Terrytown, in Jack's opinion. Though it did have a charming lake with swans.

"Today?" Jack asked. "Thirty minutes is no time at all."

"To make sure I don't have time to pack my work, I'm sure." She rubbed her brow. "I shouldn't be going to finishing school. I should be going to university. The bastard."

Her words were cold and her face red. But Jack saw the tears in the corners of her eyes. The frustration. How often had he been driven to the brink like this himself by his father's relentless demands?

"He thinks he can simply bend everyone to his will.

Does it never occur to him that perhaps we have our own lives? My work is everything to me. *Everything*, Jack."

"I know," he said.

"What you feel when you do magic—"

Free. Like maybe I'm meant for something more and not just a worthless waste of space.

"—that's what I feel when I'm inventing. When I take a beautiful idea and see it made real. If—if I can't—I can't spend three years learning about the placement of forks and spoons! I'll go mad."

She exhaled slowly, trying to calm herself.

Jack looked about the room. The bed was shoved in one corner out of the way, its rumpled form treated almost like an afterthought. Two of the walls were covered in bookcases, a large window overlooking the stables between them.

Six tables were spread about the room, cogs and metal parts scattered on their tops. Work lights angled above.

There was nothing he saw that was too cumbersome. Nothing that couldn't be packed into a trunk...

"What if I pack it all for you? Tell me what you need and I'll send it along. Whatever you want," Jack said.

"Some of it is too large."

"I'll get Albert and the others to help me."

She raised her gaze to his. "Father will beat you if he catches you."

Jack shrugged. "I can take a lash or ten for my sister."

Her eyes softened then. "You're an idiot."

But she threw her arms around his neck and squeezed.

He hugged her back.

"You'll need to find a place for it before it arrives," he said into her shoulder. "I doubt Miss Quimby will be any more approving of your work than Father."

"I am sure finishing schools are full of such places.

Anywhere women are forced to be ladies, there are secret things." She released him, wiping at her eyes with her sleeve. "If you are to be my accomplice, then let me show you what I want."

She went to the wall and grabbed the edge of the bookcase. Her fingers wrapped around one of the shelves, and a sharp click sounded. The wall between two bookcases released and opened onto darkness.

She grabbed a lantern off the closest worktable and pulled him inside.

"Close it," she said.

Jack did, and Selina turned on the lantern. They were in a stone passageway.

Jack balked. "I get a view of the garden and you get a secret passageway?"

"Please. As if you don't prefer the balcony," she said.

Two turns and they found another door covered by nine wooden cubes.

"Pay attention," she said, handing him the lantern. "You must press them in order or the door will not open for you. Even up, odd down. And the clicks descend in alternating order. Right then left."

He blinked at her. "What?"

She showed him. Then when he failed to unlock the door, she showed him again.

Her patience wore thin after the sixth attempt.

"Heaven help us, we're going to run out of time," she growled. "It isn't hard. Even up, odd down, counting in reverse from nine. Right then left. Block two, nine right clicks. Block four, eight left clicks. Block six, seven right clicks. Block eight, six left clicks. Block nine, five right clicks. Block seven, four left clicks. Block five, three right clicks. Block three, two left clicks. Block one, one right click."

Jack tried again.

The door finally opened.

"Fortune pities us. I thought it would never happen. Bodes well for keeping Father out. He's stupider than you are."

"I have packed nothing yet, little sister. A bit of kindness, please."

"Forgive me." She sucked in a breath. "Come in."

She held the lantern high as they stepped inside. The door shut behind them. He was glad to see there was no puzzle on this side of the door.

Jack gasped. Before him was an intimidating machine, its great face a hodgepodge of assembled parts.

"What on earth is that?"

"I call it a generator. It generates things."

"What sort of things?"

"Here," she said. "Let me show you."

She went to the back of the machine and pulled levers and pushed buttons. The machine whirled and clicked to life.

"Now, give me some magic."

"What?"

"Conjure something small. A bird. A rabbit."

Jack flexed his palm. Into it he imagined a dove, soft and gentle. It materialized in his hand.

Her brows lifted. She reached out and ran a finger down its spine. It cooed.

She drew her hand back. "Can you make something less substantial? I don't want to feel like a murderer."

He laughed and the dove melted away. In its place was a mouse made of little more than pink light. "Better?"

"Yes," she said, and ushered the mouse into a clear jar before feeding it into a small box on the side of the machine. Once inside, it dissolved, specks of light dispersing through the clear pipes.

One by one, the bulbs overhead lit, filling the room with brilliant light.

"My ambition is to power the whole city with magic and a few wires. It's much cleaner than the fuel we burn now."

"Magnificent," he said. "Where have you gotten the magic from before?"

He understood at least that such things require several trials.

"I've been getting samples from Silas," she said, her cheeks reddening.

"From Silas," he said with an arched brow. "Lord Silas Moranne?"

"Do you know another? Besides, he's amiable."

Jack couldn't have been more shocked. "He's *what*? You hate everyone."

"You exaggerate."

"I'm the friendly, sociable one."

"Yes, and it's exhausting," she said, tipping the glass jar into the machine's opening. "Silas's company requires very little exertion. It's one of his more endearing traits."

His company requires—? "How often do you see him, exactly?"

She didn't answer.

"Are you in love with him?" he asked.

She gave no reply to this question. Her head was behind the machine, her ears quite close to all the whining gears. Though he couldn't be sure if she really didn't hear him, or she was pretending not to.

"So," she said at last. "Can you do it?"

"Of course. I'm sure *Silas* will be happy to help should I have difficulties."

"Be sure to get the parts from the tables," she said, moving past him without a word on the subject. But the color in her cheeks had not faded. In fact, in the lingering light, it was more noticeable than ever. "And my tools here."

Five minutes later they were on the street outside the hall. The group—Jack, Selina, their mother, and Nanny—stood by the carriage. Several maids and footmen had also come out to wave their white handkerchiefs in goodbye.

With the help of the driver, Jack loaded two trunks onto the back of the carriage.

Their mother and Nanny had packed them in haste, seeming to understand that Selina wouldn't be up for the task, or perhaps even know what a lady needs to pack for a finishing school.

Jack offered his hand and helped Selina into the carriage.

"Tell him goodbye for me," Selina said through the small window.

"Father?" he asked, deliberately torturing her.

Selina rolled her eyes. "You know who."

If Jack was being honest with himself, it made a certain sense. Silas was the most bookish of his friends, the most interested in theories and ideas. He also listened more than he spoke, which seemed to be a trait his sister admired in a person.

"Give me a week," Selina said, laying her head back against the seat with a sigh. "Then send everything along."

"As you wish. Safe travels, sister." He tapped the side of the carriage, and the horses jerked forward.

As the carriage pulled away, she waved from the window, looking more than a little forlorn to be leaving.

He raised his hand in farewell. "Good luck!"

"She doesn't need luck," Nanny said from beside him. "She's a clever girl."

"Too clever," their mother said. "It's why she suffers so."

"Jacinth," a voice called. The three of them turned to find his father standing in the doorway. All the maids and footmen had stepped back from him as if he were a blazing flame.

"Yes?" Jack said, his voice cold.

"The count will be here for dinner tomorrow. I expect you to be in attendance. You too, Madeleine."

His mother dipped a curtsy. Jack did nothing.

It didn't matter. His father's back was already to them as he climbed onto his dappled gray horse and spurred it forward into the crowds, heading in the opposite direction of his sister.

"We could bring her back," Jack said conspiratorially. "We can hide her from him, and if he thinks he sees her, tell him he's going mad."

"We'd never manage it," Nanny said. "Have you 'eard all the bangin' that comes from 'er room?"

She had a point.

"Dress well for dinner," his mother said quietly.

"Why? Is the count fussy about one's clothes?" Jack asked. Lady Clara had been dressed handsomely enough.

"I don't know. I haven't met him."

"It'll be a first for us both," he said. "Perhaps Father is selling me to settle some gambling debt. I wouldn't be surprised."

"Nor I," Nanny added.

"Nanny!" Madeleine cried. "That's not true. The baron thinks only of Jack's future with the best of intentions."

Nanny and Jack exchanged a look.

"If you say so, ma'am," Nanny said. Then to Jack in a hushed whisper, "Don't be too harsh on ye mam. A lady is expected to think the best of her husband."

"Is that so?" Jack said with a bitter laugh.

It was a charming idea, though he had a feeling Clara wouldn't give him the same grace until he'd earned it.

THE EXCITEMENT OF THE AFTERNOON AND THE lingering hangover from the night before left Jack tired. He returned to his room and shut himself inside. He removed his boots and fell into his bed, surrendering to the pillows and sheets.

Nanny or a maid had been in to tidy in his absence, and it took him several minutes to rumple the sheets to his satisfaction. But once he did, exhaustion rose up to meet him. It hung off his bones like a weight.

Yet when he closed his eyes, the darkness didn't take him.

With a flourish of his hand, he conjured the cube again.

Lord Silver's lost treasure glinted in the late-afternoon light, sparking orange and gold in turn with each twist of Jack's hands.

"What are you?" Maybe if he asked the question enough, he would get an answer.

Surely it had something to do with magic. Maybe it performed its own magic? Or amplified that of the conjurers? Was this the key to Silver's success all these years?

Only one way to find out, he thought.

He closed his eyes and reached inside himself for his magic. He waited, poised, until he felt that flood of warmth rise up to meet him, a thousand possibilities rolling through the framework of his mind. He saw the cube in his mind's eye, just as it was in his hand.

He imagined it opening for him, revealing all of its secrets to its new master.

Click.

He opened his eyes and gasped.

His room was a matrix of light. Prismatic and shimmering, it cut in all directions, much like that of a bee's honeycomb. While most of the cells and compartments were empty, one was not. The one just above his right hand held his silver coin. It hovered there, floating, the cat's grin fixed on his own.

In addition to the coin, there were his two pistols that he kept for emergencies. And he also spotted a pair of black stockings—his favorite pair, in fact—hanging in a cell near the foot of his bed.

How did they get there?

He'd been missing them for nearly four months.

"That's where those got to," he said, plucking them from the liminal space and throwing them over the arm of his chair.

He marveled at the lines and intersections of light and space.

He understood instinctually that there was this other space, a layer of reality, hidden between his own and perhaps a greater existence. But he had never seen this secondary world with his own eyes.

"Or maybe this is thin air," he thought aloud.

If so, thin air was saturated with magic.

It was a wonderful discovery, and yet he was disappointed.

He'd been hoping he would find a letter.

He closed the cube and rested his hand on the coverlet. Jack fell asleep in the darkening room.

He slept hard. Stray noises seeped into his dream. Horses whinnying. Carriage wheels turning.

Then the unmistakable sound of boots scuffing against stone.

Of someone climbing onto his balcony.

It was a sound he was far too familiar with to mistake for anything else.

He woke but didn't open his eyes. His hand tightened on the cube, and with a flourish he made it disappear before the familiar creak of his balcony window opening reached him.

Lord Pickerington? he thought with a thrill of pleasure. *Did you miss me that much?*

And if not Pickerington, who?

It must be a lord. He couldn't imagine a lady raising her skirts and climbing the garden wall, let alone the balcony.

But when he opened his eyes, it wasn't Pickerington's soft caramel gaze he saw.

It was Lord Silver.

CHAPTER 7

While I will not deny my servility, tenderness does not suit me. My father's education has been rather diligent in its attempts to rid me of it. Now why have I said this? Who wants to speak of fathers now? At this rate I will be late tonight. Though I admit I like to make you wait. Little pleases me more than when I catch you scanning the crowd. It's a pleasure, that moment, when your little frown disappears at the sight of me. Perhaps then I should write more...

No. I do not wish to be too cruel. I will say only one thing more. I found your ribbons to be a clever trick. How quick they were to bring me to my knees in our last match. I dare say that was the point, wasn't it?

Do you wish to see me on my knees so soon?

— FROM A LETTER ADDRESSED TO
THE PEACOCK

I do wish it. Name the time and place.

— FROM A LETTER ADDRESSED TO
LORD SILVER

J ack bolted upright.

He pinched himself hard. "Ow."

Moonlight cut across the side of Silver's mask, making his eyes more luminescent than ever. "What did you do that for?"

"I'm not dreaming."

"Have you dreamt of this before?" Silver asked.

"Of you climbing my balcony into my bedroom? Oh yes."

Silver grew very still.

"What happens next?"

"You climb into bed with me."

Silver came to the edge of the bed, resting a hip against the side of the mattress. That was enough for Jack.

He reached up and grabbed the man with both hands, pulling him down onto the bed. As Silver hit the mattress, his whole body went soft.

Jack was unable to hide his grin. "I want to kiss you."

"You can't."

"Not with this mask on, no. May I remove it?"

Jack's hand was already on its rim, pulling, lifting.

Silver grabbed his wrist. "Don't."

Jack relaxed his grip and placed his hand on the other man's stomach.

"May I kiss you somewhere else perhaps?" Jack was unable to hide his grin.

"No." The word didn't have much refusal in it.

There was a chance, then, if Jack didn't push too hard.

He tried to conjure his willpower and self-control.

"Then what did you come for, Silver? To kill me in my own bed, perhaps?"

"Will you leave with me?"

"Leave with you?" Jack laughed. "You'd rather murder me in the woods then?"

"I don't want to kill you. I want you out of this house."

"Out of this house? Why?"

"If you go..." Silver's voice hitched.

Jack could only see the eyes through the silver mask, but the eyes can tell a man a great deal.

"Is it enough to say that it isn't safe for you here?" Silver finished. "Leave with me, Jack. Please."

A boom rocked the house. A woman screamed. Jack was already rising.

Silver seized him, holding on to the front of his shirt.

"Please, don't!" Silver hissed.

The woman kept screaming, and the smell of smoke and ash filled Jack's room instantly.

The woman screaming, he realized, was his mother.

"Let go of me." He ripped himself from Silver's grip.

"Don't!" he cried. "If you go out there, you're dead."

Jack whirled on him. "What have you done?"

Silver held a cube in his hand. Jack thought he'd stolen his trophy until he realized it wasn't the same as the one Jack had hidden. Instead of a gold face, this one was metallic. The color of Silver's mask.

He twisted its face and it opened, revealing the same prismatic light dancing across the room.

There was the cube he'd hidden, two spaces above his coin.

With a single swipe of his hand, Silver snatched it and the spectacle collapsed. His room resumed its usual play of shadow and light.

Jack seized his cloak, twisting his fists in the fabric.

"No, stop!" his mother cried, followed by a fit of coughing. "Stop, I beg you!"

Jack released him.

"Mother!" Jack, torn, ran for his bedroom door. At the last moment, he threw a look over his shoulder at Lord Silver, expecting to see him standing as he was beside Jack's bed.

But Silver wasn't there. He was jumping off the balcony and into the night, his black cloak flaring out behind him like a battle flag in the wind.

Jack made his choice and followed the sound of his mother's voice.

"Mother! Where are you?"

Flames met him. The fire licked the wallpaper and carpets, bit at the art on the walls. Jack covered his nose and mouth with his shirt and ran first to his mother's room.

She wasn't there.

He took the steps two and three at a time, missing the little pockets of flames that ripped at the carpets and had set the bannisters alight.

He ran into Nanny and Butler John at the base of the stairs.

"Get everyone out!" he shouted. "Where's my mother?"

"She ran that way," Nanny said, covering her mouth with a handkerchief and coughing into it. "Your father— your father—"

But whatever Nanny wanted to tell him about the baron was cut off by a fit of coughing.

Black smoke was filling the house. It made Jack's eyes water and his throat sting.

"Get to fresh air!" Jack commanded, urging her toward the butler. "Get everyone out of the house."

"Yes, sir."

They stumbled toward the door.

"Mother!" Jack yelled. He checked the parlor. The kitchen.

He could not find her.

He checked his father's study. His heart jerked.

It wasn't only the enormous flames and great heat that pushed against him like a furious hand. It was what he saw on the floor in front of him.

His father. Dead.

He wore a dinner jacket. His white gloves were soaked with blood. His green vest and white dress shirt crimson to the collar.

His eyes were open, unseeing.

Jack didn't need to wonder what had killed him.

A rapier thrust through his chest. Its sharp end jutted through the back of the dinner jacket.

Someone had run the baron clean through.

And the room was torn apart. Either by his father or by someone looking for something.

Money, perhaps.

One of the bookcases cracked then folded, as if snapped in half by an invisible hand. The flaming tomes rained down on his father's body, and Jack stumbled back out into the hallway and into someone's arms.

"My god," Albert said, his hands tightening on Jack's arms. He wore a simple white shirt and trousers. His bronze skin and hazel eyes looked golden in the firelight.

"You?" Jack said.

"We saw the fire from the street." The flames swelled and a wall of heat slammed into them. Albert pulled him out of its path. "Come on!"

Jack coughed, trying to ease his burning throat, as they stumbled into the foyer.

Silas's shirt was open at the collar, and he was running up the stairs two at a time.

"She's not here!" Jack called up after him. "Get off the stairs before they collapse."

Silas's face was red when he joined them by the door, though if that was because of the growing flames or the clear knowing in Jack's eyes, it was hard to tell.

Together they went out into the night.

Frantically, Jack searched the growing crowd. Maids, servants, the footmen and groomsman. Nanny and Butler John.

So many familiar faces, nearly everyone accounted for.

There was only one person he did not see.

"She isn't here," Jack said, panic squeezing his heart.

"Who?" Silas asked. "Selina? I heard you."

"No, my mother. My mother isn't here! I have to go back."

Hands were all over him. They tried to stop him by grabbing at his shirt and arms.

"I have to!" he cried. "I can't leave her!"

He wrenched himself away.

"You'll be killed! The roof is going to come down, mate!" Baz cried.

"Don't, Jack!" Nanny said, realizing what he was about to do. But she was too far away, farther even than the friends desperately trying to restrain him.

A flash of magic knocked them all back. Jack shook himself free and ran into the burning house. Something hot brushed his ear as he ducked through a collapsing door frame. He beat at it with the sleeve of his shirt.

Where is she? Where is she?

"Mother! Mother!"

A tug in his guts—a silent call—made him turn left, and as he passed an open door, he saw her and skidded to a halt.

It was the dining room. With her back shoved into one of the chairs, a gloved hand was wrapped around her throat.

A figure cloaked from head to toe in midnight blue.

His hat, cloak, vest, shirt, gloves, and boots were all the same shade, which made his white mask stand out all the more, though the side of it was charred black. And there was something familiar about it.

It's just like Silver's, he realized. The same metallic sheen and style. The same cleft in the chin and exaggeration of the nose.

He was doing something to his mother. A golden hue tinged with soft blue radiated from her. It pulsed and throbbed.

"That's it," the man murmured. "Give it all to me."

With a flourish of his hand, Jack produced one of his pistols.

The smoke in his eyes made it hard to aim, but he pulled the trigger. The bullet bit into the wall beside the man's head. He'd missed his true mark yet still clipped the man's ear.

He dropped his mother and she hit the floor in a heap of fabric. A gloved hand went up to cover it.

"Are you *Jack*, by chance?" the fiend said, with a great deal too much good humor in his voice for just having had his ear partially blown off.

"Jack! Jack!"

Then his friends were there.

"Get my mother out!" Jack yelled over the roar of the crackling flames.

Without a word, Albert and Silas went around the table and gathered her up, disappearing with her.

Jack did not dare look away from the demon looking back at him.

"Jack, come on!" Phineas cried, his hand on Jack's arm. "Jack, forget him."

Jack couldn't. There was something in the man's eyes. Something that called to him.

"You feel it, don't you," the man said, his eyes unblinking. "You can almost hear it like music. Most can't hear it, but the magic that runs through you is strong. I can feel it like a breeze in the air. Come here, boy."

Jack took a step forward, compelled.

"No!" Phineas yanked Jack back.

This broke the spell, shaking Jack from the trance the man had somehow cast over him.

Because he is not a man, Jack realized. *He is a demon.*

Jack pulled the trigger again, but this time the bullet slowed, hung in the air.

No, Jack thought. *It can't be.*

With a nod of his chin, the demon reversed the bullet, slinging it back in Jack's direction.

Only it didn't strike Jack. It hit Phineas as he stepped in front of him.

With a cry, Phineas dropped.

"You have something of mine," the demon said, and stepped toward him. "I *will* get it back."

Before the demon reached him, Albert, Baz, and Silas bounded into the room, firing their own pistols at the intruder.

It was impossible to tell if a bullet found its mark.

The demon disappeared as if into thin air. One moment he stood engulfed in the flames. The next, he melted into the smoke and ash as if he'd never been there at all. The bullets struck the dining room wall in a fury.

"What the hell was that?" Baz cried. "Did you see it disappear?"

"You two carry him!" Albert cried. "I'll get Jack."

Then the hands were on him again, hauling Jack from the dining room. He caught a glimpse of Baz and Silas lifting Phineas from the floor, and his heart clenched.

Please be all right, he begged. *Please be all right.*

"Worry about yourself," Albert barked into his ear.

Coughing, hacking, his eyes nearly swollen shut from the fire, they dragged him from the house.

He knew they were outside the moment the temperature shifted.

His skin—which felt blistered from the raging heat—relished the cool evening air.

Everyone had gathered across the street. Given the condition of his eyes, Jack could feel the night more than see it. The breeze, the whining horses. The scent of smoke. Soft crying and disbelieving murmurs rippling around him as they watched the great Ansley Hall burn to ash.

"My mother," Jack croaked out. His throat was severely abused by the smoke.

"She lives," Albert assured him. "We entrusted her to the maids' care."

"Phineas?"

They said nothing.

Jack could only watch as the ceiling of the hall, of the great house he'd lived in all his life, caved and brought the last of its walls down with it.

CHAPTER 8

*'E wen'n pressed three gold coins in m'hand 'n asked who
the two 'cross the street be. I told 'im, "That's the Baron
Siran 'n his son."*

Three gold! I'd 've done it f'ten pence!

— AS TOLD BY FRANNIE JONES,
LAUNDRESS

It was the voices that woke him. They were hushed,
and yet they buzzed around his ears like flies.

"It's the nurses who washed and dressed the body.
His parents are beside themselves. They couldn't."

"What about the casket?"

"There is a standard with the family crest. They'll use
that to bury him. We will have to carry it ourselves. Jack
can't be expected to."

I'm dead, he thought. *They're talking about putting me
in the cemetery.*

"What about the Baroness Siran? Will she be carried—"

"Mind your tongues. She isn't dead yet," a woman hissed. A cold cloth was pressed to Jack's head.

The Baroness Siran. That was his mother's title.

His mother.

"Mother?" Jack's eyes opened.

Four blurry faces slid into focus. Nanny, whose hand pulled away the cloth. Albert, Silas, and Baz. Each expression softened with relief.

He was in a small hospital room. The white curtains hanging on metal hooks surrounded one half of his bed. A crisp white sheet and blanket lay across his chest. To his left, Nanny sat in a chair, her hands in a large basin of water, clutching a pale cloth. At the foot of the bed, Albert sat on the left, Silas on the right. At his right shoulder, Baz.

"Thank God," Albert said, all the air leaving him in a puff. "You scared the hell out of us."

Jack pressed the heel of his hand to his face. Rough cloth scratched at his skin.

He frowned at the bandages.

"The doctor's been round to treat your burns," Nanny said, twisting the cloth to wring out the water. The droplets pinged musically against the metal. "How's your eyes?"

They felt puffy and his vision was blurry.

"I live," he croaked. It hurt to use his voice, every word edged in sharp fire. His hand went to his throat.

"It was the smoke. It should heal with time," Silas said, pushing his glasses up onto his face. "Your vision will improve when the swelling goes down."

"I'll keep usin' the cold cloth if it's all the same to you," Nanny said tersely.

"M-mother?" Jack rasped. He tried to sit up. Nanny pushed him back down.

"No you don't," Nanny said. "Yer eyes ain't been open a full minute yet."

It was Silas who said, "She inhaled too much smoke. Her lungs aren't in good shape and her throat—"

"That wasn't the smoke," Jack said. "There was a man."

A monster.

"He attacked her," Jack finished.

"Was no man!" Baz cried. "Looked like a demon to me."

Nanny's jaw worked. "Be he man or demon, he's gone now. I hope whatever he came for, he got it and will leave us in peace. What your father did to anger a demon, I can hardly guess."

Are you Jack by chance?

You have something of mine. I will get it back.

"Thank God your sister was sent away. Had she been home, she would've never got out in time," Nanny said, pressing the cloth to Jack's brow again. "At least she'll have made it to Edgewood by now."

Jack pictured Selina in her secret room trying to dismantle her machine while the house burned down around her. Nanny was right. She would've died trying to get all her beloved gadgets out.

She'll not be happy to know her work was lost to the flames.

And my letters, he thought bitterly. *All my letters from Silver.*

"I wrote to her already," Silas said. And when Jack turned his gaze on him, he added, "I didn't say what happened. I only told her to let us know that she arrived safely."

Us.

Silas looked away first.

"What the hell happened?" Jack asked. "I went up to rest before dinner and—"

He cut himself off. He didn't want to mention Lord Silver or his childish belief that he'd come to him at last through his window.

A fool. I'm such an idiot.

Silver hadn't come for a seduction. Silver had come to rob him blind.

"We aren't sure," Nanny said. "I was in the kitchen 'elping to prepare the courses, and then I smelled the smoke. I sent Delilah to check and she never came back. Then I went lookin' fer 'er meself and found 'er body beside the back door. Someone cut 'er throat. Poor girl. She's the only one we lost, thank the Lord. Except for the baron, of course."

My father is dead.

"Where did the fire start?" Jack asked.

"Can't say. It seemed to be all over."

Dead. Truly dead.

"Fire can jump," Baz said, his dark eyes bright. "I've seen it m'self. We had a barn go that way."

Jack felt as if he were forgetting something important. He ran through the night's events, trying to remember all that had happened, all that he saw. But his focus was still soft at the edges.

"I hate to put this on you so soon," Nanny said, touching the cool cloth to his face again, "but with your father gone..."

Her voice trailed off.

A memory came to him sharp and fresh. His father's body on the study floor, the rapier shoved through his chest as the bookcase tumbled down, red embers floating up to meet the smoke. The way his eyes had been open and unblinking. The horror in them.

The fury.

"He's truly dead?" Jack whispered. His lips were as dry as paper.

"I'm afraid so," Nanny said.

"We've made the arrangements, mate," Baz said gently.

"We're taking care of everything," Albert added. "You don't have to worry about it. The service is tomorrow, and he'll be in the ground before dark."

"You're not expected to go," Silas added. "Everyone knows you're hurt. No one will expect it of you."

His friends knew there was no love lost between Jack and his father, and he was more than a little grateful to be spared the burden of burying him.

"Was it the demon who killed him?" Jack asked.

"We can't be sure, but knowing changes nothing. Jack, with him gone it means you're the Baron Siran."

It was like someone had punched him in the chest.

The Baron Siran.

"I can't be."

"I'm afraid so, my love." Nanny's eyes were full of pity. "You have to tell us what your wishes are."

"I can't—I—"

"Easy," Albert said gently, placing a hand on Jack's leg. "Breathe."

Jack tried to pull air into his lungs, but his chest was too tight.

"What is the most pressing concern?" Silas asked from his chair.

So many people. He couldn't possibly be responsible for so many people.

"The most pressing concern is where we're to live," Nanny said. "Ansley Hall is uninhabitable. The most obvious choice would be Bloomsbury House. It's big enough for all of us and the most ready for habitation. And it's in town. Though its stables are a quarter the size of Ansley's."

"We've got plenty of room in our stables," Albert said. "Send over what you can't board."

"I'll tell Mr. Darby," Nanny said.

"Where is everyone now?" Jack asked.

"We sent them to Bloomsbury House to sleep. We couldn't very well leave them in the streets."

The panic swelled in his chest again. "How long have I been out?"

"Just a few hours," she said. "But it's very late. They needed somewhere to rest."

He could see it now, the dark circles under her eyes.

"You need to rest," he said.

She laughed. "I've too much to do, my lord."

Albert squeezed his ankle gently. "Jack, you have to give the order."

"Move everyone to Bloomsbury House," he said mechanically. "Stable the horses we can't at the Lockwood estate."

"As you wish. Thank you, Lord Lockwood," Nanny said.

"What else needs to be done?" Albert asked.

"The fire destroyed most of everyone's possessions," she said. "We need to stock the house well and replace what was lost if we can. I can take all the girls shopping, but we can't shop without money. All the accounts need to be transferred to Jack's name."

"That won't happen until he's out of the hospital and he can meet with the bankers. A week at least. What'll you have us do in the meantime?"

"I can spot you," Albert said, handing over his money pouch before she had the chance to ask.

"Me too," Baz said.

"You can't—" Jack began.

"Don't worry about it. Silas is good with the maths. Give him all the receipts and he'll keep perfect account of what you spend and we'll settle later, once the bankers have been dealt with."

"Your father had no other heirs. It should be a quick transfer," Silas said.

"There's two thousand gold in my pouch," Albert said.

"About fifteen or sixteen hundred in mine," Baz said, handing over his leather pouch as well. "There would've been more, but I was drinking this afternoon."

"I have fifteen in mine," Silas said, and placed his pouch in her open hand.

Baz and Albert gawked at him.

"What?" he said defensively. "I think it's foolish to carry so much money on one's person. What if you're robbed?"

Nanny looked properly horrified to be holding over three thousand gold in her wet hands.

"It's just a loan," Jack said.

"Aye, we know you're good for it," Baz said. "And once you spend it, don't hesitate to ask fer more, Nanny. We will cover you until Jack 'as 'is money."

"There's the matter of Ansley Hall itself." Albert crossed his leg over his knee. "It's too hot to go through now, but when it cools, do you want us to hire a crew to sift the ashes for anything salvageable?"

"Aye, but that's tricky," Baz said, leaning back in his seat. It creaked. "If they're dishonest they'll run off with all the silver they find."

"Perhaps we should select the most trustworthy men from our own houses," Silas offered, pushing at his glasses again. "I've got at least eight I trust."

"Good idea," Albert said. "I'd say there are five or six from my own."

Baz laughed. "None from mine unless I send myself."

"Baron," Nanny said.

"Don't," Jack begged. "Don't call me that. I can't bear it."

"My lord, then," she said. "As her male guardian, you are in charge of your mother's care. You must approve her treatments. Now that you're awake, they'll be asking what you want."

What I want.

Here, at least, Jack felt no hesitation. No confusion. "Save her. Whatever it takes."

"It's possible she will never wake, love."

"Try, damn it!" he cried. "Try everything!"

Tears filled his swollen eyes. Albert's grip tightened on his ankle. Baz placed a hand on his shoulder.

He was in control of himself again, but his voice shook. "Do what you can for her. Whatever it is."

"As you wish," Nanny said, and the money pouches disappeared inside the folds of her dress. "If it's the same to you, I'll get a few winks m'self and get started with all of this at first light."

His friends had the courtesy to stand as she dipped a curtsy and disappeared behind the drawn hospital curtain.

Then it was only him and his friends.

Instantly, he realized who was missing. Albert, Baz, Silas—but no Phineas.

The sight of a bullet whipping past his head and slamming into Phineas filled his mind. Of Baz and Silas lifting him bleeding from the dining room carpet.

"Is Phineas being treated in another room?"

Albert's gaze fell to his lap. Silas removed his glasses and pinched the bridge of his nose. Neither said anything.

"Where is Phineas?" Jack asked again.

It was Baz who spoke. "Phin is dead, mate."

Jack's world tilted on an axis.

Dead. Dead from my own bullet. Shot from my own pistol.

It mattered not that the bullet had been intended for the demon. Phineas was dead all the same.

When he'd woken, he'd thought they'd been speaking of his father. The baron's body that had to be washed and prepared for the funerary rites.

Now the words *his parents* made more sense. It wasn't Jack's parents they were speaking of.

It was Phineas's parents.

"His family," Jack moaned.

"They believe he died trying to help you escape the fire."

"Aye," Baz said gravely, tears in his own eyes. "They think a beam came down on him."

"He was shot," Jack said.

"There was no bullet," Albert said gravely. "It was an accident, Jack. Do you understand? Phineas died a hero. A brave man who rushed into the flames to save his friend. Stick to that."

Phineas.

"It's my fault," Jack said. "My god, it's all my fault."

"Don't," Albert warned. "You know that's not true."

But it was.

Jack was the one who had dueled Lord Silver. Jack was the one who had taken his stupid cube even though Lord Silver said that he would be sorry if he did.

Jack was the fool who thought Lord Silver wanted him

as badly as Jack did—and had wasted precious time he could've spent saving his mother, playing at seduction.

Jack had been the one to foolishly fire a pistol at a demon.

Phineas, forgive me.

Jack threw back the covers.

His body ached. His eyes and throat were raw. But he was up, his bare feet hitting the cold stone floor.

"What are you doin', mate?" Baz asked.

Albert rose to block his path. "Stop."

"Move," Jack said.

"You aren't thinking straight," Albert said calmly, his hands out in front of him. "You need to lie down."

"I want to see him," Jack said. "Where is he?"

"You're in no shape—"

"I will see him!" Jack screamed.

"I'll take you," Silas said. "If it will get you back to bed sooner, I'll get you there."

Albert's jaw worked, but he moved aside as Silas slipped his arm under Jack's and walked him from the room.

CHAPTER 9

How many times have I wished, in his miserable life, that I could stand where he stands? Kneel where he kneels and take the blows aimed at his back? That I could shield him with my own flesh? If I could have but one power, it would be this.

— FROM THE JOURNAL OF LORD
ALBERT LOCKWOOD

Slowly, they made their way through the hospital to the mortuary ward at its far end. Silas bore the burden without complaint as Jack hobbled along beside him. Jack heard the crying, a mournful melody, even before they turned down the last dark corridor of the mortuary wing.

The hallway was filled with people, their sobbing faces illuminated by the hospital's lamps. Most were wearing the crimson servant colors associated with House Gildroy. For this reason, Phineas's parents stood out in their finer garments.

Jack's heart clenched.

Phineas's mother wailed with her head in her hands as several of her maids tried to soothe her. Phineas's father stood stoically against the opposite wall. His eyes were red rimmed, wide and unblinking. Who Jack did not see were Phineas's three younger sisters. Jack supposed their parents had decided to keep them away from this gruesome sight.

The crowd parted for their quartet in a sleepy daze, until Jack stood before Phineas's father. He was a large man with Phineas's build and coloring. Only the facial features were different, sharper. Phineas had received his softer cheeks, wide-set eyes, and cherubic nose from his mother.

"Lord Gildroy, forgive me." Tears ran down Jack's face. It took all of his will to meet the man's eyes. "It should be me in there, sir."

The man looked to Jack, unblinking. He said nothing, his eyes sliding from Jack to Silas. Then to Baz and Albert. At last, he said, "He loved you all. Every one of you."

He gave Jack's shoulder a squeeze then turned away, a clear request to be left alone with his grief.

Albert pulled Jack toward the room, one hand already on the door, pushing it open.

Knowing what was coming didn't spare Jack the shock of seeing it with his own eyes.

On a metal table in the center of the room, Phineas was stretched long, as if sleeping. Someone had washed his face of all its soot and ash and put him in clean clothes. His boots shone.

The hair at his temples was still damp from the washing. His hands were folded over his stomach peacefully. Someone had even scraped his nails clean.

But his color wasn't right.

He was too pale. And when Jack reached out and

placed a hand over his, he was shocked by how cold the flesh was.

"I did this," he murmured, fresh tears filling his eyes.

"No," Albert said firmly. "It was the demon."

"I'd give anything to know why it was at your house," Silas said quietly. The flesh between his brows was pinched. "Was it after your father? Did he make a deal? I've heard rumor that half the men in town have, to make their fortunes. I've wondered about my own father, truth be told."

"I don't believe my father made a deal," Jack said.

They came for me. Because I took something that didn't belong to me.

It's my fault. All my fault.

He'd thought he'd won the match against Lord Silver.

It had never occurred to him Silver might be in league with a demon—or would have been willing to go into league with one in order to get his precious cube back.

Jack had been careless. He'd been stupid.

He'd thought it was all harmless flirting and seduction. Just a game. He'd taken the cube, hoping that Silver would chase after it.

He hadn't meant to keep it. He didn't even want it. He'd only wanted to give Silver one more reason to come into his arms.

Leave with me, Lord Silver had said.

Had he had second thoughts at the last moment? Had he felt guilty for the hell he'd brought to Jack's door? Or was he afraid the demon would kill Jack if he stayed behind?

It almost had.

I have so many questions.

He didn't believe Silver had meant to hurt his parents. He had nothing to gain from such an act. But demons have no masters. They make deals. The lend their power and strength. There was no controlling them. Perhaps Silver had said, *We go to Ansley Hall and reclaim my magic box*, and the demon did the rest.

Simple as that.

What the cube was and why it was so important—it didn't matter really.

What mattered was Phineas was dead. Before the night was through, Jack's mother might be right here beside him, on the other cold, bare slab.

Jack hung his head, overwhelmed by his embarrassment and shame.

I'll never forgive myself.

"I'd do anything to bring him back," Albert said solemnly.

"Aye," Baz said. "We all would."

An idea sparked in Jack's mind. Flint striking a rock. Once, twice.

"Anything," Jack said, mostly to himself. His head snapped up. "*Anything.*"

His conviction flexed into an iron fist.

"Help me," he said, and his grip tightened on Phineas's stiff arm.

Albert frowned. "Help you *what*?"

"Move him."

Baz snorted. "Move him where?"

"To Devil's Field."

Albert stepped back from the table as if it had caught flame. "No, you can't."

"We can save him."

"Not without damning ourselves!" Baz said. "I'm doin' a fine enough job on me own. I don't need the help of no demon."

"Fight a demon with a demon?" Silas said, his shock

apparent in his soft jaw. "Is that what you're thinking?"

"It was a demon who killed my father," Jack said. His head throbbed, but he tried to remain calm and in control of himself. "It almost—it might have—killed my mother. Phineas is dead. It'll come back for me."

"You can't know that," Albert said, throwing up his hand. "It was a random act."

"No," Jack said. He shook his head. "The demon was sworn to Lord Silver. He came to the house to get back the cube I won from him. That's why they came. I brought this on my family."

Silence filled the room.

Silas spoke first, his mind always the quickest. "Even if that were true, you can't be blamed. Silver should never have attacked you."

"Will I be blamed when it comes back and finishes my mother?" Jack growled. "Me?"

"If Silver got the cube he wanted, he won't be back," Baz said. "Why would he come back?"

"He didn't get it," Jack admitted.

"What?" they said in unison.

"There was a moment before he escaped when I grabbed him. I thought he would notice, but—" With a flourish of his hand, Jack produced the cube. Until that moment, he wasn't sure it would materialize. He wasn't sure if he'd really managed to escape the house with it in hand. Everything happened so fast.

Yet there it was, floating just above his palm in ethereal light.

Only now, upon closer inspection, Jack realized it wasn't the golden one he'd won from the duel. It was the one Silver had brought tonight. The etchings were different, its faced carved of some pale metal.

"The demon knew I had it when he saw me. He said, 'I will get it back.'"

Baz met Albert's eyes over the table. "I told you. I *said* he wanted Jack. The way he was lookin' at 'im."

"Stop! Just stop." Albert ran a hand over his face. He loosed a slow breath. Then to Jack he said, "What is your plan *exactly?*"

"You can only beat a demon with a demon. I'll make a pact with one. I'll ask that it help me kill my father's murderer and bring Phineas back."

"Bring him back? He isn't on holiday!" Albert cried.

"It's only been hours. You know it can be done," Jack insisted. "Think of Tromwell."

Timothy Tromwell. The young boy who was trampled by his father's own carriage three years before. He'd been dead for six hours when his father got the idea to carry him to Devil's Field.

They spent close to an hour on the field before Timothy emerged from the mist, alive and well.

"Tromwell's father never came back," Silas said darkly. "I'll not exchange one friend for another."

"Nor I," Baz said.

"You can't sell your soul," Albert said, his jaw working. "Phineas wouldn't want that. He'd rather be dead than have you do it, and you know it."

Jack did know it, and the fact hurt all the more.

"It doesn't have to be my soul. I have something else to sell."

"Demons don't take gold," Baz laughed. "Oh, if they did, I'd have a few less problems m'self."

Jack ignored this. "This cube is special. Very special. I'll offer it to the demon. The fact Silver had one was enough to get one demon to work with him, wasn't it? Maybe it'll be enough to convince another."

"What if it doesn't want the cube?" Albert asked, meeting Jack's eyes.

"Then we'll leave. But we have to try. *Please.* Not just for Phineas, but for my mother and sister too."

"What if the cube is worse than a couple of bloodthirsty demons?" Silas asked. "You don't know what it is or what it can do."

"That's not true," Jack said. "I know what it does, but I don't have time to show you now. Every minute we leave him like this means less of a chance we can bring him back."

They looked down at Phineas's still face. His unmoving chest.

"I would try," Baz said first, licking his lips nervously. "Nothing wrong with *asking* a demon a question. Not the same as making a pact, is it?"

"Assuming they don't eat you on the spot," Albert said bitterly. He looked to Silas. "Tell me you have a better idea."

Silas ran a hand through his hair. "We could hunt for Silver and try to give him the cube before he attacks again. Maybe that would deter the demon."

"It'll take too long," Jack protested.

Silas conceded this fact. "It would. First we'd have to find out who he was—"

"We tried that," Baz chimed in. "I've been asking around for over a year."

Silas continued despite the interruption. "—and he might not even be in town anymore. If he really did attack Ansley Hall to get this box"—he gestured at the cube glinting in Jack's hands—"there's no reason not to believe he will come again. And as Baz said, the demon might have his own interest in Jack now. Either way, do we really want Jack to face the demon a second time?"

"Which one o' us will be killed protectin' him next?" Baz asked. "I say we stay ahead of this."

Albert rubbed his brow.

"We don't have good options," Silas said softly, his eyes on Albert. "None that I can see."

"I preferred it when all you were facing was an arranged marriage," Albert said coldly, finally flicking his hazel eyes up to meet Jack's. "I prefer ladies to demons."

"Aren't they one and the same?" Baz snorted.

Silas nudged him. "Not the time, Basil."

Several beats of silence hung between them before Albert said, "Silas, open the window and climb through. Jack, I'll lift you after."

His eyes flicked to Baz. "We'll feed Phin through the window. You know we can't use the door with his family out there."

THE NIGHT WAS COLDER THAN JACK REMEMBERED. HE wasn't sure if it was his burns or if the evening had dropped in temperature, but his hands were shaking as they moved swiftly through the hospital's shadows.

Phineas's body was thrown across Albert's shoulders. Baz walked a few paces ahead, looking around corners and serving as their scout to ensure their path was clear.

Jack's arm was draped around Silas's shoulder as they stuck close to the building, where it was darkest.

"My carriage is through here," Albert said. He pointed at the triumphal arch.

"Carriage?" Baz scoffed.

"Did you seriously plan to walk the three miles to

Devil's Field with a wounded man and a dead body?" Albert asked. "And what will we say if we run into the watchmen? That he drank himself to death?"

Baz snorted. "Why not?"

"There." Albert pointed at the carriage sitting beneath the stone arch. Its two pale horses flicked their tails as the sleepy footman dozed.

They were as quiet as they could be despite the scuff of their boots against the stone path. Once Phineas and Jack were both safely inside, their backs resting against the warm padding, Albert woke the driver.

"Good evening, Charleston."

The driver started with a snort and a cry.

"Go along now," Albert said. "I need no company for where I'm going."

"I can be discreet, my lord," the footman said in a raspy voice.

"I'm sure you can, but I'll take the reins all the same."

Baz and Silas slid into the carriage and shut the door, the four of them filling the space. The carriage rocked as Albert hauled himself up into the driver's seat, its large wheels creaking.

The sound of the driver's footfall dissipated and the snap of the reins kicked the carriage into motion. It swayed with the four of them rocking inside, Baz doing his best to keep Phineas steady so his head didn't knock against the wall.

"He'll have a headache when he wakes," Baz said, and then seemed to hear himself. "If he wakes, that is."

"Silas," Jack whispered, keeping his voice low. "If this goes badly—"

"Don't," Silas warned, turning in his seat to glare at Jack.

"Marry my sister."

"Heavens, Jack. Please spare me."

"If I die, she'll inherit everything. Marry her. Let her live how she likes. But use the money to take care of my mother and all of our people."

Silas groaned as the carriage rocked again. "Can you be any more insufferable?"

"Oh, I'm sure he can be," Baz chimed in.

"And you should let her go to school," Jack said. "She got into the university. She deserves to go."

"*Let* her! Have you met Selina?" Silas pushed at his glasses indignantly. "You're assuming she'll have me."

"Unfortunately, she'll have no choice. She has to marry in order to inherit the estate. Unless you think she has other suitors?"

Color spread across Silas's cheeks. "Baz, your flask please."

Baz reached into his cloak and untwisted the cap. He took a long drink himself before handing it over. "I'd like to not be too sober when facing a demon."

Silas considered this, then took only a small sip. "I, in fact, would."

With great reluctance, he passed the flask to Jack, who drank deeply, his throat raw and burning from it. But he liked the way the warmth spread through him instantly.

"What of your engagement?" Silas asked, his tone bitter. "What will I tell your fiancée should you die?"

"You never told us how you liked her," Baz said, leaning forward, his nose redder than it had been minutes before. "Is she beautiful?"

Jack thought of her liquid gray eyes and the pout of her pretty lips. "Very."

Baz nudged his knee. "Go on."

"She's frank, blunt. She's intelligent. I think she would run my father's businesses better than I ever could."

"*Your* businesses," Silas said quietly. "They're yours now."

His heart sputtered as if kicked twice as fast as the rhythmic clop of the horses' hooves battering the street.

"If she has a head for business, perhaps you still ought to marry her," Silas said.

We're pawns. My father uses me, moves me around.

"I don't think she wants to be married," he said quietly.

"Wouldn't matter. The terms would be negotiated between you and her father," Baz said.

Silas scowled. "If Phin could hear you…"

Their eyes slid toward the corpse and darted away. They could pretend he was drunk if they did not look too close.

Maybe he can hear us. Jack didn't think he was the only one who thought this.

"I'll not have anyone who doesn't want me," he said.

The carriage lurched to a stop. The horses huffed.

The door opened and Albert appeared, his breath fogging in front of his face. "We're here."

Baz and Albert carried Phineas between them. Silas remained at Jack's side, supporting most of his weight.

It was the mist that Jack didn't like. It hung over the ground as thick as clouds. For that reason, strange shapes danced in the corners of his eyes as they moved deeper into the dark.

"Where are we supposed to go, exactly?" Albert asked.

"To the river," Jack said.

"I hear it," Baz said. "This way."

Baz was right. The mist broke suddenly and a swift river coursed in front of them, cutting off their path. It flowed from their right to the left, disappearing out of sight.

"How do you know all of this?" Albert said.

What could Jack tell them? Would he tell them that once upon a time he'd wanted to sell his soul? It had seemed like a fair trade, if, at the end of the day, his father would be gone and his mother, sister, and himself free from his anger and mistreatment.

"Lots of talk in the taverns," Jack said. "I listen to as much gossip as anyone."

The silence of the misty field unnerved Jack. Where were the crickets? The toads. The insufferable mewling cats? It was as if the mist absorbed all sound around them, leaving only an unnatural silence.

When an owl finally hooted, it only thickened the dreadful atmosphere.

"Albert, may I see your dagger?" Jack opened his palm. "The one you keep in your boot."

"Planning to sacrifice yourself here and now?" The fear in his voice was palpable.

"Easy," Baz said. "It's the mist. It'll get inside your head."

Albert lowered Phineas to the ground and turned away.

"I need to cut myself. It's blood that calls a demon," Jack said.

That's what the drunk man in the tavern had told him.

"I'm not giving you a dagger. I might need it," Albert said.

Jack opened his fist and his magic leapt forward, surging toward Albert's boot. It hit the leather and the dagger jumped out. With a flourish of his hand, Jack seized it.

"Give it back!" Albert said. "What if a demon does come? Would you have me be unarmed?"

Jack threw him one of his pistols. "If a demon comes, use this."

He handed the other to Baz.

Silas gasped, his hold tightening on Jack's waist.

Jack turned and understood why.

The mist had turned red, parting in the middle as a gust of air rushed past them.

In the center of this makeshift aisle, a girl slid forward.

Not a girl, his mind chanted. A demon.

With long flame-red hair falling down her back.

In one hand she held a gleaming sword. The other was empty yet no less terrifying, with her long nails that reminded Jack of black talons. As she advanced, her hips shifted with a cat's liquid grace, but what truly scandalized him was how little she wore.

It seemed all young ladies of his acquaintance were hidden under yards of muslin, satin, silk, or taffeta, with the exception of his sister, of course.

This one wore only leather that fit her body as tightly as the gloves across Albert's knuckles. Jack was entirely too aware of the shape of her.

The shoulders, knees, and elbows had small metal spikes on them.

Her hands too were gloved, though the fingers were exposed.

It was the golden eyes that captivated him.

"Maybe they were wrong about the blood," Silas murmured. "You didn't even have to cut yourself."

Perhaps that's why the demon looked disappointed. "Who are you?"

"Jack," he said reflexively.

She arched a brow. "*Jack?*"

She looked at each of them in turn, her eyes falling at last on Phineas. "Someone had too much fun tonight."

Her accent was strange. Not like those from town, nor from the countryside. Where had she come from?

No, you idiot, he thought. *She's from some demon world.*

"Can you bring him back?" Jack asked. He tried not to let his desperation coat every word.

She grinned. "To my place? Sure. They're as much fun dead as they are alive. Sometimes more."

Jack's jaw clenched. "Can you bring him back to *life?*"

"Why would I?" she cooed, her eyes raking his flesh like sharp nails. "What do you have to offer me for such a thing, *Jack?*"

Jack flicked his wrist and the cube appeared. "I'll give you this if you bring him back."

Her eyes seemed to brighten, nearly glowing. Was that possible?

When she spoke, her voice was low, almost a growl. "Where did you get that?"

"From the bastard who tried to kill me. I'll give it to you if you save my friend."

Please, he thought. *Please take it.*

Her sword caught fire, flaming to life. Shivering orange danced sensuously up each side of the metal blade.

Albert stepped in front of him, raising the pistol.

"It's not for you, *pigeons*," she said with the same catlike grin.

Jack pushed him aside so he could see.

The flame of her sword turned blue as she held it above Phineas's chest. She closed her eyes, tilting her head to one side as if listening for something.

A long, low whistle slid past her pursed lips, the sound

haunting. Melodic, tragic, and it seemed to ring through Jack's mind and body.

The sword flashed white, before settling to the same cerulean shade.

A blue flame separated, lifting. It pulsed in the air just above the blade.

"Go on then," she whispered to it. "They want you back."

As if it had a mind of its own, this blue flame leapt into Phineas's chest, disappearing on impact.

A heartbeat of damp silence followed.

Then Phineas moaned. Baz and Albert rushed to his side. Even Silas released Jack so that he could kneel down and inspect the result.

Jack stayed where he was, his eyes on the demon.

"Where am I?" Phineas stared up at the black sky above. "I was just—I was just in a field like this, but it wasn't dark. It was bright and there were—"

"Shhh," Albert said, trying to help him to sitting. "Don't talk."

"Aye," Baz added. "Don't hurt yerself."

The demon returned Jack's gaze. "Satisfied?"

Jack handed over the cube. She regarded it with sharp eyes, and then, much as Jack had, she flexed her wrist and it was gone.

She winked at Jack and turned to leave. "Stay out of trouble, boys."

"Wait!" Jack called after her. "There's something else."

She looked over her shoulder, the flame on her sword sputtering out. Thin gray smoke rose up to meet the mist.

"Oh?" she asked with a cocked head.

Jack wet his lips and conjured his courage. "There's a

demon that killed my father and almost killed my mother. He said he will come back for me. For that cube."

"Yes, we do that," she said. "Until we get what we want."

"I can't fight a demon on my own."

"No, you can't," she said, propping the blade against her leather-clad shoulder. "Though it might be fun to watch."

Anger coursed under his skin. He wasn't in the mood to be mocked or teased. To be belittled as his father had always belittled him. His body ran hot.

"Will you help me or not?" he asked through clenched teeth.

She shrugged. "We're talking about another bargain. Do you have a second cube in that cloak of yours?"

Her eyes fell.

"Or something in your trousers, perhaps?"

"No, but I know who does. Help me find him—"

Albert seized his arm. "What are you doing?"

Jack threw his magic out, knocking Albert back. With a wave of his hand, he cast an impenetrable protective wall around his friends. It shimmered in the mist.

"No!" they cried.

Another flick of his wrist and they fell silent, their cries absorbed by the crystalline ball encasing them.

Jack couldn't do this with their voices in his ears. He was already close to losing his nerve. One sensible word from them would be enough to ignite his cowardice.

He felt the three of them calling their own magic, fighting against his.

Jack pushed harder.

Please don't fight me, he thought. *This is my mistake. I will fix it.*

They pushed again.

He fought back, collapsing to his knees with the effort of it.

"Aren't you an interesting boy," the demon cooed. She passed Jack, crossing to the magical barrier. She ran a hand over its surface. It glimmered under her black talons, but it did not fail.

Jack was glad of that.

"I need your help," he said calmly, hoping that his fear would not betray him. "I can't do this on my own."

She leaned close to his face, so close that Jack could see now that her eyes weren't gold shining in the dark. They were flames.

Flickering candle flames.

"Be clear, Jack," she whispered to his lips. "What is it you want?"

"I want to know why Lord Silver betrayed me. Why has he made a pact with this demon? Why was my father killed and nearly my mother? What does that demon want with me?"

"You want answers," she stated plainly.

"Yes, I want answers. And I want to destroy the demon who attacked us so it can never come back and hurt anyone I love ever again."

"Do you?" she said coyly.

"Can you help me?" he asked, sweat forming on his brow. "Will you help me?"

"Sure," she said in that same playful way. "But not for free, and you have so many requests. Bring your friend back from the dead, get your answers, kill a demon. How will you pay for all of that, Jack?"

"Phineas I paid for."

"Yes, but what about the other two aims?" When she

grinned, Jack saw her fangs. How like a cat she was, even down to the pointy teeth.

"The demon we seek has another cube, just like the one you hold, but it's gold, not silver. Help me kill him and it's yours."

"And for the truth you seek? What would you pay for that?"

His heart was beating so hard in his chest he felt woozy from it. "W-what do you want?"

Her eyes bored into his. "A good meal."

He bit his lip. "I know a lovely tavern in town."

She laughed and tilted her head. "You know I don't eat what you eat."

He did. "I suppose it's me, then, that you'd like to eat?"

Her hand went to her chest in mock offense. "I haven't eaten human flesh in a very long time. Though you are right, a pound of flesh was a common enough payment, once upon a time."

"Then what is it? What do you want?"

"I want your fire," she said, and traced his damp cheek with a talon. "All that flame coursing through you. I would love to eat it *all up*."

Your fire.

She could only mean his soul. He'd seen the blue flame leaping from her sword to Phineas's chest. But *soul* was a human word. Perhaps fire was what demons called it.

"My fire," he repeated.

"Yes," she said. "Think carefully before you promise it to me, Jack. Once you give it up, you can't have it back, do you understand?"

"I understand," he said, his mouth going dry.

A surge of magic shoved against him. His friends were

working together, trying to break free. Their desperation to stop him made them stronger.

He was sweating, his head pounding. But his wall held.

Her eyes brightened, nearly glowing again. "Your fire in exchange for all the answers you seek. And I get the cube when I kill the one who hunts you. Do you agree to this price?"

Her voice was low, almost sweet. He'd talked to many a lover with such a voice.

He turned to gaze at his friends. Albert and Baz beat their fists wildly against the wall. Silas held Phineas's head in his lap, his face a mask of fear.

He could not hear their voices, but he saw the word *no* on their lips clearly enough.

Jack took a deep breath. "You can't turn on me, or hurt anyone I care about. Everyone I love is not to be harmed. If I tell you not to hurt someone, you have to obey me. That's part of our deal."

He couldn't stand the idea of losing control of his demon—*Oh god, is she mine already?*—the way Silver had lost control of his.

"I take issue with the word *obey*, but I understand. And I have a condition of my own. When I want your fire, you'll give it to me without question. *Any* time. The *moment* I ask."

He would never know when his life was to end, when this creature would reach out and suck his soul from him. He supposed that was not so different than the average life.

The time of death was always uncertain for a man.

He drew a slow breath. "I agree to these conditions."

She grabbed him with her free hand and lifted him to his feet.

Lord, how strong she is.

Will she kill me now? Will she—

But she didn't sink those fangs into his throat or rip his soul from his body.

She kissed him.

Her leather armor pressed against his cold skin as she covered his mouth with her own.

He felt the magic of the kiss, sliding over his skin, licking him like a great cat's tongue.

Then the burn came. Hot and terrible at his throat.

He opened his mouth to scream against the pain but she swallowed the sound, slipping her tongue into his mouth, caressing it with her own. One of her fangs cut his lip and the taste of blood bloomed.

She released him then, pulling herself back with effort. Her eyes were glazed with pleasure as she grinned down at him where he had collapsed to his knees again.

His fingers went to his throbbing neck and found the flesh was raised, etched with a strange circular mark.

A devil's seal, he realized. *I am claimed.*

As the demon withdrew her magic, the last of Jack's strength went with it.

His magic wall fell.

Albert was on him in an instant. He grabbed Jack's shoulders and shook him.

"You idiot!" His cheeks were wet with his tears. "You ass! What have you done?"

Then he saw the mark on his throat and his words sputtered.

"She's branded 'im like a cow," Baz said.

"And will eat him like one," Silas added.

"Demon!" Albert screamed as if she weren't right there enjoying the spectacle. "Make a trade."

She laughed. "What a profitable night this has turned out to be."

"Whatever he promised you, I'll pay and more. Take me. Let Jack be. He's suffered enough."

She arched a brow. "Has he? It must be why he's so sweet."

She made a great show of licking her lips.

"No," Jack said. "I said none of the people I loved can be harmed. No one pays but me. You swore on it. It's in the pact."

The demon shrugged at Albert as if to say, *See? Sorry I can't be of more help.*

"You promised..." Jack's voice faded. The darkness was pressing in on him from all sides.

It was the cold.

So cold.

His back hit the damp earth, exhaustion overtaking him at last.

CHAPTER 10

How well can two know each other when they speak in letters and hide their faces?

But I would know you. I would.

Give me a name. Give me a name and I will find you in the light of day.

— FROM A LETTER ADDRESSED TO
THE PEACOCK

Jack

— FROM A LETTER ADDRESSED TO
LORD SILVER

When Jack woke, he was in Ansley Hall. Specifically, he was in his father's study. Soft light poured through the open window, the noise from the street carried in on the breeze. The desk was piled with books, but the seat was empty.

His father was not here. The only sign of him was the

family ring, the gold-and-ruby crest which had split open Jack's cheek days before, resting on top of one of the linen hardcovers.

The room was whole. It was not blackened or scorched.

"I'm dreaming," he said, lifting the ring and turning it in the light. "I must be. This room burned."

"This isn't a dream," a voice said. "It's a memory."

Jack found the demon at the door.

"Whose memory?" he asked.

"Yours," she said.

"You're in my mind?"

"It's what demons do best," she said with the same mischievous grin. She holstered her sword in the sheath fixed to her back.

"I don't recall giving you permission to muck about in mine."

"You did the moment you made a pact with me." She took the ring from him and turned it in the light as he had. "That mark makes you mine. I own you until this is over. I will use you the way one uses their property, and I will protect you the way one protects their property. Do you understand?"

Mine. He supposed he did understand.

Yet it was hard to believe this was nothing but a memory. Usually his memories were hazy wisps, barely more real than dreams. Strangely colored imprints of strong emotion.

This room, however, was very real. Down to the smell of horse shit from the street. His father's lingering cologne. The dusty books. "If this is my mind, where is my body?"

"Somewhere safe," she said. "Much to your friends' dismay."

She flicked her eyes up to meet his. "Before you ask, no,

I did not hurt them. I simply took you and left. Well, I watched your friends until they were in the carriage again. Devil's Field isn't a place to leave four boys unattended. *Then* I took you and left."

"Men," Jack corrected.

"At what age does a boy become a man in this era?"

"One and twenty."

She snorted. "Forgive me. You all look quite young to me."

"You can't make deals with them," Jack said.

"I'm more interested in you, Jack. When compared to your boon companions, you're more my...taste."

She licked her lips. The flash of her fangs made his throat click.

What have you done? Albert had asked. *You fool.*

His heart ached.

How quick he'd been ready to sell his soul for Jack's.

He's suffered enough.

"I have others I love," he began. "I—"

"Rest easy, Jack," she said, holding the ring up to the light. She was distracted. "Love carries its own mark. I will know who you love even if you do not tell me. To your credit, you worded the pact well. They're safe. From me, at least."

She held the ring out toward him.

"Do you know what this is?" she asked.

"My father's signet ring."

"And this mark?" she asked, turning the red gem in the light. It brightened from a deep crimson to a ruby red.

"It's our family crest. It's an infinity symbol. Meant to symbolize our longevity."

"Is that so?"

She slipped it on a finger and regarded it.

His anger rose up in him, building to a drumbeat at his temples. "Take it off."

"Why?" Her nostrils flared as if scenting something. "Isn't your father dead?"

"It's not yours."

She grinned. "It isn't yours either. It isn't even here."

He pushed back against the heat building inside him and tried to gather his concentration. He could argue that the ring *was* his, now that his father was dead. But the truth was he would never wear that ring. He despised it. He hoped his father had been buried with it.

"Tell me about this room," the demon said. "It seems important and yet you loathe it. Why?"

"It's my father's study," he said.

"As you said. What happened here?"

"This is where my father was found dead, a sword through his chest. The demon killed him, then set fire to the room."

She shook her head. "No, before that."

"I don't—"

She snapped her fingers and the room sprang to life. One by one, each of Jack's memories in this godforsaken room replayed themselves in reverse. Jack getting slapped for refusing to be married. Jack thrown against the wall because he admonished his father for cheating on his mother. Again when his father hit a servant, and in a rage, Jack had hit him back. Only provoking a worse beating.

As each scene played, Jack got younger and younger.

"I don't want to see this." He tried to pull free from her iron grip.

"Then close your eyes."

He did. Her hand remained firm on his arm. It felt so

real. Was that a trick of the mind? Or a demon trick? Was she using magic to recreate his world?

It was a long time before she said, "I see now. So that's who's been crying. You had hidden him so deep."

Jack opened his eyes.

In the middle of the floor was Jack, eight years old, on his hands and knees beside his father's desk. His face was a mess of snot and tears.

His father was bent over him, the belt in his hand bloodied with Jack's flesh. His face a mask of barely controlled rage.

When the man moved, Jack saw the wet welts criss-crossing the boy's skin as if a giant beast had tried to tear his spine out with its claws.

That was the first time. The day everything changed for me, he thought. The day Jack began to see his father for what he really was.

"A cruel father. They're wretched creatures and yet *oh so good* for business," she said as boy Jack faded from the room, leaving the once-blooded carpet flawless again.

Jack squeezed his eyes shut until there was only silence.

He turned toward the high, sunlit window.

"What was your father's name?" the demon asked behind him.

"My father was the Baron Talbot Siran."

She snorted. "Sounds made up. He looks more like a James to me."

Jack's impatience doubled. "Don't be ridiculous."

"Or a George, maybe?" She acted as if she hadn't heard. "What was his father's name?"

"Charles."

"His father's father's?"

"Harold. Why does this matter?"

She tossed him the ring. He was forced to catch it in the air. He managed it with cupped hands.

"Look at that crest again," she said. "An infinity symbol, you say?"

Jack had never been allowed to inspect the ring so closely. He wasn't sure he believed his mind was able to reconstruct it, if all of this was in fact the creation of his mind. His father had guarded the ring the way a dragon guards its gold.

But as he squinted at the small symbol set in red, he noticed something for the first time. The symbol wasn't rounded at its edges. It was pointed.

"They're cubes," he said. "Two cubes. Stacked one on top of each other, meeting at a corner."

"Good eye, Jack." The demon's golden eyes brightened. "It seems to me that a man and a *demon* came to your house. The Day Box was taken. Only you steal the Night Box in return."

"The Day Box and the Night Box? Is that what they're called?"

She tilted her head as if he were an amusing, if stupid, kitten. "Isn't that what I said?"

"What makes the boxes important?"

"Solomon boxes can do many things. With them you can see what has been, what might be. With the two together, any dimension is accessible. Any place, any time."

"Are there only two?"

"That I've seen," she said. "Each box can open over sixty ways."

"*Sixty ways!*" Jack cried. "Impossible."

He thought of the way he'd twisted the cube in his hands, pressed its etchings to reveal the unseen pockets around him.

"I suspect you did not have the Day Box in your possession for long."

"The Day Box is gold? Then it's the Night Box I gave you."

"It's a good thing you gave it to me. Night dimensions are precarious. Had you opened the box even once, who knows what you could have let out."

"What did Lord Silver want with the boxes?"

"Lord Silver," she said with a little laugh. "Another made-up name."

At least in this point, she was correct.

"It's hard to say," she said, taking the ring and pocketing it. "The Day Box can be used for many things. I want to see this Lord Silver. When do you remember seeing him last?"

"In my bedroom."

His face felt hot.

"Don't be shy," the demon said, and hooked an arm possessively around his waist. "Show me."

The study dissolved, and in its place, Jack's bedroom formed around them. They weren't met with the same bright daylight. Instead, it was moonlight that illuminated everything in a milky glow. The bright-faced moon itself was framed by the two large windows overlooking the balcony.

Then came the unmistakable scuff of boots on stone. One of the doors creaked open and Silver slipped into the room. A chilly breeze followed him in, throwing aside the curtain.

"That's him," Jack said.

The moment froze, Silver's cloak caught mid-motion behind him as his hand left the handle.

The demon circled him, her eyes raking the young man from head to toe.

"*This* is Lord Silver?" she asked.

"Yes."

The demon sniffed the air the way Jack sometimes did outside the best bakery in town.

"*So* much magic. This one smells worse of Hellsbane than you did. Why the name Lord Silver? For the mask or the eyes?"

"The mask. What could he possibly want with the Day Box? How did he get ahold of it? What's it for?"

She raised her brows. "Let's ask Lord Silver."

Jack's hopes lifted. "Can you find him?"

A smile tugged at the demon's lips. "While they have the Day Box? No."

He frowned, stepping after her onto the moonlit balcony. "But you said—"

"The Day Box offers the advantage of remaining unseen. Our best chance is forcing them to come to us. I know who controls the roads."

"The roads?"

"You like to parrot me, Jack. Do you want a cracker?"

He scowled at her.

She placed a hand on the stone railing and peered down into the dark. "Lord Veemos makes the roads. He'll set this Silver on our path if we ask."

"Is Veemos a demon?"

"You'd best say *Lord* Veemos unless you want to meet with misfortune. And no. He and his sister are something else. Something older than demons."

"Unless he takes gold, I've nothing else to bargain with. I can't make another deal."

She threw one leg over the edge of the balcony. The shadows cut across her face, giving her a half mask of black. On that side only her golden eye shone.

"No need. He owes me."

"Leave with me, Jack. Please," Silver said behind them.

Jack's ears burned.

"Leave with me, Jack. *Please*," the demon teased in a high falsetto.

"I want you out of my head," Jack said.

She fisted the front of his clothes, balling his vest in her grip. "Then *jump*."

With a rough tug, he was pulled over the stone railing and into the pitch black.

JACK'S EYES SNAPPED OPEN. IT WAS JARRING TO BE falling one minute, then the next, find himself flat on his back, staring up at a bright blue sky, unharmed.

A river lapped gently to his left as he sat up. The grass around him was gray and faded. It bent under the weight of morning dew.

He must be awake. His body throbbed and his eyes and throat still felt tender.

"Are we in Devil's Field?" he asked.

It was too bright and there was no mist, but the river gave it away.

"Yes," the demon said. "Let's get moving. The longer we wait, the further ahead they will get."

They, Jack assumed, were Silver and his demon.

"You said Veemos—"

"*Lord* Veemos. Do you want to die horribly?"

"You said Lord Veemos was going to lead them straight to us. If that's the case, why are we in a hurry?"

She sighed, as if the task of explaining the situation to a simpleton would be too great an endeavor to undertake.

"It will take time to find Lord Veemos," she said. "He can be difficult to track down."

"What of his sister? Is she easier to find?"

"Pray you never meet his sister. It may very well be the last thing you ever do. This way."

She nodded toward a dirt path leading them away from the river.

Jack stood and stretched. The mark on his neck throbbed. He lifted a hand and traced the strange circular symbol with his finger.

"What did you do to me?" he asked.

She threw a glance over her shoulder. "Where we are going, you'll be glad to have it."

"Will it always be there?" he asked.

"Until your price is paid."

Until I'm dead, you mean.

Jack fell into step beside her. It took a few minutes for his muscles to warm and the stiffness in his limbs to abate. There wasn't much to draw his eye.

There was the demon, her hair a flare of red in this barren field, and the dark trees running along the right side.

There was also the gray river. But it grew smaller with each step.

"We're walking away from town," he marveled. "We're actually on the other side of the river."

"Did you think we would find Lord Veemos in Lunden-wick? At a tavern, perhaps?"

She tossed her red hair over a shoulder. Jack couldn't remember the last time he'd seen a woman's hair down and free. In bed, most likely.

"How long will we be walking?" he asked.

"As long as it takes," she said.

"Will it all be flat like this?"

"*Jack.*" She stopped and turned. "This may be a *very* long journey, and I'm not sure you will survive it if you are going to ask me a question every step of the way."

"Last question. I promise." He pouted his lips as he often did when he pressed his luck.

She rolled her golden eyes at him. "Ask."

"What's your name?"

"I have many names."

"What should I call you?"

"One is usually named by those who bore them. Demons bear themselves."

"Then what do you call yourself?"

"It depends," she said, "on what I'm doing at the time."

He considered this. "Fire eater, then?"

She snorted. "Sure."

"Maybe Fire for short?"

"As you wish. Neither offends me."

"Should it be Lady Fire?"

The sound that came from her made him stop in his tracks. A menacing chill slid up the back of his neck. It took several moments for him to realize she was laughing.

"There is nothing that makes me a *lady*, Jack. Only the species of man concern themselves with such empty demarcations."

"Then why is Lord Veemos, Lord Veemos. Is he a man?"

"You said no more questions. You'd best keep your promises if you want me to keep mine."

There was something about the way she said the word *promise*. The air blew harder. The cold bit his cheeks. If he wasn't mistaken, they were moving away from the cool autumn of town toward a darker winter.

It didn't seem possible that only a few minutes of

walking could change a season. But that was frost on the grass now, not dew. And with each step, the sky was fading from blue to white.

A winter sky.

He began to think of Tromwell's father. The man who never returned after bargaining for the resurrection of his son. Had he followed a demon into this wood?

Many had speculated what might be on the other side of Devil's Field. None but the most desperate had tried to uncover the truth of it, and he knew of none who had returned with a tale.

His heart clenched as three crestfallen faces flashed in his mind.

What have you done? Albert had asked, with those accusing tears in his eyes.

How could he ever explain to them that after all these years, after all the times they had rallied around him in his darkest moments, this price felt wholly inadequate.

Forgive me.

The path continued on. Fire walked the packed-dirt road as if she'd walked it a million times before. No matter how long they marched, neither her energy nor her stride ever waned.

Yet when he looked around, he saw the exact same thing. A dark wood stretched on his right, the trees dense and menacing. To his left, the river. Ahead, the worn path toward a barren horizon.

I can't stand it, he thought.

Yet they walked on.

If we don't get somewhere soon, I'll go mad.

There were no forks. No deviations. Only the sound of their boots pounding the dusty earth, powder rising with each step.

If something doesn't change—heaven help me. Please let something change. Anything.

A black bird flew over his left shoulder. Its shadow cut across the ground, wavering as if made of water. Black wings snapped open and the bird dropped down in front of them, landing directly in their path.

It was quite large for a crow, Jack thought. Maybe it was a raven.

Fire stopped. One hand went to her sword. "Hello, Malice."

The bird opened its wings and then flapped. A puff of black smoke billowed, engulfing it. When the smoke disappeared, the bird was gone. In its place was a boy, no more than twelve. His hair was as black as the bird's feathers had been, his eyes cavernous pits. His lips were thin and tucked into a mischievous corner of his cheek.

His clothes were a patchwork of black. Shades that were nearly gray and others so dark they seemed to absorb the light around them. It was as if he'd tried to repair the same shirt and trousers for centuries with whatever scraps he could find.

"Demon," he said in a boy's voice. "What do you have there? Fresh meat?"

"Do you want to pay the price for knowing my business?" Fire asked in turn.

He tilted his head much like Jack had seen the demon do.

That's how they imitate us, he realized.

From the boy's right ear, a long earring dangled. It caught the light and sparked. In fact, much of his clothing was covered in shiny baubles that flashed as he moved.

"I'm only surprised," he said with a shrug. "It's been so long since I've seen your mark on anybody."

His eyes were on Jack's throat.

"I thought you'd lost your taste for it, given what happened last time."

"Mayhem. *Don't,*" Fire said in a low warning.

"She won't hurt him," the crow boy said. "Much."

Fire turned to Jack and her golden eyes narrowed. "What?"

But she wasn't looking at Jack. Her gaze went past his right knee.

He followed it only to discover a fox, mouth open in mid-bite.

Jack jerked his leg away.

The fox's jaw snapped shut where Jack's leg had been the moment before. But the timing was so slow, it seemed as if the beast was only taunting him.

Could foxes do that?

"I never spoil *your* fun," the fox said with a flick of its tail.

"She's had no fun to spoil," said the crow boy.

"As dull as I remember," said the fox. It trotted to the crow boy's side, blocking the path.

"It's talking," Jack said, inching closer to Fire. "Why are they talking? Are they demons?"

"You've always had a soft spot for the bright ones," the fox said. Its tail curled around one of the crow boy's legs.

"We'll see if he's bright," the crow boy said, and then laughed, loosing a high cackle.

From his pocket, the boy pulled a clear sphere. His fingers pressed against its iridescent surface. When he turned it, it caught the sunlight until the sphere seemed to glow.

No. It *was* glowing.

Fire sighed, clearly annoyed. "Jack. I hope you know how to listen to your heart."

"What?" Jack's stomach tightened. He didn't like how still she'd gone beside him. "This hardly seems like the time for worldly wisdom."

Fire stepped toward the fox and crow boy menacingly. "I'll remind you both of what will happen if you damage my prop—"

Fire's words were cut in half as the boy lifted the sphere and she disappeared in a puff of smoke.

"What have you done with her?" Jack demanded.

The crow boy showed too many teeth. "You can have her back. We haven't hurt her."

"I doubt you could," Jack said imperiously.

At this, the fox's fur bristled. The crow boy put one grubby hand on its shoulder for comfort.

"Are you sure you want her back? Maybe we just did you a favor," the boy said.

"I need her," Jack countered. He had the dagger he'd stolen from Albert, but he wasn't sure what good it would do against these demons.

"Need her for what?" the fox asked.

"She's so *expensive*." The crow boy's fingers twisted a bauble on the front of his shirt. "Perhaps we can help you for less?"

"For *much* less," the fox repeated. "And there are two of us. That doubles your bargain."

Jack's hand went to his throat. "No."

"We haven't even named our price!" the fox protested. "How do you know you won't prefer it?"

"I'll do it for your eye," the crow boy said. "I love eyes."

Jack's stomach twisted. The sphere in the boy's grip was red and glowing. Was Fire really trapped in there?

"I'll not give you my eye," Jack said.

"It's only one!" the boy protested. "How many can you possibly need? You'll still have the other."

"I'll help you for a leg," the fox said, her grin cheerful, almost like a dog's. "The left or the right. It makes no difference to me."

"If not the eye, perhaps that branded bit of flesh at your throat. Oh, I'd love to get my hands on that!" The boy bounced up and down delightedly. He came up onto his toes. "Say the word and I'll take it right off you. Then you won't have to worry a bit about her."

The boy lifted the sphere a little higher.

"*Yes*," the fox said encouragingly. "Solve all your problems, that would."

"*No*," Jack said again, more firmly this time. "Give her back now. Please."

The fox flicked her tail. "How about if it were just a *bite* of leg?"

It was true that Jack had little experience with demons, and all of it acquired in the last few hours of his life. Yet something told him they needed his consent. They needed him to agree to this game somehow.

Jack opened his mouth to refuse them a third time, but the crow boy stopped him with a raised hand.

"Think hard before you say that." His eyes were wet black. Jack saw his own face reflected back at him in miniature. "We won't hurt you half as badly as she will. What we will do will feel like a mercy compared to what she has planned for you. Do you have any idea what she is?"

"A demon, same as you."

They laughed. "Not like us."

There was something in his tone that rang true. Something that convinced Jack that yes, actually, he would rather lose an eye or his leg than have Fire devour him. That their teeth—both of their jaws combined—might not be *half* as sharp as hers.

But Jack did not relent.

"I won't make a deal with you," he said, and with a flourish of his hand, he produced Albert's dagger and pointed it at them. "Now give her back."

He knew his blade was unimpressive compared to Fire's flaming sword, and yet he hadn't expected them to look positively excited to see it.

The fox's tail went rigid. The crow too was unable to hide the gleam in his eye.

"I won't hurt you unless you give me no choice. I only want you to give her back."

The boy croaked another laugh and tossed the sphere into the air. "Give her back? No, no. You must *win* her back."

The fox leapt and caught it in her mouth, before landing on soft black paws.

Then she was off, running as fast as her four legs could carry her. To Jack's dismay, that was very fast.

"Stop!" he cried. "Come back here!"

It was too late. The fox was halfway across the frosty field, her nose pointing straight at the menacing woods ahead.

In another flash of black smoke, the boy disappeared from the road, leaving no trace that he'd been there at all. A shadow cut across the sky above Jack and a single black feather floated down to the grass.

Jack had no choice but to run after them.

CHAPTER 11

The most terrible part of it is that in my weakest moments I believe him. I believe he would take me, as I am. His heart is a true one. You can see it in the way his friends look upon him. How all draw near him like a warm fire on a cold night. And he offers such warmth to me?

Me? Of all creatures?

I do not deserve it. He will know this, should he ever discover the depths of my treachery.

— FROM THE PERSONAL DIARY OF
THE ONE CALLED "LORD SILVER"

Jack ran until his lungs burned. He bent, coughing between his legs. His energy was leaving him too quickly. The perspiration was already wetting his brow. Every direction he looked, he saw only the crowded trees, the damp ground, and shifting shadows.

I should still be in the hospital, he thought. *Not chasing demon children through the woods.*

I can't stay here either. I need to get Fire back, his mind countered.

He began walking again but more slowly now, his breath still puffing laboriously in front of his face.

He hadn't imagined the cold or the sudden onset of winter. Perhaps the demon world spun faster than Jack's and their autumn was but a heartbeat.

Or maybe it was always winter here.

He strained to hear anything that might let him know where the fox and crow had gone. Only the whisper of branches and rustle of leaves answered back.

A flash of a red tail caught the corner of his eye and he whirled, running before he even fully saw the fox leap from behind a mossy tree trunk.

When he reached the spot where he'd seen her, only her laughter remained.

A crow cawed, its cackle joining the fox's gleeful yip.

A black feather drifted down and struck the shoulder of his cloak. He brushed it away.

I need only catch one of them. If I do, I can bargain for the sphere.

A crow's strident caw filled his ears as he bent to pick up a second feather.

Another flash of fox tail pulled him deeper and deeper into the woods.

As the shadows grew thicker, so did Jack's certainty that there was something else in the forest with him.

He stopped, three feathers in his grip, and listened. It was his heart hammering in his chest.

Or the trees? No.

Not the whisper of leaves... *Whispering.*

The building murmur grew with each of Jack's steps.

Louder and louder until it was no longer the unintelligible raucous of a tavern hall but a distinct voice.

This way, Jack. This way!

It was Fire's voice.

She must be trying to help me, he thought, and darted toward the sound. He dodged the trees as they leaned toward him.

Over here, Jack. Over here!

Now she was back where he'd come from. He retraced his steps, trying his best not to stumble over lifting tree roots and snapping undergrowth.

Here!

No, here!

This way!

With each urgent call, Jack darted off onto a new path. He followed each voice in turn, each voice that seemed to know better than he did where he was going and how to get what he wanted.

He went on like this until his face and neck were damp with sweat and his chest burned.

Through here! Fire said, or a voice just like hers.

"I can't!" he cried out. He collapsed onto his knees in the middle of a beaten path. "I can't. I'm exhausted."

He used one corner of his cloak to wipe the sweat from his eyes. His lips were salty with it and his chest hurt from the effort of breathing.

The cool air was a blessing for his sore eyes, but not for his cheeks, which felt red and chapped under its assault.

Jack, hurry!

"I can't," he said again, and collapsed onto the flat of his back.

He had no choice but to rest. He'd become useless on his feet.

He closed his eyes, putting his head against the dirt.

When he opened them again, the forest was no longer bathed in afternoon light.

It was night.

Cold white moonlight fell across his boots, his hands, his clothes.

He sat up with a start as an immediate dread filled him. How long had he slept? How in the world could he have fallen asleep in a strange forest? Even a child knows better than to do such a thing.

"Oh no," a voice said. "Oh, you've really gone and done it now."

Jack twisted in each direction, expecting to see either Malice—that's what Fire had called the crow boy, wasn't it? —or Mayhem, the fox with a fondness for human legs.

But it was neither. It was a tall thin girl with a gaunt face. Her pale hair looked as if it hadn't been washed for many days. As if she had no time for such frivolous things.

The same could be said for eating. There wasn't much meat to her bones at all. It seemed her body was little more than a thinly wrapped skeleton that had covered itself shabbily and only out of the barest sense of politeness.

"You're lost," the girl said, her large eyes bright and unblinking.

"I'm not," Jack said reflexively.

"You are," she countered. "*Here* of all places."

"It's not like I want to be here," he argued.

"You lay down, didn't you?" she asked with an arched brow.

"They took my—" He broke off.

What could he call Fire? Not his friend, since she was most certainly going to eat him alive. Associate? Seemed odd, given the intimacy of their relationship.

"They took my demon," he said.

"Your demon?" She laughed as if he'd just said the most ridiculous thing. "Would it also be *your* hyena? *Your* lion? *Your* bloody Jack the Ripper?"

"I have to go after her." He pulled himself to standing.

"All right. But she isn't in there."

"Of course she is. I heard her."

She laughed, humorless. "Shoddy ears you have then."

"I know what I heard."

"You heard a trick," she countered.

"Of course it's a trick. They're demon children. I imagine they're a thousand times more tricky than human children."

"No, what if your demon set you up," she said. "What if this whole 'let me help you get revenge' was a lie to get you into this forest, exhaust you to weakness, and then eat you while you screamed to death."

Jack couldn't tell from the expression on the girl's face if she was excited or horrified by the idea.

He shifted uncomfortably in place. "Do I know you? Why are you even here?"

She looked properly offended at this. "Just because you're lost in the woods doesn't mean you have to take it out on *me*."

Jack drew a slow breath.

"I'm Jack. It's a pleasure." He extended his hand.

"You're shaking hands with someone you aren't even sure you know in a dark, moonlit wood. It amazes me you aren't dead yet."

He let his hand fall. "What time is it? It feels quite late."

She harrumphed. Then her eyes doubled in size. "Shhh."

"I didn't—"

"It's starting again," she said, waving away his words. "Do you hear it?"

Jack stopped knocking the dirt from his clothes and strained his ears.

It was the whispering. It began again as a low hum, growing and building until it became the din of any tavern come supper time.

Jack! Jack, hurry!

Jack turned toward the voice—it was so close now—only to feel a cold, bony hand seize his arm.

"Don't go in there," the girl said. Her eyes were so large and close that Jack felt he was looking into a skeleton's deep black sockets.

He tried to pull his arm free, but he couldn't.

She's not human. She's not a girl at all.

Fear iced his spine.

Yet she didn't let go. If anything, her fingers bit deeper into his arm. "You know some demons bite humans on the neck and a venom goes into their bones, melts everything down to goop, and then they drink you. Like a beer."

"What do you know of beer?"

"Then they sell your skin at the auction. Some demons like to wear human skin, you know."

"Which are you?" he asked. "The skin-wearer or the biter?"

She pulled her hand back as if burned. "How dare you! I don't *wear* people. Though I do make my own clothes. You just can't trust anyone else to make them properly."

Given the state of the garments she was wearing, Jack believed her. Her tattered dress reminded him of the crow boy, with its strange patchwork of colors and patterns, overlaid without much care to its structure.

"Aren't you a demon?" he asked. "How do I know you

aren't trying to talk me to death so you can make a pillow out of my innards?"

She rolled her eyes and threw up her hands.

Jack! You're losing me.

Jack took a step away from his temporary sanctuary toward the woods.

"Listen to me," the girl insisted, her eyes reflecting the moonlight like a cat's. "You can't find her by following that voice. If you do, you'll only be lost again. Do you want to be lost in a demonic forest at night?"

"No," Jack said.

"Do you want to be eaten by a very hungry linden tree?"

"Well, *no*," Jack said.

"A werewolf? A witch? A wendigo?"

"I don't want to be eaten by anything," he said.

"And what if you cut yourself on a tree or something—you'll bleed."

"Hardly the worst—"

"The smell of blood will have a hundred demons on you before you can say, 'Which way would the witch wave if the witch wave could wave which?'"

Jack's head was buzzing. "What?"

"You have to think, Jack! Do I really have to spell everything out for you? Think of all the horrible things that could happen to you if you go blundering around in a dark wood at night!"

"Why should I when you're thinking enough for the both of us," he said.

The more she talked, the more he felt as if a current of electricity sputtered beneath his skin. Invisible ants ran up and down the back of his neck.

At least she didn't seem to want to hurt him. She only wanted to keep him here, safely on the path.

"But Fire—"

"You're not listening." The girl shook her head. "It's not her."

"But—"

"Try again. Listen with all your powers of concentration."

Jack rubbed at his forehead. A headache was forming behind his eyes. If this girl didn't leave him alone, Jack was going to lose his mind.

Jack.

Jack.

He strained, concentrating on the voice echoing through the trees.

Jack.

The voice warped, grew strange.

She was right. That wasn't Fire. There was something off about the cadence. Now that he heard it, he wasn't sure how he'd been so convinced before.

"They want to pull you off the path," the girl said, seemingly relieved that he was listening to her at last.

"Then how do I find her? I know that Malice and Mayhem have her."

"Listen better. And know what you want."

What I want.

Fire's face flashed in his mind, as she had looked in the moments before Malice pulled his little disappearing act.

I hope you know how to listen to your heart, she'd said.

"How does one listen to their heart?" Jack asked.

The girl smiled. It was a terrifying sight, all those teeth stretched in a near manic grin.

"Now you're asking the right questions."

Jack began by listening to his literal heartbeat, though he was certain this wasn't what Fire had meant. And yet, as he did, he felt something strange stir inside, moving and alive.

My magic.

He still had his magic in this weird place.

Could he use it to find Fire?

When he used magic, he usually visualized what he wanted clearly in his mind first. Down to the smallest details, and then after he held that image tight in his vision, he let go. The moment he released his hold on his desire, it sprang forth from him, fully formed and alive.

"I want to find Fire," he said, and lifted his hand.

Light golden and bright built in his hand.

He imagined a torch, its firm and steady wooden handle, its head ablaze.

A torch that will find Fire, no matter where she is.

The light twisted and grew in his grip until it thrummed against his palm. With its gentle warmth in his hand, he felt stronger.

"Show me where Fire is," he told the torch.

A gentle tug against his hand pulled him forward off the path.

In the light, the trees seemed to move back and away from him, shrinking as if the light offended them.

"Hurry!" the girl said on his heels. "You have to hurry!"

He quickened his pace.

"Watch out!" she said, and pointed at the ground in front of him.

A tree that had been trying to escape had lifted its roots, and Jack was about to trip on them.

He slowed, stepped over it. "Thank you."

She didn't respond to this. Already her wide eyes were scanning the dark around him. He didn't miss how she too shrank from the light, keeping her form just on the edge of its boundary.

The torch tugged against his palm again. Left, right, left, left, forward, right.

"Duck!" she cried.

He did in time to feel something with sizable wings fly overhead. Far too big to be a crow, and the wing beats didn't sound feathered like a bird's.

It was more akin to the sound of leathery flesh.

"That was close," the girl muttered. "You need to be more careful."

With his heart hammering in his throat, he rushed faster and faster through the trees, aided by the girl's marvelous vision.

Then the woods broke open and there was a clearing, encircled by trees on all sides. It wasn't much larger than the dueling ring beneath Oxley's Inn.

A grinning boy looked up from the rock on which he sat. "Took you long enough."

"You little bastards."

"That was fun." The fox stretched on the mossy forest floor at his feet. "Let's play another."

"Yes," Malice agreed, his crow grin bright. "In this one, let's—"

"No!" Jack yelled. "I'm done with games. You've had me running around these woods all night."

They both burst into laughter.

"Nappin' round these woods all night is more like it!" the fox chided.

"You will give me back my demon, or I will take her!"

"I'd like to see you try," said the fox with a flick of her tail.

His anger rose like a wave. His face burned with it. He could hear his jaw clicking in his ears as his teeth ground together.

I want them both wrapped in chains, he thought.

The magic unfurled with a whipcrack across the clearing. Twin flames of magic, red as his fury, snapped at the two demons. The boy squawked and lifted off the ground a second before the chain slammed into the rock he'd used as his perch.

The second chain hit the fox in her right hindquarter. Her scream folded into a snarl as the chain wrapped around her leg, tightening.

The more she squirmed, the tighter it curled, until her entire body was wrapped in the glowing metal links.

She transformed, shifting from fox to girl, no more than six or seven years old.

Her hair was the same color her fur had been, and her eyes shifted from their inhuman gold to a dull brown. Across her smudged cheeks was a smattering of red freckles.

She squirmed through the temporary gap made between her larger fox shape and that of a small girl. Jack's surprise at seeing her with flesh recovered, and the chains snapped back to life, latching on to her ankle.

Not a fox, he told himself. *A demon. She'll kill you just as well as the other one would have.*

His chains tightened on her.

They will not take you seriously unless you hurt them.

"Stop!" Malice cried. The black wings he'd used to escape the first snap of chains slid out of sight. He was a human boy again. Or at least, he looked like one.

Jack hesitated but did not retract his chains.

"I'll give you the sphere," Malice said. His voice was no longer that of a mischievous boy. It sounded far older and graver than his youthful form should have allowed. "The game's over."

"Swear it," Jack said. "Swear it on something that matters to you demons."

"I swear it on her life," he said in a low voice.

The chains fell away, and she wasted no time. Mayhem snarled and sprang at Jack.

Mid-air, she transformed into a fox once again.

"Enough!" Malice grabbed her tail, pulling her back down to a crouch.

She turned on him, growling as her four paws hit the dirt.

"He isn't playing anymore." Malice released her. "He'll hurt you."

She flicked her tail as if shaking him off. But she didn't charge Jack again.

Malice pulled the sphere from his pocket. Its bright surface darkened. Then, slowly, smoke filled the clearing.

When the smoke cleared, Fire stood there with her sword propped against one shoulder.

However, the crow and the fox were nowhere to be seen.

Fire looked around and arched her brow. "I admit I didn't know if you'd make it this far."

The chains dissolved, and with them, the last of his composure.

"Where were you!" he yelled, his anger fresh and hot. All his exhaustion, fear, and frustration crashed down on him. "You abandoned me when you're supposed to be helping me."

"*You* called them."

"The hell I did!" He felt close to tears.

"*You* wanted something to change," Fire said. She stepped toward him. "When you wish for change, you get it. Remember that."

It came to him then. He remembered walking the straight path and nearly dying of boredom. When step after step had seemed just like the one before. When he thought he'd go mad if it continued on as it always had.

"Do all demons read minds?" he asked bitterly. "Is there nothing like privacy in your world?"

"Take a little responsibility, Jack," she said bitterly. Being trapped in a sphere had put her in a bad mood.

"Responsibility!"

"We are all responsible for our own minds and what we make of them."

His ears were hot. The very word *responsibility* brought his father to his mind.

"What about your responsibility? You're supposed to be helping me." Jack tossed his cloak over one shoulder with an angry shrug. "How will you fare against Silver's demon when you can't take on a couple of children?"

Fire arched a perfect brow. "Children?"

"The crow turned into boy, the fox into a girl, but they were children. Even demons must have once been children, I suppose."

"They see nothing," Fire muttered to herself. "What are their eyes even *for*?"

"I could've left you in that sphere," he said. It was nonsense, of course. He couldn't have and they both knew it. He needed her to finish this, but he wanted her to feel as useless as she was making him feel. "Aren't you even remotely grateful that you're free?"

She snorted. "Malice can't hold me for long. The moment you gave up, I would've been freed."

"That's not true," he said. "I gave up. I fell asleep on a dirt road in the middle of nowhere."

"That's not the same as giving up." She tapped the side of her skull. "To give up in here."

He was exhausted from the ordeal but more than a little relieved to finally have her standing before him again.

Even if the direct stare of her golden eyes unnerved him.

"How did you manage it on your own?" she asked.

Then he remembered the girl. He'd forgotten all about her when fighting Malice and Mayhem.

"Oh!" He whirled. "Because she helped me. She—"

His voice died in his throat.

She wasn't there. The clearing was empty save for Fire and himself. The purple twilight of the coming dawn made the trees glow white, but there was no girl.

"Where is she?" he asked. "She was just here."

"A girl? Or a demon?"

"I'm not sure," he admitted, realizing now she'd never answered his question.

"A ghost?" Fire offered. "These woods have more than a few."

"These are haunted woods?"

"With the spirits of those who've never escaped them."

"Demons and ghosts. What will I see next? Harpies?"

The smile on Fire's face could only be described as wicked. "We have many things here, Jack. Keep your eyes open."

As Fire turned away, he searched the clearing, hoping to catch sight of the ghost girl. Perhaps she was hiding behind a tree.

But there was no one, even as the shadows grew thin at first light.

"Thank you," he whispered, before turning to leave.

He hoped somehow his gratitude would reach her.

CHAPTER 12

I wish he could hear my parents, the way they speak of him. Lord Siran might as well be the Lord himself in their eyes. It isn't enough for me. He must come back. He must. So that I may thank him with all of my heart.

— FROM THE JOURNAL OF LORD
PHINEAS GILDROY

"Where are we going now?" Jack asked once their boots were back on the path. He suspected it was the road he'd slept on when the girl—or ghost—had found him. It was hard to be sure when the woods looked quite different by the light of day.

"Have you forgotten already? Before we were detained, we were looking for someone." Fire craned her neck from one side to the other. Perhaps being trapped in an orb was hell on one's neck.

"Veemos," Jack said. "I remember."

"*Lord* Veemos," she corrected. "And no. We seek

someone who will know where Lord Veemos is. He keeps his schedule."

"Like a personal secretary?"

She snorted. "No. Like a nosy busybody who can't mind his own business. He deals in information the way you humans deal in money. He desires to know everything about everyone."

"And where will we find this busybody?"

"Hellebore," she replied.

"What is that? Is it a proper city?" Jack asked. "Because I would fight a street rat for a scone right now."

"Yes. It's a city."

"When will we reach it?"

"Nightfall."

"*Will* there be food there? Or do I get my hopes up prematurely?" His stomach had been rumbling since he woke.

"If I were you, I wouldn't eat it. I'm not sure it will agree with you."

"You realize that humans must eat."

She looked him over. "How long before you die?"

"Without water? Another day, maybe two. I've heard that a man can go at least a month without food."

"I have time then." She turned away.

His shoulders sagged. It felt as if there was lead in his boots.

"I don't think I'll make it to nightfall."

She rolled her shoulders, giving Jack the impression that she viewed him as little more than a whiny child. The way his head buzzed, he felt like one.

Then her magic rushed over him.

"What are you doing?" He tried to step back, as if her

magic were a substance that could be dodged, but it was too late. Her power was all over him.

"I'm sharing my stamina with you. You're welcome."

Stamina?

It felt like someone had plumped his muscles and made him six inches taller.

"Incredible." He flexed his arms. A large, goofy grin spread over his face.

She arched a brow. "That's enough then."

"Is this how you feel all the time?" He jumped to one side, surprised by the distance he covered.

She watched him. "Like dancing? No. I dance only when moved."

He put his feet together and jumped again, once, twice, each time getting higher. When his feet came down the third time, he lost his balance and fell forward onto his hands and knees, laughing.

"Will you please get up and walk?"

"Sure, sure." He pulled himself up and dusted himself off.

With his exhaustion and hunger forgotten, Jack was able to keep pace with her now.

He couldn't stop grinning, and sometimes he fell into humming a tune until Fire demanded silence.

As the hours passed, something grew on the horizon. Dark shapes formed, swelled. The sound of music floated toward him on a breeze as the last of the forest disappeared behind them.

She'd told him it was a city, but nothing could prepare him for the experience of stepping from the forest and seeing Hellebore for the first time.

Like his Lundenwick, it was true there were cobbled

streets, lit lanterns, and buildings that lined the thoroughfare.

Also like his town, men and women strolled down the streets arm in arm, in quiet conversation that could not be heard over the rumble of wagon wheels or clopping horse hooves.

But that is where the similarities ended.

In Hellebore, raucous laughter spilled into the street. Music unlike any he'd ever heard leapt from open windows. Colorful banners and sigils of all shapes and sizes swung in the air.

Many of the creatures looked unlike anything Jack had ever seen. Leathery skin, horns, tails, and wings. Some with two eyes, many with more. Some walked upright. Others crawled.

Quite a few had human shapes like his own with smaller or larger heads. With others, only the glow of their eyes or the claws extending from their fingers or the sudden flash of fangs in a laughing mouth gave the game away.

Girls danced in the open air, their stomachs, arms, and bare feet exposed. Jack caught the eye of one beauty whose blond hair swung loosely around her shoulder. She returned his smile.

She wasn't the only one. Most of the demons who caught sight of him smiled, started his way.

That was until they saw Fire walking beside him. Then they pulled back as if their hands had struck a flame.

"Stay close to me, Jack," Fire said, and took his arm. "You have a tendency to find trouble."

"Are you sure she's trouble?" he asked as an especially beautiful pixie winked at him.

"Yes," Fire said, unamused. "And not the kind you're looking for."

Without releasing him, she scanned the banners hanging from what could only be thought of as shop windows.

"Stay here. Speak to no one." She stepped through a doorway, the smell of incense and spice striking him before the door swung shut.

A moment later she returned. "I'm told he's in East Quarter tonight."

She pulled hard on his arm, removing Jack from the path of a galloping—what? He couldn't be sure what he was looking at. A giant red lizard?

"A baby dragon. A hatchling in its first month," she said. The creature garbled a cry and bounded up the road, snapping at the colorful banners as it went. "And in sore need of training, by the look of it."

"Hey now!" a man cried. Or perhaps a beast that could pass for a man, if one overlooked the small horns fixed to his skull. "Come back here!"

Panting, the man with the orange beard ran past them, making apologies as he traced the creature's path.

"The father, I presume," Fire said. She tugged on his arms. "This way."

"How did he father that?" Jack laughed.

"I believe you understand the basic mechanics," she said flatly, and pulled his arm again.

"I thought dragons laid eggs."

"Not all," she said plainly.

The streets grew narrower with each turn. The walls of the buildings moved closer and closer together as if for warmth, the lanterns farther and farther apart, until they found an alleyway barely lit and with only enough room to walk single file.

Jack was trying to keep his balance on the unsteady road when Fire stopped abruptly, and he bumped into her back.

"Here we are," she said, and pushed open a rough wooden door.

Jack pressed a hand to his chest as he peered inside.

It was even worse than Jack had imagined. The room was small and musty. A single green lantern in one corner gave the space a sickly glow. Another corner held three sofas surrounding a lit fireplace. The opposite wall was consumed by a bar. Behind it, a thin man with almost no hair brightened at the sight of them.

Fire pushed Jack down on a hard stool.

"Good evening!" the barkeep called out. It was hard to tell if this was false cheer or if he truly was grateful for newfound company.

"Are you human?" she asked him.

"I am, milady."

She put three silver coins on the bar top. "Then feed him. Whatever he can safely eat."

The man's eyes slid to Jack's throat and saw the mark burned there. At this, his cheer wilted at the edges. "As you wish, milady."

Fire leaned down and put her mouth quite close to Jack's ears. "Stay here until I come back."

"What? You can't leave me here!"

"I can. And you will leave with *no one* and speak to *no one*, if you can help yourself."

Jack scoffed. "I don't talk that much."

She reached for his shirt and undid the first two buttons on his collar, opening the shirt wider at his throat.

"What are you doing?" He grabbed for her hands and missed.

She ran a hand through his hair, tousling it.

He tried to ignore the delicious rake of her nails across his scalp. It was easily done the moment she slapped his cheeks lightly on each side.

"Hey, stop it!" He reached for and missed her hands for a second time.

"For a bit of color." She stood back to admire her work and nodded. "Good enough. No, wait."

She pressed her fingers into the mark on his throat. The sensation wasn't nearly as pleasant as having his hair combed. His skin felt as if it wanted to crawl off his bones.

She pulled back and inspected him again.

"That'll do. Stay here, do you hear me? I won't go far."

"Wait! How long will you be gone?" he asked.

He twisted on the stool in time only to catch sight of her red hair before the door to the bar swung shut.

"What the hell was that?" he muttered, touching his hair and bare throat self-consciously.

Her rough handling was immediately forgotten when the barman returned with a small tray balanced on one hand and a large carafe of wine in the other.

"I'm sorry, we don't have water," he said straight away, as Jack's eyes fixed on the wine. "It's hard to come by here."

"The wine will do. Thank you kindly," Jack said in grateful anticipation. His stomach twisted in on itself as he took several greedy gulps.

On the tray were two plates.

The smaller of the two held a lump that looked very much like a bread roll, if misshapen. The larger plate held boiled potatoes, a side of wilted cabbage, carrots, and a wedge of what Jack hoped was cheese.

"It's not much," the barman admitted. "There aren't many of us around these parts."

"It's beautiful," Jack said, his stomach rumbling again.

He wasted no time at all forking the potatoes into his mouth. They needed salt, but they did the task of easing his bellyache well enough. The cabbage and carrots went down after.

"Hungry, were you?" The barman poured Jack a large glass of wine.

"It was a long walk," Jack complained. "My *feet*."

His eyes cut to Jack's throat again. "What did you offer up?"

"My soul," Jack said. "I had nothing else to sell. What about you?"

"Labor. I'd already given my soul to God."

Labor, Jack thought. Why hadn't he thought of that?

"So you have to work as a barman? For all of eternity?" Jack found this funny but did not dare laugh, no matter how the wine warmed him. He drank down the first glass nearly in one go. The barman immediately refilled it.

"Until I die, I suppose." The man shrugged. "But a life for a life seemed fair enough."

Jack thought of Phineas cold on the slab in the hospital's mortuary. "Who did you save?"

"My boy, Timothy."

Jack's head snapped up, half the bread roll in his mouth. "Timothy? Timothy Tromwell?"

"Do you know him?"

As the man leaned forward into the light, Jack could see it now. He was pale and his face gaunt, and most of his hair gone, but he knew the man all the same.

"Mr. Tromwell. Forgive me," Jack said. "I did not recognize you, sir."

"The lighting is terrible in here," he agreed, but waved the thought away. "Tell me of my boy. How is he? How long has it been?"

How long has it been? Does he not know?

"Three years," Jack told him, the half-eaten roll forgotten in his grip. "Timothy is eight now."

"Eight years old," the man marveled. "How is he? Tall? Handsome like his mother? Healthy?"

The desperation in his voice nearly broke Jack's heart. It mirrored his own too closely. More than that, it was the pain of seeing a father whose eyes were filled with love. A father who would give anything for the happiness and safety of his son. Even his own life.

A father so unlike his own.

"He is well," Jack said, despite his tightening throat. "Very well, sir."

The man touched his knuckles to his eyes. "And his mother? Has she forgiven me?"

"I'm sorry, I cannot say, sir."

Jack had heard rumors that Mrs. Tromwell had vowed to never marry again, holding out the hope that her husband would one day return to her. But knowing now that it wasn't possible, that she would wait all her life in vain, well, Jack didn't want to burden the man with that knowing.

"But she is well," he said. "I've not heard otherwise."

"Thank you." The barkeep's shoulders shook with relief, his hand relaxing on the neck of the carafe. "What about you? Your situation must've been grave if you were willing to sell your soul."

Jack told him an abbreviated version of the night the demon came to his house, killed his father, and wounded his mother. How he carried his friend's body from the mortuary to Devil's Field even while the flames of his house still burned. He let the story imply that he only sought to save Phineas's life. He made no mention of cubes or magic, or of the beautiful boy he was searching for.

His guts tightened as the image of Lord Silver flashed in his mind. The way he looked when he took the fighting stance across the ring from him, sliding one foot back behind the other, lifting his chin defiantly.

You don't know if he's beautiful. You've only ever seen his mask, he chided himself.

But he felt certain all the same that to see Silver's face would undo him with desire.

"And does he live?" Tromwell asked at last. "Your friend?"

It took a moment for Jack to realize that he meant Phineas and not Silver.

"He does," Jack said. "Though I worry his parents might reject him for what I did. Maybe they'll believe he's damned or—"

"No," Tromwell interrupted with a hard shake of his head. "No father would reject a lost son returned. He will be the first on his knees to thank you, if you ever see him again. I'm sure of that."

Silence hung between them as Jack finished his cold bread roll and lump of cheese.

Jack grappled with the image of his father run through by the sword, his body collapsed on its side in the burning study.

Could my father be dead? Truly dead?

"Are you all right?" the barman asked.

"Yes," Jack lied. "I'm only tired. It's been a difficult few days."

He could still hear the music and laughter from the streets, but it was muffled by the wooden walls and thick door.

He reached for the wine.

"No, wait. Let me," Tromwell began, but another voice cut him off.

"What do we have here?"

It was a slow, melodic voice that slid over Jack's skin like the cool belly of a serpent. A man settled down onto the barstool beside him.

He was easily the most gorgeous creature Jack had ever seen. He was tall, with dark hair pulled back from his face and tied with a blood-red ribbon at the base of his neck. Wisps of hair curled around his jaw and cut beneath his eyes. His long slender throat was exposed by his open collar, and the sight of this delicious stretch of skin made Jack think of kissing it, almost against his will.

His jaw was strong and his eyes seemed to be several colors at once, shimmering now somewhere between blue and violet as his gaze raked over Jack.

"My lord, I—" Tromwell began.

"That's enough," the stranger said. "Go away."

Tromwell's mouth snapped shut, and he whirled as if spun by an invisible hand toward the door. He left without glancing back.

"Now," the stranger said, smiling, "where were we?"

The man's lips were the darkest pink Jack had ever seen, nearly red, beneath a generous nose. While Jack stared dumbly at his face, the creature reached out and placed a finger on the mark of Jack's throat.

"You're already spoken for," he said with a tsk. "What a pity. I would love to have something as handsome as you."

Jack shivered at the touch, feeling drunker now than he had moments before.

He didn't think it was the wine.

There was a heady fragrance in the air, like the sickly-sweet smell of lilies that his mother sometimes carried in from her garden.

The man placed his chin in his hand and pouted. "What could he possibly want you for? You aren't even his type."

He?

Jack frowned.

"Perhaps I can work something out on your behalf," the man cooed, rolling his eyes up to meet Jack's. "Or if not, then I might simply borrow you for a while? Would you like that?"

The way the light played across the surface of the man's eyes mesmerized him. They were edging toward a dark blue now.

Jack found himself leaning forward.

"Oh, too easy, Jack," he said, his laughter trailing over Jack's cheeks. "Fight me a little, will you? I enjoy a bit of resistance."

"Who are you?" Jack asked. He sounded dreamy even to himself. Maybe he was dreaming. Certainly when awake, he'd never felt as if he could fall into a voice and drown.

"Give me a kiss and maybe I'll tell you." His eyes raked across Jack's lips and throat again.

Until Fire's voice cut right through the magic. "You're as shameless as ever, Raz."

It was as if someone had snapped their fingers and Jack's senses returned to him, the drunkenness falling away like a blanket snatched from his body on a cold morning.

The man laughed and ran a hand over the front of his suit. "I should've known this was a trap set for me. He's too perfect."

Fire wrapped her hands around the back of Jack's neck. Her fingertips brushed the surface of the demon seal. It tingled again, that terrible flesh-crawling sensation causing him to crane his neck away from her.

"There's truly a mark." The man's eyes shifted toward a vibrant green. "Pity. I don't suppose you're interested in a trade?"

"Maybe," she said with a tilt of her head.

"Hey!" Jack knocked her hand away. "I'm not cattle."

Fire rolled her eyes. "Pretend you don't love the idea of a night with Raziel."

At this Jack shut up. Had his thoughts been that obvious? What a stupid question. Of course they were. The demons of this world had been reading his mind as clearly as one hears a conversation. Now that he thought of it, he wasn't sure he'd ever said his name, and yet Raziel had known it.

He wished he could blame it on the wine. Or the strange, heady perfume wafting off the demon that made it so hard to think.

But both had dissipated and Jack's desire had not.

With great reluctance, Raziel pulled his hungry gaze from Jack's face and looked to Fire. "What do you want?"

"Where is Lord Veemos?" she asked.

"As if he's taking appointments."

She was undeterred by this rebuff. "Where is he?"

"You can't take him to Lord Veemos," Raziel said. "He *reeks*."

"That is unkind!" Jack cried. "I've had a very difficult night in the woods, I'll have you know, and she hasn't offered me so much as a glass of water, let alone a bath."

Jack's outrage only seemed to delight Raziel. He grinned at Jack the way one grins at a puppy.

"You reek of *magic*, darling. Nothing more," Raziel said

gently. Then to Fire, "You never understood their needs. I see you still don't."

To Jack he said, "You don't want to work with her. Tell me what you need, and with a snap of my fingers I can give you the world."

Raziel tilted his head, deliberately giving Jack a lovely view of his throat and exposed chest again.

"He won't give you the world," Fire countered. "Just raw knees."

Raziel glared at her.

"Do I lie?" Fire demanded.

Raziel turned away from her. "What she *means* is that when I'm finished with you, you won't care one bit about whatever it is you're after."

Raziel winked and bit his lip.

Something in the air shifted. Jack felt it like sparks along his skin.

"What's—" he began. He'd wanted to ask, *What's happening?* But he'd seen Fire's eyes and knew it was her doing.

"Tell me where Lord Veemos is or I will hurt you," she said in a low growl.

Raziel's eyes were the deepest green yet. "Is that a promise? It's been a long time since someone has done it properly."

The sparking sensation built, doubling then tripling until a small whine escaped Jack. He grabbed the bar top to prevent himself from collapsing.

He smelled smoke.

"Enough." Raziel's hands were in Jack's hair. "You've singed his locks. How could you? Do you know how hard it is to find such thick, beautiful curls?"

"*Raziel.*"

"I'll tell you if you give him to me."

"No."

"A night, then?"

"I need him functional," Fire argued.

"Define *functional*," Raziel countered.

That mind-dampening fragrance filled the room again. Jack's drunkenness returned.

"Has his senses. Remembers his name. Can walk on his own two legs," Fire said.

"Walking, no," Raziel conceded. "But you could carry him."

"I really can't."

"Of course you can, you just don't want to." He pouted his full lips.

"*Where?*"

Raziel's grin returned. "My payment first."

"Functional," Fire said again. "You agreed."

"It'll only be a kiss. Given the mark on his throat, you've already had yours, so don't be stingy."

After a moment, Fire's shoulders relaxed.

"Jack," she said, looking at him at last. "You have to consent to this or there is no deal."

"To what? A kiss?"

"The best kiss of your life," Raziel said, wetting his lips.

He waited to see if this was a joke, if they were both going to start laughing diabolically at his ignorance, but no one moved.

"What is it with demons and kissing?" he muttered.

Raziel's fingers slid across the side of Jack's throat and clasped the back of his neck.

His breath was hot against Jack's mouth. "Just a taste."

"You may kiss me." Jack closed his eyes.

The brush of lips was hardly felt, the probing tongue that followed an afterthought.

It was the energy that overtook Jack like a wave.

And that sickly-sweet fragrance crashed into his body, warming his every nerve.

He felt naked and exposed as the overwhelming sensation of dozens of hands traced his warming skin. Fingers trailed over his arms, his legs, his buttocks, his cock.

He tightened then softened as something clicked within him, opening, loosening. His magic was laid bare, responding to some unseen caress.

They were one and the same—his magic and his desire. He realized that now.

And perhaps that was why Silver had spurred him to greater and greater heights when dueling. For who else provoked such desire in him?

Not a soul.

Raziel pulled back, red-faced. His eyes were pinched closed. He was biting his lip so hard it had turned white.

"Vanity, hedonism, and *so* much lust," he moaned, reluctantly relinquishing his hold on Jack's neck. "Are you sure I can't have him? I'd pay almost anything."

"No." Fire hooked her arm under Jack's, hauling him to his feet. "Now, where is he?"

Raziel struggled to compose himself. He ran a hand through his hair, tugging it free of the ribbon. "You'll find him in Fireside. At the northeast entrance."

Fire stilled. "You're lying."

"Would I send something so handsome into the flames?"

He pulled at his buttons, widening his shirt even more. He looked a little drunk himself. "If you insist on going, you'd better manage it. If you waste something so"—his eyes flicked to Jack's—"*precious*, I'll never forgive you."

She pulled on Jack's arm, tugging him toward the door.

"And if Lady Vee catches scent of him—"

"She won't," Fire said, but even Jack saw the momentary unease in her face before she pulled open the door. "Come on."

"Jack," Raziel called.

Jack turned, feeling steadier on his feet now that there was some distance between them and that fragrance was fading, feeling more and more like a dream.

"Open your hand. Hold it up. Yes, like that."

Raziel waved his hand, and in Jack's flat palm, a gray-white feather appeared.

"Call me should you ever need me." Raziel took the glass of wine Jack had left behind and threw it back in one gulp. Jack noted that his eyes were deep violet again. "No matter where you are, I will come."

CHAPTER 13

Dear Lord, protect m'boy Jack. I miss 'im. And I want to see 'is face again.

— FROM THE PRAYERS OF LORD
BASIL LANCASTER

"You would be an idiot to use that feather unless your only other option was death," Fire said after Jack waved his hand and hid the feather away in his nowhere place.

Her stride picked up pace as soon as Jack's legs allowed it.

"Even then I'd reconsider," she added.

"What was he?"

"Hungry and bored," Fire answered. "Luckily for us."

"If you didn't want me to get involved with him, you shouldn't have used me as bait."

"*Involved.*" She snorted. "It was only a kiss."

It felt like a great deal more, he thought. "Where is Fireside?"

"Ten or eleven days' journey."

"Eleven days!"

"If we were walking. We're not."

"How will we get there then? Do demons ride horses?"

"Do we ride—?" She sneered. "Of course we ride horses. Dragons, helljacks, and prairie fae too."

Jack had zero interest in riding anything that wasn't a horse.

"But we aren't riding," she said.

"Then how—"

"Hush, Jack. You'll know soon enough."

The crashing of cymbals, the blare of horns, and the ruckus of strange string instruments hadn't died down even though the hour felt infinitely later than when Jack had entered the bar. Still they walked away from the town, toward its dark borders.

Then the alley they traveled ended abruptly.

What stretched beyond was only a moonlit field and the shadowed outlines of mountains in the distance.

In a quick motion, nearly too fast for Jack to see, Fire drew her sword and hurled it into the night.

Something screamed.

"Heavens," he swore as she ran into the dark after her prey.

When she came back, she held a bleeding rabbit in one hand and the sword in the other.

"That was cruel."

"Its death will buy us passage to Fireside. Wrap your arms around my waist."

He didn't want to while her arms were slick with blood. He could smell it, gamey and rich.

But he hooked an arm around her waist, the hard leather unforgiving against his forearm.

"Count to three and close your eyes," she said.

"All right. One..."

She broke the rabbit's neck with a quick twist of the hand, then held its tender head.

The night fell away, and it was as if someone had shoved a poker through Jack's abdomen.

Where the moonlit field and the edge of the city had been moments before was now a cauldron of fire. Black, jagged rocks steamed as rivulets of lava flowed around them on all sides.

Jack staggered against the heat, and rough hands seized him.

"What's wrong with you?" Fire asked, dropping the rabbit. Its body was consumed by the flames. "Stay on the rocks."

"It's too hot," he said. "My eyes are burning."

He felt the surge of her magic again, enveloping him.

When he opened his eyes, they no longer burned.

"Your flesh is so delicate," she said. "What's it even for?"

"Keeping our inside bits on the inside?" Jack ventured.

"It's not even good at that. One little cut and—" She made an explosive gesture with her hand and sputtered her lips. She looked sadly at where the rabbit had disappeared. "Thank you. You've bought us a great deal of precious time."

Jack too said his own little prayer. "Can Lord Veemos really be here?"

She pointed her sword toward the mountain before them. "The entrance is here. We just have to get to the door without being eaten."

"Eaten?" He started. He'd expected her to say burned alive. "Eaten by what?"

A screech echoed through the air, blistering Jack's eardrums and rattling his chest.

"What the hell was that?" he asked.

"Fireflies."

He frowned. "Fireflies? Those delightful little insects that we catch as children?"

Another gut-rattling scream shook his body.

"No," she said. "That."

She pointed her sword at the sky. In the ashy gray air was an enormous bird. The creature was made entirely of flame, and when its wings beat, Jack could see through it to the sky beyond. Soot scattered with each powerful thrust of its wings, and its mouth, a cone of fire, opened again only to unleash another unearthly cry.

It was no insect.

It was fire. That could fly.

And it was hurtling toward them.

"Run." Fire's sword began to glow. "Get to that ledge there as quickly and safely as you can. Keep the inside bits on the inside."

Jack didn't look back. He began clambering over the rocks as fast as he could. He did his best to stick to solid ground, avoiding anything that wavered with heat or smoked with ash. She had removed the searing temperature, but Jack was still certain a misplaced boot or hand would melt all the same.

As he hauled himself up, he cut his hand on a rock and cried out. Blood ran down the flesh of his palm.

He turned in time to see Fire run her sword—now burning an ethereal blue—through the creature. A blood-burst of red light followed its death.

But where she cut one through, three sprang up from the ashes to replace it.

"Keep moving, Jack!" she yelled.

He wrapped his cloak around the palm of his cut hand and obeyed her.

When he finally reached the ledge that was meant to lead them to the northeast entrance, he pulled himself up with shaking arms.

Only to find himself staring into the eyes of a beast, larger than any Jack had ever seen, made of the same fire as the birds but with the body of a bear and the head of a lion. Its taloned paws were only inches from Jack's gaping mouth.

It opened its jaws to swallow Jack whole.

That's that, he thought.

This would be the end of him.

"Down!" Fire screamed, and Jack felt the swing of the sword inches above his head as he crouched.

The beast erupted into light then was gone.

She wasted no time in hauling Jack into a dark crevice between the rocks. The light of her sword illuminated a path in the narrow space.

"Are you all right?" She slapped at his cloak, knocking the ash and smoldering rock from it.

"I'm fine," he said, but his face felt hot. The way it did whenever he fell asleep too close to the fireplace reading.

"Then why are you holding your hand?"

"I cut it on a rock, but it's fine," he insisted. He pointed at the end of the path, at the somber door that stood there. "Is that it?"

Because he wanted more than anything to get out of this hellscape.

She held her sword in front of her as she approached the door. She squared her shoulders, steadied her stance.

She looked ready to fight. There was far more concern

and concentration in her face now than she'd had for those flying monstrosities.

What was on the other side of that door?

"Should I be worried?" he asked, taking an instinctual step back. "Is Vee—*Lord* Veemos a terror?"

Instead of answering, she used the tip of her blade to rap on the door three times. Then she assumed her fighting position again.

Nothing.

"If you could just tell me if I—"

"Hush," she said. "Stop your relentless questions for two minutes. I beg you."

The door began to creak open slowly, squealing on its ancient hinges.

On the other side stood a man, a good head taller than Jack. A cheerful, jaunty feather jutted from his hat, which sat tipped over one eye. The one eye he could see was as fathomless as a black sky, and painted to match.

In his left hand, the one not holding open the door, was a half-eaten apple. With his cheek bulging, evidently full of fruit, he didn't *look* very dangerous.

Lord Veemos frowned. "Have I offended you?"

"Where is your sister?" Fire asked.

He relaxed at this. "She isn't here."

Fire slid her sword back into the sheath on her back, but nothing in her posture suggested she was relaxed.

"I know this one," Lord Veemos said, his gaze sliding from Fire to Jack. "But not you."

"I'm Jack," he said, and because he was unsure if a bow or a handshake was more appropriate, he did an awkward motion that was a bit of both.

"Well met, Jack." Veemos too slid one heel back, dipped forward, and took Jack's hand.

Jack hissed at having his cut pressed open.

"Oh my," Veemos said with a nervous laugh. "They are so delicate, aren't they?"

He inspected his nails, which were perfectly neat and trimmed. "Perhaps I should give these more attention?"

"It wasn't you. I cut it on the rock." Jack gestured over his shoulder at the smoldering ledge.

"Well then. You'd better come inside and let us clean it."

And at that, Lord Veemos opened the door wider and offered them passage into the otherworld.

Jack wasn't sure what he expected to find when they finally caught up with Lord Veemos, but he had not expected this. The walls were not walls at all, but spheres that glowed and spun in place like stars. From the floor to higher than he could see, they were stacked in rows and columns.

Then there were the strings. They stretched in all directions, a light luminescence brightening the filaments.

Mesmerized, he reached out to pluck a line just above his eyes, and Veemos said, "Don't touch, please."

"I'm sorry." Jack pulled his hand back. "They're just so beautiful."

"They are," the man agreed, the feather in his hat trembling with the turn of his head. "Every one of them. There isn't one, no matter how it ends, that I don't love for its beauty. Come along."

Because the black floor reflected the glowing orbs, Jack felt as if he were walking on the night sky itself. A very orderly night sky, true enough, but no less entrancing.

"This way," Veemos said, and turned right, cutting

down a new corridor. "Here we are. You can clean up here, and when you're done, meet us in the study."

Jack stepped into the bathroom and the door shut behind him.

Then he was alone.

Was it his imagination that Fire had seemed all too eager to step away from him?

Don't be paranoid, he thought. *Perhaps she only has business to discuss. We did come here for a reason, after all. She has no reason to abandon you.*

Before him on a vanity table was a large pitcher of water and a deep basin. Beside the basin, a clean rag. Fortunately, there was also a mirror, so Jack was able to see himself for the first time in days.

Granted, he didn't look his *best*. Not by any measure. His hair was a mess. His cheeks and hands were covered in ash as well as his clothes. But he did what he could with the cool water and the rag. Then he used Albert's dagger to scrape beneath his nails. Once his hand had been cleaned and the blood stopped, he took a good look at his hand.

The cut was shallow. It would heal quickly.

He frowned into the mirror. "I wish I could change my clothes."

As if by magic, a door on the wall opened and a rack of white shirts and a variety of vests and riding trousers exactly like what he wore slid out to greet him.

On the hook, a little note that said, *Free of charge. Please help yourself.*

He snorted. Free of charge. He supposed that in the demon world that was a very important clause to include in one's fine print.

He chose dark riding trousers, a crisp white shirt, and a

purple velvet vest, all of which fit him well. Washing his feet and changing his socks was also a delight.

Feeling infinitely better, he stepped out of the bathroom, and instead of finding the same dark hall full of luminescent orbs he'd left minutes before, he found himself in a study.

He turned back, confused.

"No, you're in the right place."

Veemos stood by a fireplace, a drink in his hand. The glass sparked with the firelight.

His red-headed guide was curled in an oversized chair with her legs slung over one arm, her eyes fixed sleepily on the flames.

"But—" Jack began, yet he didn't know how to finish.

"He can move the rooms of his palace around," Fire said, taking another drink from the glass in her hand.

Veemos tsked. "It's not a *palace*. You exaggerate."

"I use the word *palace* only because there is none greater." She held out her drink so that he could refill it. He did so from a flask inside his breast pocket. "What do you call a place that holds an infinity of worlds within its walls?"

Veemos motioned for Jack to come forward. "You're safe here, Jack. I promised your patron that I guarantee your safe passage while you're here with me. Now I make the same promise to you. You need not fear me."

"It isn't you we fear." Fire seized a piece of ice from her glass. "It's your sister that concerns me. I was hoping to find you alone."

Veemos shook his head. "I'm never *alone*. But she sleeps. You may put your fears to rest."

"Come here, Jack. Be a good boy," Fire said, and at her urging, Jack realized he still remained frozen in place outside a bathroom that wasn't a bathroom anymore. The door was gone.

Reluctantly, he obeyed, and stopped just a few paces short of them.

The firelight played across their features.

Veemos stared at him for a long time, craning his head this way, then that. His brow furrowed as he considered Jack's features.

Then he broke into a generous grin and said, "I like your face, Jack."

"Am I still bait?" Jack asked. He was tired. He felt cross.

Lord Veemos frowned, looking from Jack to Fire.

"He's met Raziel," Fire explained.

Veemos laughed. "No, *no*, my boy. I want nothing from you. I meant only that I like the look of your face. It's an honest face. There's a great deal of heart in it. Even if a bit guarded."

Jack took a step back.

Something softened in Veemos's gaze. "For good reason, I'm sure. I understand you need help finding someone."

Fire arched her brows, nodding to suggest this was the moment Jack should plead his case.

"A demon came to my house and killed my father. I believe he's linked to..." His voice trailed off. "Another man I know. I want to find them. Kill the demon, save the man."

Veemos and Fire exchanged a glance.

"I do not control the roads for demons," Lord Veemos said. "By their very definition, demons no longer *have* roads."

"Only humans have roads?" Jack was surprised.

Lord Veemos grimaced. "It's a bit more complicated than that. There are non-human creatures that *have* roads, while a few humans destroy their roads and forge new paths."

His gaze slid to Fire. She said nothing.

"But in general, humans have roads and demons do not. Your friend, he is a human?"

The word *friend* stung.

Had they been friends?

It was true they had never dined together, nor did they meet outside the filthy walls of the Oxley Inn basement. Yet Jack had thought there was an understanding between them.

Had he deceived himself?

But the letters had felt so honest. What was written in those pages was as intimate and loving as any sentiments he'd shared with his closest companions.

It was all in your head, you idiot, and look what it got you, Jack thought bitterly.

And now the letters were gone. More than two hundred of them consumed by the flames. Jack wouldn't even be able to reread them, looking for clues or hints of Silver's deception.

Jack's gaze fell to his feet. "He is human, as far as I know."

"Then I can put you on his path. I'll cross your road with his."

"That will be enough," Fire said. "I'll do the rest. How long do you need for the task?"

"Tomorrow should do fine. You can be on your way the morning after."

Fire rose from her seat, placing her empty glass on the lacquered tabletop. "I'll have a shower then, if you don't mind. My hair itches."

"And you, Jack?" Lord Veemos asked. "What do you need? Sleep, I wager. I can see the exhaustion in you."

Jack's eyes were quite heavy. The fire's warmth was making him sleepy. "I wouldn't mind a soft bed, if you have one."

A sound caught Jack's ears. A turning. It reminded him of the gears in his father's clock, the one that had undoubtedly burned with the rest of the study.

A door to the right of the room creaked open.

From where he stood, Jack saw the foot of a bed awash in candlelight.

"May sweet dreams find you," Lord Veemos said as firelight danced across his face.

"Thank you," Jack said. To Fire, "If I need you...?"

"I'll know. You think loud enough." She stepped into the bathroom and shut the door behind her.

A soft chuckle escaped Veemos.

Jack hesitated at the doorway. He didn't enjoy being laughed at, but he also wasn't going to start a quarrel with the man of the house. Not after he'd been shown so much generous hospitality.

"Forgive me," Lord Veemos said, with a little frown on his lips. "I mean nothing by it. I have a funny sense of humor."

Jack straightened. "Is there no way to hide my thoughts from the lot of you?"

Veemos's lips twitched. "Of course there is. Shall I show you tomorrow? No, I would never charge for something like that. You would be indulging the professor in me. It is a gift to me, when I can make myself useful."

Something in Jack's heart lifted. "I would appreciate the help. Anything that would make me feel more..."

He searched for the right word. He didn't like feeling like a child. Incompetent. It brought up in him a smallness he detested. His father had always made him feel that way. Small.

Lord Veemos's face was soft when he spoke. "You would like to feel safer, I imagine."

Jack was relieved to be understood. "Yes, please."

"Very well. I'll find you after tea. We will work on that together."

"Thank you," Jack said with great relief. "Good night."

Veemos touched his hat and turned away, his eyes fixing again on the swirling flames. Jack barely noted the four-poster bed and inviting pillows before he fell into it.

He slept deeply and without dreams.

CHAPTER 14

The poets say luck favors a fool in possession of more heart than brain. I pray that this be true, and that Jack will return safely to us.

Selina will say I should have never let him go alone, that if I were his true friend, I would have followed Jack to Hell and back.

She thinks me braver than I am.

— FROM THE PRIVATE JOURNAL OF
LORD SILAS MORANNE

When Jack woke, it was still night. He sat up, rubbing his head with confusion. How could it still be night? He was certain he'd slept a long time.

"Because there is no day here. With Lord Veemos, there is only endless night."

Fire sat by the window in a highbacked armchair that Jack didn't remember seeing before he tumbled into the bed hours before. The opposing chair was empty, and between them, a tray full of food rested on an ornate table of gold.

"How can it be always night?" he asked, watching her lift a cup of warm tea to her lips.

The steam caressed her face.

His mouth was dry and in desperate need of water. His throat ached from its absence. Watching her made him very aware of this fact.

"All creation is born of darkness," she said plainly. "Eggs?"

He pushed back the covers and slid from the high bed.

"The water is here."

A large glass and a carafe of water waited for him. Not to mention the generous selection of thirteen dishes. Eggs and sausages. Bread and cheese. Three dark puddings. Fruit. Olives. Fish. Cold meats. Porridge and real butter. Proper salt and pepper.

"This is a feast." He grabbed the glass of water she offered and drank it down without breathing. It was cold against his lips and tongue. Once it was gone, he refilled it from the carafe.

"Lord Veemos must be quite happy to have us." She speared a sausage with her fork. "I suspect it's been a while since he's had visitors."

Jack froze, his fork poised above the dish of glistening fruit. "Lord Veemos isn't a fairy, is he?"

She arched a brow. "What have you got against fairies? Many would say they're better company than demons."

"I only ask because we hear stories, where I'm from. If you dine with fairies or if you eat anything they give you, you cannot leave their realm. Is this a trick?"

"Be easy, Jack," she said, slipping the final crust of toast into her mouth and brushing her hands free of the crumbs. "Lord Veemos will play no tricks on you."

She sat back in her chair, clearly satisfied with her meal.

"Do I need to tell you what an honor it is for you to even be in his presence? I know it is hard for you to understand the magnitude or significance of this moment, as small-brained as you are—"

He scowled.

"—but do try to act grateful if you cannot manage pure delight."

"I am grateful." He speared a dark cherry with his fork and lifted it to his lips. "You mentioned a sister. What of her?"

"That one has the teeth of a jackal. Let's not speak of her lest she wake." She sipped her tea again.

"I—"

"*Don't.*" She pointed her fork at him. "Don't even think of her. Your thoughts are a great deal too loud in general."

Emboldened by how well the cherry went down his throat, Jack heaped two boiled eggs, three sausages, and two slices of toast onto his plate. It was far too much for a breakfast, he knew. Oh, how his mother would scold him if she could see him.

But he felt as if he'd walked a thousand miles on little more than a prayer.

He was hungry.

"What is he, Lord Veemos?" Jack asked between bites. "What does he do? What is this place?"

Fire picked her teeth with her tongue. "You always have so many questions."

Something about seeing her rake her tongue over her pointed teeth made his stomach twist. He imagined those sharp points sinking into his flesh, ripping his soul from his body.

She flicked her eyes up to meet his. "No, when I eat *you*, I won't use my teeth."

He wasn't sure if he felt better or worse about this. "What will you use?"

"I haven't decided." She shrugged. "My hands, most likely."

The food in his mouth turned to ash. "I'm to be torn apart then?"

She rolled her eyes. "I'm not an amateur. Give me more credit, Jack."

But there was something in her voice he didn't like. Sympathy? Pity? Disdain? It was hard to place.

"Will it hurt?" he asked while buttering his toast.

"Living hurts. I thought you knew that well enough."

He put the knife down, his half-eaten plate forgotten.

"I've soured your mood." Fire tapped her nails against the cup in her hand, her gaze heavy on his face. "Do you still want me to answer your questions about Lord Veemos, or would you rather be rid of me?"

It was true that he didn't want her company anymore. Not with his burning awareness of the mark on his neck and his impending fate. But his curiosity burned brighter even than the flames dancing in her eyes, especially with no other diversions present.

"I still want answers."

She placed her cup on the table beside her half-demolished plate. "*What* is he? It's hard to say. *Old* is accurate. Ancient, more so. Older than anything else I've ever met. Skilled. He possesses talents I've seen in no other creature."

"He's not a demon?"

"No, not as you mean it," she said. "I would say he's

closer to a god. Or perhaps he is *God*, if there is such a thing."

He started at this. "Can God and demons really keep company with one another? Did God make you?"

She snorted. "No one makes demons but themselves."

He considered that while she refilled the teacups.

"As for *what* he can do, I would not pretend to know the extent of his abilities, but for our purposes, he is the keeper of the roads. All comings and goings are by his design. For nearly all creatures in this world and others, he makes their paths."

"Except for demons." Jack remembered that much at least.

She nodded, conceding the point. "Except for demons. We make our own designs."

"Humans have no free will then. We walk only the paths he puts down for us?"

"I didn't say that. I mean only that if you meet with fortune, you have Lord Veemos to thank for it."

He thought of his bloodied back. His father's cruel words. Of Silver's betrayal. The fact that he would certainly die when Fire ripped his soul from his body. A day that might come quite soon indeed.

"No," Fire said firmly. "What your father did to you was his own doing. You cannot blame Lord Veemos for the cruelty of men. But remember this, Jack. What appears as misfortune is often the most generous of gifts."

His skin prickled.

She gestured to the room around her.

"As for this place, it is a no place."

"A no place?"

"A convergence of many places which is thereby a no place," she said.

He pinched the bridge of his nose. "It's too early for riddles."

"Then be satisfied with this: this is where Lord Veemos resides. Where he works. It moves with him and shifts to suit his needs. You may call it—as you've done in your head twice already—the Palace of Eternal Night. A bit dramatic but true."

She rose, taking her tea with her.

"Where are you going?" he asked.

"I want to explore. And I want to visit Lord Veemos's library. It really is something to behold."

"I'll come with you."

She held up a hand. "We've had enough of each other this morning. Besides, I'm sure you'll have more questions for me by tea."

The door clicked shut behind her, and in her ringing absence, Jack found he could eat again. Not much, but enough to quell the hunger that had left his limbs weak and mind cloudy.

Stomach full, he collapsed into bed for another round of drowsy sleep.

I am not an amateur, she'd said.

But even a skilled butcher still used a blade, did he not?

Jack knew her abilities would spare him none of the pain he'd promised to pay.

Still, he thought. *For their safety—*

For Silver.

He knew he'd have paid even more.

WHEN HE WOKE, THE FOOD TRAY WAS GONE AND JACK'S bladder spoke to him with desperate urgency. He rose and opened the door only to find a closet. Another door led to a dark hall with more of those glowing suspended orbs. It was so immense he dared not start off down it, knowing he would certainly get lost.

He shut the door again.

"Where might a man find a bathroom?" he begged the thriving darkness.

Wheels turned. He cocked his head, putting his ear against the wall, and *yes*, things moved behind the rich wood paneling pressed to his cheek.

Jack listened to the mechanics whirling until there was a click and the closet he'd opened the moment before was a closet no more. It was a bathroom again.

"Why, thank you," he said to the house, as he wasn't sure who else he should thank.

He thought suddenly of his mother, her gentle voice saying, *These walls have ears.*

In that instance, she'd been referring to his conduct and how he must guard it even in his own home, in case a servant should pay service to his father rather than himself.

Now he wondered what creatures might live in Veemos's walls. Surely he had servants to care for such a fathomless place. Though they must not be humans because, as Mr. Tromwell had pointed out, *There aren't many of us around these parts.*

Perhaps like Fire, Veemos made his own pacts and deals, and if Jack wasn't careful, he could find himself sentenced to a life of servitude between two claustrophobic slabs, pulling the great levers that governed the rooms' placements.

He shivered, shaking off the thought.

He used the toilet, brushed his teeth, washed himself, chose clean clothes. *Free of charge.*

He took his time fussing over his curls, which had never been fond of travel.

When he was satisfied with the look of himself freshly scrubbed and handsomely dressed in the mirror, he seized the handle again.

"I want to see Lord Veemos's library," he announced to the door.

He felt a little silly doing this, stating where he wanted to go before he actually started off there.

Yet the turning of unseen wheels echoed behind the walls, and then the handle twisted in his hand.

He pushed against the door.

The view staggered him.

When Fire had said library, Jack had imagined walls of books. Perhaps a grander version of his father's own study. Maybe even like the great hall at the university where Albert spent four weeks roaming before taking his barrister exams.

But no. The word *library* didn't begin to describe such a place.

There were books, true. But there was so much more.

It was an immense space, so high that Jack couldn't see where it ended, no matter how he craned his neck.

In the air around him were more of those dazzling, glowing orbs.

In addition to the orbs moving lazily past, he found floating maps and papers. Telescopes and ticking clocks. Pocket watches and small, whirling devices. Stray books flapped by like strange, misshapen birds.

There were armchairs and sofas large enough to seat twenty. Some with their feet firmly on the floor. Others upside down, giving the sense of a false ceiling above.

He was so busy looking up he tripped. His knees

connected with a precarious pile of books and he was pitched forward. Pinwheeling his arms, he righted himself.

He apologized for the mess he'd made, but the books were still unhappy. They ran from him like crabs on a beach, trying to escape his hands.

"Try not to make a mess, Jack. Lord Veemos is very fond of his library."

He searched for the voice but didn't see her.

"Up here," Fire said.

A staircase folded above him, and Fire stood upside down on it, her body impervious to the usual effects of gravity. Her hair didn't fall away from her in a rain shower of red, as good sense would dictate. It remained perfectly at ease about her shoulders. No color had rushed to her cheeks.

"How are you doing that?" he marveled.

She looked up from the book and closed it.

"Stay there, I'll come down."

She disappeared through a darkened doorway—also inverted—and a wall of books swung open beside him.

"How disappointing," she said, and tossed the volume she'd been reading on an armchair as it floated past. "I thought they'd be doing better. Alas. They're as idiotic in 2042 as they are in 1842."

Jack frowned, feeling as if he'd just walked into the middle of a drunken conversation.

"Who?" he asked.

"Go easy on them," Lord Veemos chided. "Not everyone can be as evolved as you, my dear."

Fire snorted.

Jack found Lord Veemos in an armchair with a paper suspended over his crossed legs. His shoes shone and his trousers had not a single crease.

Beside him was a cup of tea on a table, dark and steaming. All of this would be well and good if the armchair and table and even the tea itself were not completely upside down as Fire had been.

Lord Veemos's one exposed eye lit up upon seeing him. "Oh, hello, Jack!"

He folded the paper once, twice, until it was a quarter its previous size. "Stay there. I'll join you in your dimension. Much easier for you."

He rose from the sofa, and there was a strange bending of light that Jack's eyes couldn't quite follow.

Then Veemos was beside them, as tall and cheerful as he'd been the night before. "How did you sleep?"

Jack placed a hand on the back of his head as if to make sure it was not spinning.

He remembered Fire's insistence on gratitude. "Very well. Thank you, sir."

"Good, good. And breakfast?"

"Wonderful, sir. I feel very welcome here."

Lord Veemos straightened at this, his smile bright. "Most excellent. I'm so pleased to hear it."

The feather in his jaunty hat also trembled with pleasure.

"Tell me about the salt," he said.

Jack frowned. "The salt, sir?"

"Yes! The salt. The very notion that you humans thought to pull it from the sea, dry it, and then put it on your *food*. How clever!"

"The salt was good." Jack wasn't sure what else could be said about salt. He certainly had nothing to match Veemos's exuberance on the subject. "It's essential to taste."

"Imagine that." He seemed to genuinely marvel at the idea.

"Sir," Jack said, his eyes straying to that upside-down world above. "What is all of this?"

"A convergence. It's lovely, isn't it?" Veemos beamed. "Here, I'll show you around. Though I can't take you into the higher dimensions. I'm afraid your mind might pop if I try."

"My lord, if it's all the same to you, I'd like to tend to some errands. May I leave Jack in your able care? It shouldn't be more than a few hours."

"Of course! It would be my pleasure."

Fire pressed two fingers to her throat, indicating the demon mark on Jack's neck. "If you need me, I'll know."

And with that, she was through a dark doorway and gone.

"Now, where were we?" Lord Veemos said, his feather trembling with each twist of his neck. "Ah, *yes*. Let me show you the roads."

Veemos cut a path through the winding stacks. At one point the books grew so high on either side of them that Jack saw only the wisp of Lord Veemos's white feather as he hooked a right then a left, at the edge of Jack's sight.

"You have so many books," Jack said.

Veemos threw a look over his shoulder then waved a hand at the passing stacks. "Oh yes, they like to huddle together like this for warmth. I let them arrange themselves as they like, of course."

He stopped abruptly.

"Ah, here we are."

They stood in a circular opening between rows of books. It was a sort of crossroads, with at least four other paths veering off from this central pit.

Veemos chose none of the diverting paths, his attention

fixed instead on the tangle of lines in its center, suspended just above his head.

"You see, everyone has a road, Jack," Veemos said. His slender fingers tripped wildly over the strings, reminding Jack of a skilled harp player.

Then Veemos began to float above the ground, rising smoothly as his hands continued their work, higher and higher.

"You are all connected," Lord Veemos called down to him. "Every single one of you. Even the most distant can feel the tremors from its furthest kin. Not that many notice. It's very consuming, I suspect. Isn't it?"

"Isn't what?" Jack asked, feeling as though he were trying to converse in another language.

"Living," Lord Veemos said, his one visible eye fixed on Jack. "Does it take up all the space of one's mind?"

"Yes," Jack said, feeling that this was the right answer even if he didn't fully understand the question. "It does."

"Perhaps you need bigger minds," Lord Veemos said. "But here, yes. This is where your roads run the closest."

"I'm sorry, but I'm not sure I follow you, sir." Jack squinted up at Veemos, trying to see which of the lines he was referring to.

Slowly, Veemos's feet returned to the floor, and in his hands were two silvery threads. They glowed, quite a bit brighter than most of the lines around them.

"This is your road, Jack," Veemos said proudly, indicating the line pinched between his right fingers. "Isn't it beautiful?"

Jack touched it gently.

"Well, it's a representation of your road," Veemos said as a matter of correction. "An image your mind has conjured to comprehend it. Actually, can you tell me what it is that you see?"

"A cord? No, not so thick as a cord. A string? A thread?"

Veemos turned his head as if to see it from another angle. "Ah yes, I can see the reasoning there."

"This is mine?" Jack said, feeling a small shiver in his stomach as he plucked the glowing filament gently.

"Yes."

"And the other?"

"The one you seek," Lord Veemos replied, his dark eyes reflecting the light from the glowing threads. "I believe you called her Silver?"

"Him," Jack said.

"Him, yes." Veemos dipped his head. "My apologies."

Jack reached out to touch Silver's thread, but Lord Veemos pulled back. "I wouldn't."

Jack let his hand fall. "How will you cross our paths then?"

"Interestingly enough, it seems your roads have crossed before. They've run together for a few years already. It is years? Human time is a bit strange to me."

Jack thought of the first time he'd seen Silver in the basement of the inn, the boy's haughty stride and straight shoulders.

"We made each other's acquaintance about two years ago," he said.

"And your paths were destined to cross again in the future," Veemos said, looking down the line where Jack could not see. A stack of books blocked his view. "But I can force an encounter sooner."

Jack's heart leapt. "Yes, thank you."

Again those slender fingers danced along the line. This

time, it was less like a harpist and more like a spider with its many legs hard at work.

After a moment of pinched concentration, the lines in Veemos's face softened.

"There. In just a few days, you shall meet again. It couldn't be sooner, I'm afraid. I have to allow space for natural movement, you understand."

Jack didn't understand, but it hardly mattered.

Days. Just days and I will see Silver again.

His memories conjured Silver's face, his body, his heat. That sweet, commanding lilt of his voice.

Leave with me, Jack.

Jack's face burned.

Veemos watched this with rapt amusement. Then he said, "I should warn you that it may not be the most happy of reunions. Silver travels with another."

The demon. Silver still traveled with the demon.

"Lord Veemos," he began cautiously, "is there a way to break a pact with a demon?"

Lord Veemos frowned.

"Not for myself," Jack was quick to add, in case he would speak to Fire about his inquiries. "The one I'm looking for is in league with a demon. I believe it's out of control and making him do things he doesn't want to do. If I could free him, I would."

Lord Veemos lifted Silver's strand to the light. "There is no demon bond on this strand."

Jack's throat tightened. "There isn't? You can see that?"

He held Jack's strand up to his face and turned it ever so slightly.

"Do you see something like a red thread here?" he asked. "Or perhaps a faint red hue radiating from your line?"

He did.

"That is your pact with Fire. This is the only way I can ever see the demons, actually, when they bond with another. It's why they don't do it as often as your stories suggest. They're quite vulnerable when they throw their lot in with those who walk the roads. You're still so fragile in that state. If you die before your pact is complete, she could perish with you."

"Fire could die?" Jack couldn't believe it.

"They're bound to you by their word. She would have to find a way to fulfill her promise without you, which given the wording of some bonds is impossible to do. She loses a bit of her freedom when she makes a pact, do you understand? Demons exist for freedom."

"And Silver has no such bond?"

Lord Veemos squinted at the line again, but after a closer look, he shook his head firmly. "No. There is no pact. It's possible he has paid his price since you saw him last."

If so, and Silver was still alive, he hadn't sold his soul. Had he sold labor as Tromwell did? Or something else?

Veemos tilted his head, his feather brushing Jack's cheek. "Though I do feel a sense of duty and loyalty from this line. It's quite heavy. A burden. Silver must feel very beholden to someone."

Jack's throat tightened. "Could Silver be in love with the demon?"

It was hard to say the words against his pounding heart.

"There is certainly love, yes. But a great deal more than that."

Jack wasn't sure he wanted to hear more.

Veemos released the strings. They both watched as the lines rose again, floating up to where the others crisscrossed the twilight sky above the stacks.

Lord Veemos's eyes were round with pity. "If you want to free your friend, you may have to change Silver's heart. Love is a sort of contract of the heart, if you know what I mean. That's really the only way to break such contracts."

A hand fell on Jack's shoulder and squeezed.

"Don't look so glum, my boy."

"I'm not," he said, forcing a smile. "Thank you for your help. I'm very grateful."

When Jack lifted his eyes, Veemos's tender expression hadn't faded. He nodded toward one of the tunnels between the stacks. "Come along. I've something else I'd like to show you."

Beholden.

There is certainly love.

Jack tried to shove back against these thoughts.

He didn't like the twisting jealousy that rose up in him at the thought of Silver in love with someone else.

There is certainly love.

Hearts make their own contracts.

What is love anyway? Weren't there occasions when he'd whispered *I love you* into the soft curve of an ear and had not entirely meant it?

In those moments it was just something pretty to say to urge a climax higher or to deepen a lover's surrender.

In other moments, *not* saying *I love you* meant more than saying it. He'd never said the words outright to his friends, for example, but he certainly loved Albert, Baz, Silas, and Phineas. It was above question.

"There's lots of kinds of love," he muttered to himself. "It doesn't have to be romantic."

"What was that?" Lord Veemos called, turning to look over his shoulder

"Nothing," Jack said, trying to shake off the sulky feeling chilling his bones. "I'm only thinking."

"Ah, careful with that," Veemos said with a knowing nod. "Too much thinking carries one to dark places. Don't I know it."

It seemed like a long time before the book stacks finally broke open and Jack found himself in a cathedral-like room.

His heart skipped a beat, a small gasp escaping him.

"What's the matter?" Lord Veemos asked.

"It's so beautiful," he confessed. The sight of the burning orbs in the darkness hurt his eyes. "Sir, what are these spheres? I've seen so many since we arrived."

"They are the ghosts of worlds past." Veemos motioned him forward. "Here, I'll show you."

In the center of the room, far below the glowing spheres floating slowly past them, Veemos pointed to a golden stand. He reached up and seized one of the orbs and slid it down into the holder.

His hand slipped silken over the smooth surface.

"Ah, yes," he said. "I remember this one."

His fingers dipped beneath the surface of the ethereal sheen, and from this invasion, images projected up into the air above.

Creatures galloped across a plain. They ran like horses, but instead of manes whipping in the wind, there were several erect antennae that only folded and bobbed with the movement. The eyes were two, fortunately, but the legs—if Jack was counting them correctly, difficult to say with how fast they moved—were at least six in number, if not eight. There were five of these creatures together, each one bumping into the rump of another playfully.

"What are they?" Jack asked.

"There is not a word in your language for them, nor for

this world, I'm afraid. But it was a fascinating place. It had two suns and eight moons. Very little water, all of it fresh. It was why it didn't last, unfortunately."

He lifted the orb from its cradle and sent it back into the sky, grabbing another as it passed.

Once this one settled into place, he dipped his fingers beneath the surface again, the way one might test the water of a river.

He sighed fondly. "Abylonia."

Jack watched as the surface shifted and shone with light reflecting off the water. And above the water, two moons.

"It's an ocean," he said.

"Yes, quite contrary to the first, this world was made entirely of water. There was no land except that which was underwater. And the life..."

He wiggled his fingers and the surface of the water disappeared. In its place was a chaotic menagerie of creatures Jack had never imagined. Fish, he'd seen. But also creatures with long slender bones and eyes along the entire length of their spines. A gelatinous blob of a creature that seemed to warp into and out of itself as a means of propulsion. Something with very human eyes, but no nose or mouth and a body only of tentacles. Yet another that almost looked like a bird, except the wings were used to propel it out of the water to snap at small insects floating on the surface.

"Abylonia perished because the oceans became too warm. As its sun aged, it grew hotter, and that was that."

With a deep sigh, he lifted the globe from its cradle and sent it floating into the sky too.

The third orb, Veemos only frowned at before shoving it way.

"What was that?" Jack asked.

"A gruesome world," he said simply. "Not something you want to see if you hope to sleep tonight. You humans do sleep every night, am I not mistaken?"

"Can you at least tell me what lived there?"

"Blood drinkers. And the poor creatures they bred to feed that hunger."

So many, Jack thought. *More than I could ever see.* "This is how many worlds have *died?* How many still survive?"

"Even more," Lord Veemos said with a knowing grin. "Easily a hundred times what we see here."

A hundred times! Jack pressed a hand to his forehead. "Are you joking?"

"No."

They were ghosts. Ghosts of entire civilizations, continents, planets—destroyed. And when they passed from existence, they came and wandered these halls.

Maybe even Jack himself would be a phantom in this endless place one day.

"Yes, one day Jack Siran will be but a ghost," Veemos said with a sympathetic tilt of his head. "But likely not in *these* halls."

"Why would you show me this?" Jack asked. "It's... it's..."

Overwhelming? Terrifying?

"To remind you that what you fear isn't as large as you make it. While it's true your life is precious, absolutely unique, it's rarely so for the reasons you believe."

Jack's mind struggled against this.

"Simply put," Veemos said, releasing the orb he held and watching it rise toward the dark ceiling like a balloon, "everything is going to be all right. You may rely on your magic to see you through your difficulties. You can and should trust yourself more."

Jack stilled. Wasn't he supposed to hide his magic while they were here? Had he revealed it in some way? Would it escape the sister's notice?

Panic scratched at Jack's mind. "If I—"

Veemos held up his hand. "My sister sleeps."

"What if she wakes?"

"She hasn't for a long time," Lord Veemos assured him. "Fire told me of your abilities as soon as you arrived so that I could take precautions. I have."

But he'd known that Jack was thinking of magic. Of ghosts.

"Can you still teach me how to guard my thoughts?" he asked.

"You made a shield around your friends that night of the pact, did you not?"

"I did." How much had Fire told him?

"Do the same for your mind. A sort of helmet to guard your inner counsel. You can even make it invisible. But don't do it now. I do want to be careful," Veemos said. "It's best that you do not do magic in my presence. For your own safety."

"Yes, sir."

"You can do this," he assured Jack. "You need only believe in yourself. You do not need anything else to make it right."

CHAPTER 15

Does it matter that I have wanted to tell him the truth from the moment I met him? I fear it will not. It is the truth, not the intention of telling it, that matters.

— FROM THE DIARY OF LORD SILVER

In his bed again, Jack cried himself to sleep. It reminded him of his mother.

When his father beat him, she would carry him to his room and lay him face down on the mattress. She'd put warm rags on his back and cleaned each cut. It did not matter if his father had used his leather belt or the horse's whip—her diligent care was the same.

While she worked, he'd pretend to sleep.

He would pinch his eyes closed, tears drying on his lashes, and listen to the soft prayers she whispered to Nanny.

What can I do? If I interfere again, Talbot will only hurt him more. He's sworn as much. What is better in that man's eyes than to see not one suffer but two? I do not know how to protect him. I cannot send him away. Nor can I stop my husband. He swore to hit Jacinth twice as hard for my efforts should I do so again.

It broke Jack's heart to turn over and see tears in her eyes and how hard she worked to still her quivering lip when she asked, "How are you feeling, my love?"

After that, he pretended not to be so bothered by his father's beatings. He knew that any pain he showed would be another blow to her own heart.

So he acted indifferent. He put the pain away.

He put *all* of it away. The sense of betrayal, rejection, heartbreak, and confusion. It bred in the unventilated dark. Together they became another beast entirely.

His anger was born.

As he lay in Lord Veemos's palace, one arm thrown over his wet eyes, Jack was furious.

How could his father die like that? How could he be killed so easily? And before...before... what?

Why did the thought of his father dead anger him so? Jack should be relieved, over the moon, and yet, he was angry enough to strike something.

How could he? How could he before—

Before he could apologize to Jack for all that he'd done?

Before Jack could tell him exactly how every cut, bruise, and insult had ruined him for happiness? How his self-doubt and the unease festered inside him all because of what he'd said to him, done to him, asked of him?

Or was he angry because his father had died before he could take responsibility for what he'd done and now never would.

Despite the heat of his anger, dreams overtook him. Dreams of strange sea creatures and a sky full of moons, lost and looking for a planet. They wandered Veemos's endless halls, searching, waiting for another chance to be born.

Something clicked and his eyes snapped open, the uneasy remnants of a dream clinging to his collar and chest.

He sat up to find Fire at the foot of his bed.

"You've been crying. He showed you the worlds, didn't he?" she asked.

Jack pressed a palm to his forehead. "He did."

She rolled her golden eyes. "I told him not to do that. Of course he waits until I leave."

"Why did you tell him not to?"

"I knew you would have nightmares." She sat on the foot of his bed, one hand wrapping around the dark wooden poster. "He thinks it's inspirational. He calls it *perspective*. He has no idea how fragile you are."

"Wait, how did you know I was having a nightmare?"

She snorted. "Your thoughts aren't the only thing you share. Did he at least fix the roads for us?"

"Yes," he said. "Yes, I saw him do it."

"Then we should go. We've been here too long. I'd rather not tempt Fate longer than I have. She doesn't care much for me."

Jack wanted to ask if Fate was truly a person, and how one could slight her.

Fire rose from the bed and went to the table.

"I've cheated her more than once. No one likes having their hard work undone," Fire said. She grabbed the bread rolls from the fresh breakfast tray and began stuffing them in her pockets. She got three into the right pocket before slipping a fourth in the left. "Now get up. We're leaving."

"Where? Back to the demon world? To Hellebore?" Jack asked, rising from the sheets.

"We'll retrace our steps. How many of these do you think you can eat in a day?"

He frowned at the roll she held up. "Do we have to leave?"

"Don't tell me you're fond of this place already. True enough, you are outside of time. No wrinkles will form on that pretty face of yours as long as you're here. Though I don't know what your kind has against wrinkles. I find them interesting."

"That's not what I meant. I haven't even said goodbye or thank you."

"He knows your sentiments, and more importantly, he understands our urgency. Come on."

Jack followed her from the bedroom into the dark hall.

They went the way they had come, passing the floating orbs and cathedral ceilings as they approached the outer rock wall. Instead of going right, she went left. At the end of the hall there was a white door. She opened it on pitch-black darkness.

The nothingness filled him with dread.

"Are we going in there?" he asked hesitantly.

"I'd rather not go through Fireside if it's all the same to you," she said.

He remembered the way the heat blistered his skin and burned his eyes. Not to mention those ravenous, fire-breathing creatures so innocuously called *fireflies*.

"Where will this take us?"

"I will ask it to take us to Hellebore, at the edge of Thought."

Jack frowned. "The edge of thought?"

"Thought is the forest where you were carried off by Mayhem and Mischief," she said. "Hellebore is the city."

"I remember the city!" he said defensively. "I just didn't know that was what the forest was called."

"All the same, we're going. Are you ready?"

No, he thought. He wanted to say goodbye to Veemos, to thank him for his kindness. It was the proper thing to do. And he wanted to put a shield around his thoughts before they stepped out into the world again. He didn't want to worry about demons like Mayhem and Mischief deterring them.

"Before we go," he said. He opened his hand and closed his eyes. There was his magic. Cool and bright. He touched it.

Click.

"What are you doing?" she asked.

"I'll use magic to mask my thoughts so—"

She grabbed him, squeezing his arms hard enough to make him yelp. "Ow!"

"Don't!" She shook him. "Do you have any idea what you've done?"

"It's all right!" he cried, trying to shake her off. "Lord Veemos said as long as I wasn't in his presence I could."

"This whole palace is his presence, you idiot!" she spat.

Jack only blinked.

"It's not a real place. It's a convergence, it's a—Oh, *hell.* Never mind."

She seized his arm and pulled him forward.

But the outer door meant to serve as their exit slammed shut. Fire grabbed the handle and pulled. She yanked, and cursed to no avail.

Thunderous footsteps echoed down the hall toward them.

"Look what you've done," Fire hissed.

Jack's veins filled with cold water.

The creature marching toward them radiated menace. She might have been the same size as Veemos, but she seemed taller. Her dress, a thin slip of black lace, billowed like a flag in the wind, though no wind could be felt. Her legs were muscular from pelvis to knee, what he could see of them before the black stockings began.

Her hair was white—no, not white. It was the luminescent shade of moonlight, the same ghastly glow of the ghost worlds which seemed to flee her path and presence.

Everything about her facial features was tight, as if a great hand had grabbed the face and pulled back, stretching it thin across the bones.

Something caught the light and gleamed. Jack thought the woman carried blades tucked between each of her fingers and that perhaps he needed to prepare himself for flying knives, but then the light shifted again and he realized they were not blades.

They were her nails, crystalline as ice and filed to a point.

"Daimona!" the woman called out with the haughtiness of the richest lord. In her mouth she too had fangs like Fire's, and eyes that swirled not with molten fire but liquid moonlight. "You dare? In my own house!"

"It is regrettable, Lady Vee," Fire said with a disturbing level of deference. "But we wish you no further insult. We will be going now."

Fire tried again to pull at the door. It would not give.

Lady Vee, he realized. *Veemos's sister. This is Lord Veemos's sister?*

She was intimidating to be sure, but he wasn't sure how afraid he should be.

"That's what makes you stupid," Fire said under her breath.

"What about Lord Veemos?" Jack called out. Maybe if they summoned him, he could pull his sister back.

"You dare to come into my home, sleep in my beds, and yet do not pay me for such hospitality?"

"I wanted to say thank you," Jack said.

The lady turned on him then, her eyes flashing like an animal's in the dark. "You should. Come here, boy."

Fire grabbed hold of his wrist. "Don't. Stand behind me."

"I can help you," Jack said. "I know how to fight."

"And what would you say if a little boy with a wooden sword ran out onto the battlefield, Jack?"

"I'd carry him off before he got killed."

"I'll be carrying you off now," Fire said, her muscles tense. "Do not cross me."

"Lord Veemos!" Jack called again. "We need you!"

"Jack, be quiet."

"Jack is his name?" Lady Vee cocked her head to one side like a hawk sighting a mouse. "Come here, *Jack*. I want a better look at all that pretty magic in your veins."

Something warm and sweet, not unlike the fragrance that had wafted off Raziel in the demon city bar, coiled around his arms, his legs.

He found himself stumbling forward, his vision softening at its edges.

A sharp elbow in his guts winded him.

He coughed, the spell broken.

"I'll not apologize for that," Fire said. "If you walk right into her arms, you'll kill us both. Pull yourself together."

"I won't hurt you. Come here, Jack," Vee said again, another coquettish tilt of her head.

"No," Jack said firmly.

The creature's entire face transformed. The tight

features turned monstrous, the mouth rounding into a row of sharp teeth.

"You will not keep me waiting!" she seethed. Her words melted into a furious scream.

The whole house rattled. Dust floated down from the ceiling above. A crack split up the side of the hall, and from the woman herself—if she could be called such a thing—a burst of red light sprang forth, barreling toward them.

Fire's sword was out of her sheath and struck the light, parrying it away before Jack could comprehend what was happening. The blast knocked back his hair and pulled tears from his eyes.

Fire's hair too whipped wildly about her face. She did not wait to lift the sword above her head and slice through the air. A return arc of blue fire exploded from her.

The ground rippled and cracked, the marble rupturing along a jagged seam.

Lady Vee stumbled on her feet but did not fall. On her lip was the thinnest trickle of blood.

"Why go easy on me, daimona? I know what you're capable of."

"I do not wish to offend your brother."

"My brother!" Lady Vee's face contorted with rage. "Worry about offending me!"

Jack thought she would attack them then. She bent her head, leveling her shoulders for the charge. But she staggered, her head snapping back to reveal a thin, exposed throat.

It did not remain a throat. It bubbled and blistered, contorted and reshaped itself.

The body rippled until where there had been black lace and stockings and hair made of moonlight, now emerged the perfectly tailored coat Jack recognized.

The hair turned dark once more.

It was Lord Veemos. Or half of him.

The right side of his body had become Veemos again. Without his hat, true. Jack realized that the eye he'd covered before was Lady Vee's eye now. Had it always been hers? Was covering that eye the way he made her sleep?

Jack could do nothing but watch the struggle between the two beings for one body. The throat as well as the right arm belonged to Lord Veemos. The left arm and leg, however, were still Lady Vee's, half of her black lace dress stretching over her exposed leg.

The crystalline talons on the hand still belonging to Vee tore at Veemos's face and throat. He held it with the gloved hand he controlled, even as Lady Vee's features began to creep in and claim more of the face. Lord Veemos's left eye lightened and darkened in turn, the lips on that side stretching back.

"I'm terribly sorry," he said, his one eye filled with immeasurable sorrow.

"We need a way out," Fire said.

Veemos staggered. A guttural, feminine cry full of rage ripped from his throat.

"How dare you!" his sister screamed.

"Stop it!" Lord Veemos said. "I *beg* of you."

"A door, my lord, we need a door." Fire wrung her sword handle in her grip.

Veemos let go of his sister's wrist long enough to throw out one thread of magic. With this simple twist of his wrist, doors appeared. Up and down the hallway, door after door after door after door.

Then the talons slashed him, cutting deep cuts along his face and throat. Liquid starlight welled up instantly, filled the cuts, and ran down the front of his clothes.

With tears in his eyes, he looked to Jack. "I'm so sorry."

"No, it's my fault. I didn't know you meant—and now —" Jack didn't know what to say. He only wanted Lord Veemos not to be so sad. So obviously disappointed in himself. Jack knew that feeling. "Forgive me."

Lord Veemos's grip on his sister's arm tightened. His eyes widened.

With a panicked breath, he said, "*Run.*"

CHAPTER 16

What is creation without destruction? What is magic without madness? The problem is not her manner or her means. She is only what she must be so that all of this may exist. Without her, nothing would be born at all.

The only problem truly is that I love what I create. And my affection does not provide immunity to destruction.

— OBSERVATIONS MADE OF HIS
SISTER FROM THE JOURNAL OF THE
ONE CALLED LORD VEEMOS

F ire grabbed Jack's collar and shoved him through the first door that would open. Together, they tumbled into the darkness.

"What the hell just happened?" Jack said, panting, his curls falling into his eyes.

She shoved him forward. "Less talking, more moving."

There was another white door at the end of the hallway. She threw this one open and they walked through.

This time they dropped from a ceiling and hit a pile of hay.

Jack spat stalks from his mouth. "They share the same body? How can they share the same body?"

She hauled him out of the pile. "You do realize she will follow us?"

"What?"

"We have to keep moving if we hope to throw her off our trail."

As soon as she said this, the door in the roof of the barn opened and Lady Vee fell from the rafters into the pile of hay just as they had.

Fire pushed him toward the door in the barn's wall.

"Open it!"

He did, but not before Fire threw a second blast of blue light in Lady Vee's direction. One, two, three slashes from her blade created arc after arc after arc.

The hay caught fire.

Fire tried again. And again.

Lady Vee seemed not to care. She was out of the hay and advancing. She seized the sword, cutting her hand on the blade.

More silvery blood trailed iridescent over her skin. She grabbed Fire's hair and yanked it backward.

"Go through the door! Go through it and keep running," Fire called over her shoulder. "Run through every door you see!"

Jack did the opposite. He called his magic.

It rose up in him, fueled by his fear and panic, and formed a large phantom light over his head. He could see it, the rock hard and misshapen in his mind.

Bigger, he thought, *bigger and bigger and heavy enough to keep her down.*

He hurled it in Lady Vee's direction and it slammed into her, knocking her back into the hay.

Fire's knees hit the dirt floor, but only long enough for her to pick up her sword.

Then she was shoving Jack through the door, slamming it closed behind them.

"Are you all right?" he asked. "You're bleeding."

He was surprised to see her blood coursed as red as a human's.

"Don't do that!" Fire hissed. "She will track you by your magic. The more you use it, the better she will know it. Then she can find you anywhere."

"But you could've—"

"*You will die!* I can heal myself. You cannot. Don't you understand? What *I* am going to do to you will be a pleasant river cruise compared to how she wants to undo you. There will be nothing left of your soul or your mind if she catches you. *Nothing.*"

He didn't even have time to process how Lady Vee might undo him before Fire spun him and pushed him through the next door. And the next. And the next.

They ran.

Jack could hardly see the landscapes they passed. Waters and skies of every imaginable color. Deserts, forests, frozen tundra. Mountains and villages. As soon as one door closed, she pushed him through another, sometimes pulling him sharply left or right. Up or down.

"Run," Fire said.

"I am!"

He was exhausted from it. Panting. His lungs ached. His breath was sharp. But he kept his legs moving.

Then a door opened on a bookshop. It was like Everdeen's except he didn't recognize the language printed on any of the spines crammed into the stacks or burdening the tables.

"Through that door." Fire pointed her sword. "Go on."

Jack obeyed her, barely trailing his fingers over the dusty jackets as he passed. The shopkeeper, a short bespectacled woman, called out to them in a recognizable merchant voice. But when Fire propped her sword against her shoulder, the merchant fell silent.

Jack opened the door expecting to find a city street.

What he found was Lady Vee grinning down at him. Her hand shot forward lightning fast and seized his throat.

"Got you," she said.

A terrible pain ricocheted along his bones, from his toes to the top of his head. His skin vibrated.

"Where do you keep it?" Lady Vee moaned into his ear. Her body pressed the full length of his. "Some keep it in their minds, others in their hands or sex or..."

She sniffed him like a beast might, raking her nose along the skin of his jaw, his ear. Then pulled back, her eyes sliding to his chest.

"The heart. You're a romantic."

Her hand fisted the front of the beautiful clothes Lord Veemos had gifted him and shredded the fabric with one rake of her nails.

"A heart is easy enough to take," she said with a ravenous grin.

Jack knew this was the end. He knew this was the moment this monstrous creature would plunge her sharp fingers into his chest and rip out his heart.

The mark on the side of his neck flared to life, and Jack wrenched his head to one side in an attempt to escape this greater pain.

At the same moment, a sword slid right past his ear,

slicing the lobe before slamming into Lady Vee's chest. Her hold on him loosened and Jack's knees buckled, his hip colliding with a table.

The books piled there tumbled to the floor.

Vee staggered, her hand on Fire's blade. Fire placed one boot on the woman's abdomen and pulled, wrenching the sword free.

With the same blade, Fire cut her hand and threw the red blood on the ground of the shop. In its place a door sprang up.

This door was not white, but red.

Without a word, Fire shoved Jack through this red door. He landed in a dark place, his body striking a hard surface. Through the open door, Fire was silhouetted, looking down on him from where he stood.

The shop, which had seemed dim before, blazed behind her.

"What are you doing?" he asked her, the fear rising up inside him.

"Stay there. *Don't* move," she told him, and kicked the door shut.

Around the frame of the door a purple light grew brighter and bolder. Then the door exploded as if destroyed by a great blast. Fragments of its wooden frame rained down onto his hair, face, and clothes.

When he looked up, the door was gone.

Jack was alone in the dark.

CHAPTER 17

I don't like to be alone. It is the thing I hate most in this world.

— FROM THE JOURNAL OF LORD
JACINTH SIRAN

Jack tried. He *really* tried.

He understood now that when Fire said, *Don't move, stay there,* those were not guidelines. It was an ironclad rule for the sole purpose of keeping him alive in this vexing and menacing world.

For that reason, Jack swore he would not leave the spot where she'd left him.

He would wait here, on this very meter of earth, until she threw Lady Vee off their trail. Once it was safe again, she would come and retrieve him.

It didn't matter that it was too dark for him to see more than vague shapes moving in his periphery.

It didn't matter that all he could hear was the panicked tenor of his own labored breathing.

He was going to stay put. For however long it took, he would obey her.

That was, until the woman with the club came.

He heard the shuffling of feet first. Her soft crying.

He worried it might be Fire, hurt somewhere in the dark, then dismissed the idea completely. Fire would not be whimpering even if both her arms had been cut off. She'd be screaming bloody murder and spitting cold rage.

That left Lady Vee. Could she be down here in the dark?

Perhaps this was a trick. Perhaps she was only feigning a wound so that he would call out and reveal his location.

He said nothing. He only listened to the footsteps coming closer, the crying growing louder.

If I don't move, he realized, *she is going to trip over me.*

Did he dare to use his magic to give a bit of light to the space?

A light only I can see, he thought. *A magic only I know about.*

A soft glow sparked in his open palm, hovering like a lantern.

He loosed a breath. It wasn't Lady Vee.

It was a woman. A blindfold was tied tightly over her eyes. Clutched in her hands was the handle of a club, three feet long and fatter on one end.

She wrung the thinner handle the way nervous ladies and gentlemen sometimes wring their handkerchiefs.

He rose from where he was crouched and stepped out of her way. He didn't speak to her. He only took in the details of her dress, her face, the club in her hands.

She didn't look like a threat. In fact, she only looked scared.

Terrified out of her mind.

"My lady?" Jack asked.

She stopped at the sound of his voice, cocking one ear in his direction.

"My lady, are you all right?"

Her crying did not cease, nor did she answer him.

The blindfold was a funny thing. It reminded him of a game he played with his friends when they were children. One would cover their eyes with such a cloth and the others would run about, trying to distract him by throwing their voice this way and that. The object was to catch someone, even with your eyes closed.

"My lady, I'm right here."

Nothing.

She did not reach for him. Her feet shuffled forward again.

"Don't be afraid," he said. "I'm here, too. Perhaps we can figure this out together. You can look at me. I promise I'm—"

He was going to make a joke about being easy on the eyes.

But when he reached out and his fingers were about to pull off her blindfold, that was when everything went terribly, *horribly* wrong.

The moment his fingers brushed the fabric, began to lift it from her face, the woman lost what little control she still had of herself.

She pulled back the club and swung, howling. Her mouth contorted into a feral scream.

She swung again and again.

Each time, Jack managed to step just beyond reach, until the edge of the club struck his elbow and made him wince.

He hissed with pain, his feet tangling. He went down.

The air left him as his back made contact, but he didn't have time to recover because she was lifting the club over her head and bringing it down on him like an axe.

He rolled, feeling the wind on his face the moment before it slammed into the floor. He needed to get out of here. He needed a door.

"Light!" Jack yelled, the fear riding him now.

His magic doubled, brightening beyond the sphere of a lantern to that of a streetlamp.

His limbs grew heavy.

The room was full of these wanderers.

Creatures like this woman, eyes blindfolded, small clubs at the ready. Most stood perfectly still, as inanimate as a doll left in a corner.

A few others wandered slowly, cutting an unknowable path through the darkness.

His attacker swung at him again and Jack ducked, mostly, taking only a glancing blow to his upper arm.

But she was pulled forward by the force of her swing and stumbled into a man, his black hair placid against his head, trapped beneath the scarf tied over his eyes.

The moment she touched him, he sprang to life. His club came up and he swung.

Only he did not hit her. He struck another—man or woman, Jack could not tell in the shifting shadows—and this one too awoke, furious.

He could do nothing but watch the center grow. One combatant became two, then three and six, eight then ten.

"I have to get out of here," he said. He ran from the fight, pushing his way further into the dark. Where there were bodies he turned and twisted, doing his best not to disturb the air around him as he passed. To touch them would be to activate another nexus.

Behind him, the anger grew in its cacophony. The sound of clubs connecting with flesh made his teeth hurt. Angry snarls built to a fever pitch.

Away, he thought, *away, away, away.*

He hit a wall. Black and impenetrable. He followed it, running one hand along its surface until it connected with another. Jack pressed his back into this corner, sliding down to the floor with his knees to his chest, panting.

He could do nothing but watch the bodies before him jostle and swing. Absorb the music of their fury.

It's madness, he thought. *All of it is madness. They don't even know what they swing at.*

He considered extinguishing his light, but he did not dare. To see the madness was better than not seeing it, not knowing what was there in the dark, sharing his air.

So he watched. He waited.

Until his breathing slowed, his heart returning to its normal rhythm. The cold sweat in his palms began to dry.

And slowly, one by one, the bodies began to still again, resuming their doll-like stasis.

It could have been ten minutes, an hour, or a day. Jack didn't know how time passed in such a place. But time must have passed because everything was still again.

All that was left was the soft crying he'd first heard.

It was as if the frenzy hadn't happened at all.

Jack had almost fallen asleep when a door opened suddenly in the wall and Fire stepped through.

"Thank God!" he exclaimed. "Do you have any idea what it's been like in here? You left me in a cave of *insane* —Fire? Are you all right?"

Fire took a staggering step forward. Then another. There was something wrong with her gait.

He rose from his crouch.

"Are you—"

That was all he managed to say before she fell forward, nothing but dead weight in his arms.

CHAPTER 18

What could I tell him of her? Of what she was and what she became? Of her great history, its losses and triumphs?

    Nothing he would believe.

    I know no other creature so well acquainted with death.

— FROM THE PRIVATE JOURNALS OF
THE HISTORIAN RAZIEL DE PLAISIR

Fire's sword clattered to the floor, snapped cleanly in two. Jack wasn't sure how many times he said her name. As he turned her over, as he inspected her armor and limbs for deep cuts. There was blood. A great deal of it. He could see that even in this shadowed place with only his magic as a light. And an ugly gash across one cheek that made that side of her face seem painted as if for war.

But he couldn't find a fatal blow. Nothing to stanch or stitch.

"Fire! Wake up. We can't stay here."

She made no response. Her breath labored.

"What can I do?" he whispered. Only soft crying and moaning from the wanderers answered him. "What can I do for you?"

He looked around but there was only darkness. Only a smooth wall where the door had been.

We need a way out of here, Jack thought, trying to use his own magic to make one.

Nothing happened. The door he envisioned did not appear.

A magic potion to heal her then?

Again, his palm flexed around nothing but air.

His magic was there. He felt it coursing, seeking for some way to make it out into this world.

Only it could not fulfill his requests.

Her breath worsened.

"What do I do?" he asked again, pressing a hand to her cheek, the side not covered in her blood.

It was so cold. Too cold. He took off his cloak and wrapped her body in it.

She'd used her blood, hadn't she? To make the door that led him here. Jack wet his finger with the blood from her cheek and scrawled a door shape on the floor beside him.

Nothing. Whatever magic Fire used was out of his reach.

"What else do I have on me?"

With a wave of his hand, two things appeared. There was his dueling coin. The marker that gave him permission to visit the dueling den. It turned in the air in the soft glow above his lit palm. One side a cat, one side a snake. It shimmered and floated but was otherwise useless.

He could not save Fire with this.

The other item was a long gray-white feather.

Raziel's feather.

Should you ever need me. No matter where you are, I will come.

He looked at the feather for a long time, tracing its soft edge with his finger.

He understood what he was considering. To summon Raziel would be to summon another demon. *Was* he a demon? He wasn't even sure he'd received a clear answer on that.

He remembered also Fire's warning that death might be a better choice than asking for his help.

But Jack had no other options. There was nothing else he could do. He had no other way to help her, and each of her labored breaths seemed worse.

"You'll hate me for this," he whispered to the half-dead thing in his lap. "But I can't let you die before we finish this."

He took a deep breath and held the feather up rather ceremoniously.

"Raziel," he said clearly, being sure to enunciate. "Raziel, I need you."

He waited.

Nothing happened. He frowned and held the feather up a little higher.

"Raziel, I need you. *Please.*"

It felt as if something had changed with the darkness. There was a velvet sensation sliding over his skin. But Raziel did not appear.

He lowered his hand, defeated. "Why didn't it work?"

"Oh, it worked," a saccharine voice said in his ear. Hot breath slid up the side of Jack's neck and coiled around the inner crease of his ear. "I just wanted to hear you say it again."

Jack swore and twisted his ear away. "You scared me."

"Not my first choice, but a racing heart is a racing heart."

Raziel stood and came around them, stopping in front of the pair. His body and face were little more than an outline in the soft glow of the palm light Jack was using as his lantern.

When he crouched down to inspect Fire, Jack saw the beautiful curve of his jaw, the other half of his body remaining in shadow.

"Nearly dead at the bottom of a pit. Just as I expected, you *idiot*."

He was clearly speaking to Fire.

"It's my fault," Jack said, his shame heating his cheeks. "Lord Veemos told me not to do magic in front of him, but I was trying to shield my mind as we were leaving so I wouldn't attract so much attention. I thought that's what keeps slowing us down and getting us into trouble, me blasting my thoughts everywhere, and if I could just not be so stupid and—"

In a whirlwind, Jack told him everything that had happened.

When he began to repeat himself, Raziel grabbed the tip of Jack's chin with his fingers. "Stop that."

Jack's words broke off. "What?"

"Beating yourself up. Blaming yourself for everything. Who taught you to do that?"

Raziel released him.

"You're human. A very beautiful, very gifted human, but human nonetheless. By that very definition you will make mistakes."

"But Fire—"

Raziel cut him off for a second time. "I've known this

one for a *very* long time. I can assure you she has made plenty of errors of her own. Many of them far more consequential than you awakening a wrathful goddess."

He looked around the dark cavern.

"In fact, this isn't a bad place to hide you. Lady Vee would never come down here. As disgusting as it is, Fire did well. She must have a great deal of affection for you or be very committed to your quest."

"She's going to eat me," Jack said simply. "She can't possibly have affection for me."

"You'd be surprised." Raziel met Jack's gaze. "Now. Would you like to get the hell out of here?"

Jack hesitated. "What will it cost me?"

"Do you really want to negotiate down here in the dark with these cravens or can we do it somewhere more comfortable?"

He'd already summoned Raziel. Whatever the price, it couldn't be higher than his own soul, could it?

"All right," he said, too tired to put up a fight.

That was all the invitation Raziel needed to lift Fire from Jack's lap and throw her over one shoulder. Then he gathered the two broken pieces of Fire's sword and waved them out of sight before extending a hand to Jack.

"Come around behind me," he instructed. "Put your hands around my waist."

Jack did as he was told.

"Close your eyes and hold on tight."

Raziel was warm, his clothes soft. Jack placed a cheek against the fabric of the man's shoulder and breathed in the scent of his hair.

Raziel chuckled. "Open your eyes."

He did, and found the darkness was gone.

They were in a bedroom.

It was splendid, done up in a rich red with a large four-poster bed in its center. Sheer curtains were pulled back and tied, and a mound of pillows lay against the headboard.

Around the room were hundreds of soft candles burning, and a luxurious sofa in one corner. Beside it, a wall-sized bookcase and a desk piled with papers. It looked as if Raziel had been in the middle of writing a letter when Jack summoned him.

"I'm sorry if I interrupted your correspondence," he said. "When I called for you."

"I don't write letters," he said. "I keep records. And it's no matter. There is nothing that won't keep."

Raziel placed Fire on the bed with surprising gentleness, then moved around to the other side. He waved a hand from her head to her feet and back. Fire's body glowed.

When he lowered his hand, her breathing had improved.

He pulled two glistening vials from his pockets. One was full of a bright red elixir, the other with something as black as night. He uncapped them and tipped them both into her mouth, rubbing her throat with his thumb to coax them down.

"Will she be all right?" Jack asked from the armchair where he'd placed himself.

"What I've given her will heal the wounds, but she's depleted herself. I say give her a day, maybe two, to replenish her energy, and she'll wake."

"Thank you," Jack said.

With a wave, the vials disappeared and he turned to Jack.

"As for you..." He pulled Jack from the armchair and inspected him. "Your clothes are ripped. Your hair is a *mess*. And what's happened to your ear?"

"Fire cut it accidentally when stabbing Lady Vee."

Raziel ached a brow. "Something I'd have liked to see."

He ran a thumb over Jack's jaw, tipping it up so Jack had to look into his eyes.

"What to do with you?" he said darkly.

Jack's stomach tightened. It was that gaze that did it, and the memory of Raziel's lips on his.

Tonight his eyes were mostly gold, with a hint of green in them.

The corner of Raziel's lips quirked. "I think a bath is in order."

"How much will that cost me?" Jack asked.

"The price...You will join me for dinner. I'll make it a proper meal, I promise."

"Hardly a price."

"Yes, well, it's for my own peace of mind," Raziel said. "It hurts me to see you so poorly cared for."

His thumb trailed over Jack's sleeve.

"Though these clothes are very fine. Or they were in their former life."

"Lord Veemos gave them to me."

Raziel nodded as if he'd suspected this. "He has good taste. May I draw your bath now?"

Jack's eyes slid to Fire sleeping soundly in the large bed. Her face was soft. The pained lines between her brows had smoothed out.

Jack felt for the first time in this whole blasted journey that he'd made the right decision.

"She'll be safe here," Raziel promised. "My home is as well guarded against wrathful goddesses as anything else."

Jack didn't want to imagine all the threats possible in a demon world. "I'll have that bath, thank you."

"When you're finished, we'll dine."

Jack laughed. "Does the meal also have a price? It seems there are no ends to prices with you demons."

"You're smart to ask." Raziel leaned toward him. "We are capitalists. That's true enough. So yes, there will be a price. A small one. If I may be so bold as to assume you'll pay it."

Raziel's warm mouth covered his. Lust stirred in Jack's groin and abdomen, his limbs growing heavy.

Raziel's body shifted forward, making contact with Jack's from chest to hip, the tight flesh of his quad pressing against Jack's. This full-frontal pressure and all the delightful little shifts and friction it created made Jack's skin come alive and his breath catch even before Raziel's fingers came up to twine in his hair.

But there was no magic in the kiss. It was hot and deep, but there was no spreading apart of his mind.

This is not like the first time.

Raziel pulled back with a smile, his fingers lingering on Jack's jaw. "No. It's only a kiss. But for it, you may enjoy the full extent of my hospitality without concern for prices."

Jack closed his eyes and savored the last of it. When he opened them again, they were in a bathroom. The tub was already full and steaming, a large soft towel waiting on a chair. The light from a hundred candle flames danced off the water's surface and walls.

"I'll see you for dinner," Raziel said, and tugged on Jack's chin playfully.

Then he was gone.

CHAPTER 19

Ask me when I came to love him and I could not tell you. Ask me instead to detail the moment I first noticed the stars in the sky. Perhaps I will recall that more clearly.

— FROM THE PRIVATE JOURNALS OF
HISTORIAN RAZIEL DE PLAISIR

The bath was exactly what Jack needed. Hot enough to redden his skin and loosen his muscles as he leaned back against the tub's rim. It was scented with something. There were hints of lavender, which he recognized from home. His mother also perfumed his baths, especially those given to him before bed, with sachets from her garden. And there were other familiar floral scents. Lilac, lily, freesia, and rose. But there was also something else he didn't recognize. Something that made him think of the incense used in church on Sundays and also the woods behind Albert's house where he ran with his friends first as boys but even now as grown men, when the mood struck them.

Albert's face sprang to mind. Again, that terrible refrain: *Whatever he promised you, I'll pay it. He's suffered enough.*

He saw all of their faces: Baz. Silas. Sweet Phineas.

He missed them. He wondered what they were doing now. What they would think if he told them about Lord Veemos and the Palace of Eternal Night. Of the forest of Thought. Of the city of Hellebore. Of his strange and bewitching host.

What would they make of such an adventure?

Would they praise his bravery? Condemn his stupidity?

They had been so quick to rally around him at the idea of an arranged marriage. How small a matter that seemed now, a forced union. Lady Clara had been kind enough, and she might even have been a bit fun. He did feel that given enough time, they could have been truly friends if nothing else. Now, it mattered not. Jack was the Baron Siran.

As such, he would never have to marry.

He wanted to see them, his friends. He longed for the moment he returned and they would pounce on him and squeeze him until he couldn't breathe.

I don't deserve them.

That isn't my life anymore. It belonged to someone else.

A different Jack who'd spent his nights drinking in bars or dueling for trinkets. A Jack who fell into the arms of anyone pretty enough and willing enough to have him. A Jack whose father was as terrible as his mother was loving. A Jack with a brilliant and obstinate sister and patient nanny.

A Jack with the best friends in the world.

None of that felt real now, not a single aspect of that life, save one.

His desire for Lord Silver. Silver was the only piece of that life which had crossed this strange veil with him.

Silver.

If only Jack could talk to him, to understand what was happening and to finally see his face. To look upon each other for the first time.

As much as he longed for that moment, had longed for it even before a demon stole into his house and burned his life to the ground, he understood that it was an encounter he might not survive.

Silver might be ugly.

He laughed at such a silly thought. It could not be true. No matter what features were under that gilded mask, Jack knew he would adore them.

The real danger was the very possibility he would never make it back to that life at all. To his mother or sister. To all the people who were now counting on him.

He'd always known his ability to survive was in question, but for the first time, he also doubted Fire's.

After their encounter with Lady Vee, Jack realized Fire was not immortal. It was possible she wouldn't—*couldn't*—defeat Silver's demon.

And then what would they do? Die?

He would have bet everything he had and failed.

He placed his hands over his face and sighed into the cupped hollow of his palms.

This has to work. It has to.

He stayed in the water until it began to chill and bumps appeared on his arms.

Scrubbed and clean, Jack rose from the bath. He toweled himself dry and put on the clothes waiting for him. Layers of soft silk and a golden vest. Polished boots and a belt. A fine dinner jacket made of gold silk.

He put it all on and used the mirror to comb his damp hair into place, wrapping strands around his fingers to create the curls he wanted. He caught himself thinking of Raziel, and that he hoped Raziel found his curls in an acceptable state again.

When he opened the bathroom door, Raziel was leaning against the bannister opposite.

His eyes raked over Jack's body, inspecting him the way one would a horse. He tugged at Jack's cuff and collar. He lightly slapped at his lapel.

Then he nodded. "Very good. Are you comfortable?"

"Yes, thank you."

"Hungry?"

"Yes."

Raziel gestured to the staircase. "Then let us dine."

The dining room was small with only a table for two, which Jack found very strange.

"I suppose you do not have many visitors?" he asked, finding himself more than a little nervous as the waiter, a silent man in a servant's livery, pulled out his chair for Jack to sit.

"On the contrary," Raziel said, taking the seat beside Jack and allowing it to be pushed in by a second servant. "I keep a great deal of company, but tonight I wanted something more intimate."

"You changed your table for me? You didn't have to go to the trouble. I'm very easy to please."

Raziel's lips twitched as if Jack had made a joke, then, realizing he hadn't known the effect of what he'd said, the grin only deepened. It seemed to Jack that he wanted to say more.

Instead, he pressed his lips together and motioned for the waiters.

They disappeared through a door, only to return with their dinner plates.

A young man in the corner began to play a lilting tune on his violin.

"That's a beautiful song," Jack said.

Raziel lifted a wine bottle. He filled Jack's glass first, all the way to the top.

"I hope you have an appetite," Raziel said.

"I usually do."

Another twitch of the lips.

"Excellent to hear."

The courses began. A loaf of fragrant bread glossy with butter brushed over its surface was placed between two bottles of red wine.

On the plate itself, the first course consisted of beef in gravy and golden potatoes.

Jack took a bite of each in turn, accepting the slice of bread cut and buttered for him by Raziel. He chewed slowly.

Raziel drank his wine, watching Jack. "Is your food not good?"

"It's very good," Jack said.

"Then what troubles you?" Raziel returned the butter knife to the table beside his plate.

"I admit, it's difficult to enjoy this after everything that's happened. It's strange to be here after being in that dark place."

Raziel sat back in his seat, his gaze heavy on Jack's face.

"I also worry about our aim," Jack went on. "Lord Veemos promised to help us, but what if Lady Vee undoes that promise?"

"She can't." Raziel tipped his glass in the light. "She has no power over the roads. Isn't that what you went to see him for?"

"How did you know?"

Raziel shrugged. "Fire has little else she might need him for. My point is, you can rest easy here, Jack."

"I don't know how to relax," he said, meaning it as a joke. But the voice was too small and frightened.

It was true, wasn't it? He was always waiting for the next slap across his cheek. For the next belt to come down. It was difficult to relax when that was the atmosphere of his life, all he'd ever known.

Raziel put his wine glass on the table and dabbed at his lips. "Perhaps we keep saying it because you don't seem very adept at it. Was that your father's doing as well? Did he train you to carry this perpetual sense of unease?"

My father.

He's dead. He can't hurt me anymore.

Raziel's gaze had darkened, his eyes nearly black. "Is he still alive? Your father?"

"No. A demon plunged a sword through his heart."

"Oh, good." Raziel looked impressed. "Though a pity. I'd have liked to have paid him a visit. I can think of more than a few good tortures suited for such a person."

Tortures. Pleasures.

Jack could see how sometimes they were one and the same.

"May I ask..." Jack hesitated.

Raziel only smiled. "Yes, you may ask."

"Are you a demon or a god or some other manner of creature?"

Raziel gave this more thoughtful consideration than Jack had expected. Finally, he said, "It is hard to answer that when your own understanding, your human understanding, of those words is so limited. At the most basic level, I am a historian. I keep thorough records of all that has been in this world and others. I have lived and will live for millennia, barring misfortune, so I am well suited to this task. I see much and know more."

A historian. Not the answer Jack had expected.

"All right, but how do you survive? What do you eat?"

"I gain my strength and power by consuming the pleasure of others."

"You steal pleasure from others?"

Raziel pursed his lips. "*Share* in it, is more like it. Pleasure has an energy that sustains me."

Something moved in Raziel's eyes then. A subtle shift in light captured there. Jack felt it like a hand caressing his throat.

Then the spell broke and Raziel said, "It's why I wish you'd enjoy this meal more. Perhaps this course doesn't suit."

He motioned for the waiter standing by the door. He took Jack's half-touched plate of beef away. A second waiter immediately replaced it with a slice of juicy roast pork.

"Perhaps some jams." Raziel touched his temple. "As the bread is the only thing I've seen you enjoy."

"All of it is very good," Jack said. "I'm simply a slow eater."

Raziel scowled. "This will not do. I can tell the difference between genuine pleasure and feigned delight. You need only tell me what you want, Jack."

"Can you not read my mind like all the other demons?"

"When I saw you first, easily. Now, no. The trick that Lord Veemos gave you is quite effective. Was it difficult to master?"

"No," Jack said. "I'd done it before, or something like it."

"Interesting. I can catch snippets of thoughts and I can still feel your emotions clearly, but you are decently guarded."

"Then I've achieved my aim," he said, spreading jam across the bread.

Raziel tapped his nails against the wine glass. "That still leaves the matter of you telling me why the meal doesn't suit. I cannot sit here and watch you eat a loaf of bread."

"I love bread."

"Please tell me what else I can give you."

Jack regarded the beautiful table and all of its elegance. There was nothing unpleasing to his eye, not a single detail. And yet...

"Usually this would be exactly what I want." He fingered the edge of a candlestick. The flame above tremored. "A grand dinner with beautiful company."

"But?" Raziel pressed.

"But when I was in the bath, I was thinking of my friends and my mother and sister. I suppose I'm homesick."

"What cures your homesickness?" Raziel asked. "Apart from going home."

Jack took a drink of the wine. It was very good wine.

"When I come home from being far away, my mother always serves me three things. Vegetable pie, lemon short-bread biscuits, and a cup of tea."

"Vegetable pie?" Raziel marveled as if he'd never considered such an idea.

Jack's cheeks flushed from the alcohol. Raziel was right. He hadn't eaten enough if he was so affected. "I don't even know all that was in it. Some herbs and cheese perhaps, and definitely a sweet squash."

"Can you picture it for me? In as great detail as you can," Raziel said. "Close your eyes."

Jack frowned.

"This isn't a trick to steal a kiss. Though be sure you direct the thought at me so it will pass your shield."

Jack closed his eyes. First he saw his mother. Her soft, gentle face and deep brown eyes. He smelled her perfume and felt her cool hand pressed to his forehead. The way she always did when he came home after being away. The way she checked him over, inspected him for fatigue or fever.

Then there was Nanny. Round and urgent, pulling him out of his coat and boots and into the dining room. There was his sister, her brief acknowledgment before she returned her attention to whichever book she was reading. Nanny pushing him down into the chair where there, before him, was the pie. It smelled of sage and thyme. There were potatoes in it and some sort of bitter green. Sweet winter squash, bright and orange. The whole thing oozed of butter and steamed when his fork slid through the browned crust.

Then there was that first, delicious, soul-warming bite. How it filled him.

"I see," Raziel said. "Now the tea."

"What about the biscuits?"

"I know biscuits," Raziel said indignantly. "But tea is trickier."

Though Jack could not separate them. The lavender and lemon twined in his memories.

Raziel snapped his fingers, breaking Jack's trance.

Jack opened his eyes to find the pork was gone and in its place was a thick slice of vegetable pie. Beside it, a little saucer of flower-shaped biscuits, sugar shining on their surface. And between them, a steaming cup of lavender tea.

"Is it an illusion?" Jack asked.

"Try for yourself."

Jack forked a bite of the pie into his mouth. It was as buttery as he'd remembered. The crust had a savory crisp to its flaky edges, and even from the first bite, the warmth of it filled his chest. Then the biscuits, tart with that delicious tang of citrus. The sugar coating his lips was a treat savored twice, when he took a drink of the lavender tea.

"I don't know how you've done it," Jack said, his happiness blooming like a spot of sunshine after the rain. "But this is exactly right."

Raziel sat back in his chair, his smile that of a contented cat.

"Good. Now *please*. Enjoy yourself."

So Jack did.

He ate to his heart's content while Raziel dined with his eyes. Then when sleep crept in, his limbs heavy with it, Raziel said, "I think it's time I show you to your bed."

With heavy legs, Jack was led up the stairs. Raziel held open the door and Jack crossed the threshold first.

It was another sumptuous bedroom with a large, inviting bed.

He stripped himself of his belt and dinner jacket, laying them both over a velvet chair. Then he undid the buttons on his vest and shrugged out of it.

When he sat on the bed to remove his boots, Raziel placed a dressing gown beside him.

"Is this your bed?" Jack asked. *Of course it's his. Everything in this house must be his.* "The one you sleep in?"

"No," Raziel said, leaning against the wall opposite. "She sleeps in it."

Heat filled Jack's cheeks. *Are you going to watch me undress?*

Raziel's lips twitched. "As tempting as that may be, no. I want only to know if you need anything else before I leave you."

When a panic began to rise up in him, Raziel raised a hand. "I won't be far away. I'm not sure what else I can say except that you are safe here. Lady Vee isn't going to kick down the door and take you."

"How can you know that?" Jack asked, hating himself for sounding like such a child.

"Because I cannot sense her in this world."

"What do you mean?"

"Either she's gone to another or Lord Veemos is himself again. It's impossible to say. Given Fire's condition, I'd wager she put up a good fight. Perhaps it was enough to subdue the lady and give the lord a chance to reassert himself. All that matters is that she is gone and you are safe."

Jack's shoulders relaxed.

"So I ask you again, is there anything else you need in order to sleep?"

Jack considered this. "I need to know what my debt will be. I don't know that I can sleep without knowing. I'll lie awake wondering what to expect if you don't tell me."

"Very well."

"And I want to know why you haven't done the flower thing."

Raziel arched a brow. "Excuse me?"

"When you're...I don't know. When you're—" *Dear God, do not say inside me.* Instead, he gestured from Raziel to himself and back again. "There's this scent. It's like the lilies from my mother's garden. It makes it difficult to think."

"How unfortunate that my seduction makes you think of your mother."

Jack laughed, and Raziel seemed pleased to hear it.

"I only project my scent when I'm actively entrancing prey," he said. "In those moments, I'd rather you *not* think. It works better for me when you surrender entirely to your desire. But in truth, I had other reasons to act as I did the night I met you."

"What reasons?"

Jack put his back against the headboard, and Raziel leaned against the post at the foot of the bed.

He is very beautiful. A thought Jack did not direct at Raziel.

In the candlelight he looked more human than he had in the strange light of the tavern. There he'd seemed other-worldly and almost ethereal. Now he just looked like someone Jack would be very happy to wake up beside.

Raziel examined his nails. "I was a bit jealous, if I'm being honest."

Jack started. "Jealous of what?"

Raziel shrugged nonchalantly. "It began as an innocent enough inquiry. I wanted to know who and what you were, why you were here in Hellebore. I'm no better than the crow or magpie when I see something new and shiny."

"But what made you jealous?"

Raziel pulled one knee up to his chest. He rested a wrist on it. "Fire, as you call her, has only ever made a pact with one other, and it did not end well."

"When was that?"

"Many human years ago. It nearly killed her. So you can imagine why I believed I'd *never* see her link her fortune with another's for as long as I lived. Yet here you are. Curious, isn't it? Why she took the risk. Why she cares for you. What's so special about *you*?"

Nothing, Jack's heart said. *Nothing at all.*

Raziel frowned. "I was a little insulted that I took the bait, but not surprised. Only someone who knows me as well as she does could have managed it. All the same, I'm beginning to understand her affection for you."

Jack snorted. "You're mistaken, sir. She's looking forward to tearing me apart with her bare hands. She's told me as much. There is no affection between us."

Raziel tilted his head. "Is that so? We will see."

Jack looked away first.

"Regardless, I do not use my power on you because this time is different. She isn't awake. No amount of prodding or pushing will irritate her, which is something I rather enjoy doing, so there's little point. And I want you to relax, so I can better measure you. Once I understand your desires, I'll know how to best enjoy you."

Jack's heart skipped a beat.

Raziel tilted his head again, inspecting Jack as if from another angle. Or perhaps he only enjoyed giving Jack a view of his long throat and chest where the shirt lay open.

He must know what thoughts that conjures.

Raziel certainly smiled as if he did. "The bath, food, and care were paid for with the kiss and the pleasure of your company. In fact, you may consider all further hospitality, clothes included, to be complimentary. I only ask that you keep those curls beautiful for me."

"Do you think them beautiful now?" Jack asked.

"Very."

"I haven't done anything to them."

"Even better," he said. "That leaves only the matter of the rescue that is unpaid."

He clicked his nails together.

Raziel leaned forward then, crossing the bed and putting his face quite close to Jack's.

There was no kiss. He was only searching Jack's face. His eyes settled on his mouth.

"There are limitations to what we can do," Raziel said regretfully.

"I've done all of it," Jack murmured softly. "If you're wondering."

And Jack, feeling more than a little bold to have such a handsome face so close to his, shared some of his most favorable experiences. Nights he'd spent with both lords and ladies. Sometimes both or with two of the same.

All the moments he kept and replayed only for himself when alone.

His most adventurous and avant-garde acts.

In short, he sought to impress Raziel with the thoughts he directed toward him.

"What a lovely little flirt you are." Raziel ran a thumb over his lips. "You are experienced for your age, yes, but I assure you that there are things I want to do with you that you have *never* done before. I am not sure you've even considered them."

With Raziel's warm breath on his lips, Jack's desire warmed. The ache in his lap stirred, building to a dull throb.

His eyes, which he didn't remember closing, fluttered open.

I want you, he thought. But he dared not move.

Because Raziel remained still, he wasn't sure the thought had passed through.

Again, he thought, *I want you now. Here in this bed.*

Raziel licked his lips, fire dancing in his dark pupils. Not reflected fire, but a golden flame from within.

The sight of it reminded Jack not to play games.

This wasn't a gentleman who would roll out of his bed in the morning. This was a demon. And if Jack was not careful, he would get eaten alive.

Raziel pouted, sitting back on his heels. "I've scared you. A shame. I like you bold."

As his eyes searched Jack's face, they shifted to a soft violet hue.

"What about dreams?" he asked finally. "Do you dream, Jack?"

"For the last few years, all I've wanted was to be rid of my father and to be the greatest conjurer in the country."

And Lord Silver, he thought. *I still want Silver.*

Raziel smiled. "I meant when you put your head on your pillow at night. Do you dream?"

Jack's face burned. "Oh yes, of course."

"May I have your dreams?"

Jack frowned. "Like take them away? When I sleep I'll see nothing?"

That would be a shame. Some of his dreams were quite lovely. When he dreamed of the sea or as if he were flying like a bird. Or when he rode Starlight so fast the horse began to lift into the sky.

"I will not *take* your dreams," Raziel said. "But I will own them. I can enter when I like, and in those dreams we can do anything we want to each other without fear that I will hurt you. Would you like that?"

The throbbing ache in Jack's groin said *yes*. He would like that very much. But also, it wouldn't be so terrible to do whatever he liked in this very bed.

Right this very moment.

"And this may be preferable—"

"It's not," Jack blurted.

Raziel bit back a laugh.

"Preferable in the *long* term," Raziel finished. "Regrettably, I agree with Fire that you will not be very functional should we pair in the conventional way. And in the future, should you marry or love another, it will not matter. You cannot be unfaithful in dreams."

Lord Silver flashed in Jack's mind. Inconvenient. Jack pushed it away. "Are there consequences to such a pact?"

"Even in dreams I could exhaust you, if I am too attentive," Raziel admitted.

"A premature death then. Or a life I'm too tired to live?"

"No, that won't do. How about, I will visit your dreams, but only as much as your health allows," Raziel amended. "I promise never to deplete or harm you."

Jack looked into those eyes, but there was no terrifying golden fire. They were soft. Hopeful.

"Yes," he said. "I would agree to that price."

Raziel licked his lips, coming forward again. "Shall we make it official? It is still a pact."

"Another kiss then?" Jack asked, and already he was smiling. "Truly, what is it with you demons and kissing? I don't understand it."

"This one will hurt a little more."

"I don't mind a bit of pain."

"By the gods, I think you were made for me," Raziel said.

Jack closed his eyes, expecting to feel Raziel's mouth brush against his for the second time that night. But there was no press of lips to his.

Instead, there was a brief caress of a tongue on the side of his throat beneath his ear, and then Raziel bit down, hard. Jack's erection was immediate, and Raziel was kind enough to press a hand against it as he held Jack's throat in his mouth, sucking.

Here the flower fragrance came at last, sweeping away the last of Jack's pain.

He surrendered to it, overwhelmed by the heady scent as before. Though his movements felt heavy and slow. It was like trying to make love while very drunk.

There was only the vaguest understanding that Raziel's fingers were unfastening his trousers, removing all layers of fabric that separated them. That there was a warm hand, taking hold of him. With that first delicious pull, Jack moaned into an open mouth, wrapping his arms around Raziel's neck, as the weight of the demon's body settled down on top of him.

Just a little taste. Raziel's voice was silk in his mind, but it was a voice Jack would recognize anywhere. *Something sweet to send you off to sleep. Then the real fun will begin.*

The real fun.

Raziel was not wrong about that.

CHAPTER 20

It is said the boxes are extraordinary because they were made through the twin powers of love and sacrifice. Their creator killed his only children, and through the expanse of their souls, bound the dimensions of time and place to his will. The Day Box was born of the spirit of his son, paid for by the flesh and blood of this son. The Night Box was born of the spirit of his daughter, paid for by the flesh and blood of this daughter.

It is also said he killed himself for what he had done. That in the last days of his life, he claimed that whenever he opened the boxes, he heard only his children crying.

— FROM THE ENTRY "THE SOLOMON
BOXES" AS RECORDED BY THE
HISTORIAN RAZIEL DE PLAISIR

When Jack's eyes fluttered open, he was alone in the bed. He lifted his head to find the room empty and darker than he'd remembered. The candles had burned down. For a moment, he felt as if he were back in Lord Veemos's palace of night. But despite the momentary twinge of sadness he felt—he always felt sad when waking alone—Jack smiled.

His body was a pummeled waste of flesh. He felt as if every inch of him had been pounded and caressed in turn.

He rolled onto his back and stretched contentedly. It was curious. How could his body feel so completely used if it had been only a dream?

And if it were only a dream, how could it have been the greatest pleasure Jack had ever known?

Perhaps because there were limitations to physical intimacy. No amount of enthusiasm could erase the fact that a body tired. Limbs failed. Only so many orgasms could be achieved, and even then, each one was slightly more strained and less satisfying than the last.

Pleasure eventually surrendered to raw exhaustion.

It had not been so in his mind. In his mind, the dream body never tired and the pleasure did not diminish. With each cresting release, he found himself pushed higher and higher into ecstasy.

"How will I ever exceed that?" Jack whispered.

"I'd rather you not."

Jack lifted up onto his elbows to find Raziel placing a cup of tea on the bedside table.

"At least not for the sake of my ego." Raziel sat on the side of the bed. "How do you feel?"

"Amazing." Jack rolled his eyes up to meet Raziel's.

Raziel pushed his fingers through Jack's hair. "You did seem to enjoy yourself."

"That thing you did with the—"

"Yes."

"And then with the—"

"Jack, I was there." Raziel was clearly amused.

Jack sat up, placing his back against the headboard. "It all felt so real. Sometimes my dreams are no more than hazy bits, but with you they were crystal."

"With me they will always be real."

Jack took the tea and sipped it. It was strong and black.

He gathered his nerve to ask the question that plagued him. "Were...were you satisfied?"

A blush filled his cheeks despite his efforts to maintain his dignity.

"I am very satisfied," Raziel said, his eyes mischievous. "Can't you tell?"

Could he? There was more color in Raziel's face. A healthy glow. And his eyes seemed brighter. Not to mention they were a deceptively calm shade of baby blue.

Somehow, despite all possibility, his beauty was even more distracting.

"I never tire of hearing that you find me beautiful," Raziel said.

"Am I sharing again?"

"Only a little."

"Perhaps I am too tired to shield."

"How tired? Can you walk?" Raziel's voice filled with concern.

Jack rose and found he was only in a nightshirt that he didn't remember putting on. He felt steady enough on his feet to complete a course around the bed and return to it.

"Well?" Raziel asked, demanding his report.

"I feel a little sore, a little sleepy, but nothing serious. If I'd been riding all day, I'd feel much the same."

What we did wasn't so different than a long day in the saddle, was it?

Raziel laughed.

"You should rest today. Fire will wake soon, and she will not want to linger."

Raziel put his lips to Jack's wrist again, watching him with upturned eyes.

"I saw something last night," he said cautiously. "In your dreams."

"In my dreams?" Jack asked between sips of tea. "Many strange things occur in my dreams."

"Yes, but it is a wonderful way to get to know someone, by knowing their mind."

"You were snooping, were you?" Jack asked.

Raziel had a strange look on his face as he leaned his back against the post.

"What is it?" Jack asked, his wrist falling to the covers. "What did you see?"

"It was fragmented, but I saw your father in the burning study. And the night you were in the field with Fire. It seems you made a deal with her because you wanted to lure the demon away from your family and friends."

"Yes," Jack said. "And?"

"Are you sure you sold your soul?" Raziel asked.

Jack frowned. "Of course."

Raziel tilted his head and squinted. "What did Fire say *exactly* when you made your pact?"

Jack threw his mind back to that dark night on the field. To Phineas waking on the cold earth and the cube turning in Fire's hand.

I want your fire, she'd said as she'd traced his cheek with a talon. *All that flame coursing through you.*

"But she did not use the word *soul,*" Raziel said.

"No. But isn't that what fire is? It had been fire she'd called back to save Phineas. I saw it jump off her blade."

Raziel considered this. "Has she ever used the word *soul* with you?"

"No." Jack scraped his mind again. "You don't think it's my soul? But she said she was going to use her hands to eat me!"

Raziel tilted his head. "I seriously doubt she means to use her hands to *literally* tear you apart. She wouldn't do that unless you'd truly offended her. I can think of only one creature who has earned such a death. *Him* she would tear apart."

"Who?" Jack asked, his curiosity piqued. "What offense did he commit?"

"Betrayal." Raziel's gaze was far away. Jack let it wander, hoping he'd get the answer to his first question. He did not.

"It remains that there is no mark on your soul, Jack. I looked carefully. I don't believe it's what she will take."

"Then what is my fire?" Jack asked.

Raziel exhaled slow and deep. "It could be your magic."

His magic?

"She deals in magic. She knows more about it than almost anyone."

Jack's spirits sank. "If she takes my magic..."

Raziel seized his chin yet again. "You are a fountain. She can scoop all the water out of you, but it doesn't mean you can't be filled again. It may be painful to lose it. And harder still to learn it all again. But it's not something someone can take all of. In fact, it's not such a terrible price. You must've given her something incredibly valuable."

"The cube," Jack said without hesitation. He was cheered a little by Raziel's attentions. "I gave her one and promised the other."

A life without magic! How terrible. Would Silver even want him if he was no longer his equal in this way?

An inexplicable sadness rang through him at the very thought that without his magic he had no chance of winning Silver's love.

He hated the very idea.

Yes, but you will have your life, another voice said.

"Tell me about the cube," Raziel said, his expression dark.

"I won it from Lord Silver in a duel," Jack began, and told Raziel of the events leading up to his pact with Fire. "Then she noticed my father's signet ring had two cubes in the gem. Stacked atop of each other, meeting at a corner. Perhaps my father knew something of the cubes."

Raziel's brow came together. "A curious idea."

Raziel left him then. Not in body, of course. His fingers played absently in Jack's hair, but his thoughts were elsewhere.

"Where've you gone?" Jack asked into the hollow of his throat.

"Forgive me," Raziel said.

"It's all right. You must have something on your mind. My friend Silas thinks too much as a rule," Jack said. "And he still finds me good company."

Raziel smiled. "Does he? And do you let him play with your hair?"

"Lord, no. He prefers my sister." He almost laughed. "No, when I'm with him, I read books. If you must spend the day thinking, I could spend the day reading. Or we could do other things?"

Jack gave him a meaningful look.

Raziel's eyes shifted from baby blue toward gold. "Do not tempt me more than you already do."

"Are you saying we can't make love in the daytime? Are you truly worried you will hurt me?"

"Yes," Raziel said without hesitation. "I could put you to sleep, but even then it's too soon. I must discipline myself and let you rest between."

Jack wrinkled his nose. "You don't *really*."

Raziel pulled him into his arms and kissed him. No floral scent or caresses of the mind. Just warm, hungry lips. "I beg you to stop, for both our sakes."

Jack fell back against the bed and covered his face with his arm. "You'd best give me a book then. A large stack of them. Have you any books here?"

"Have I any books?" Raziel snorted. "What do you like to read?"

This was a twenty-minute explanation that Raziel had not been prepared for. But he bore it patiently, and based on Jack's descriptions, set off to procure what would most please him.

Jack, in the meantime, breakfasted, changed his clothes, and shaved. He brushed his curls, taking a bit more care with them. All while enjoying the wonderful ache of his body.

A move here, a twist there, and the tenderness would bring with it some bright and delectable memory from the night before.

Once he was presentable, he found Raziel in his bedroom.

Fire still slept in the bed, her mess of red hair spread over his pillow. Raziel was at his desk, his hair brushed and tied with a new emerald-green ribbon. In his left hand, an ink pen hovered above the page.

"I've set you up there," he said. He pointed at the large sofa against the wall. Beside it was a little table with six or seven books piled on top of it. And beside that, fresh tea, and another plate of his mother's lemon-lavender biscuits.

"Thank you," Jack said, and was so bold as to slip an arm around Raziel's neck and kiss his ear.

He glanced at what Raziel was writing but could not read it. It was in a language he did not know. But he saw the diagrams of the cubes.

"Funny writing."

"I write in the demon standard," Raziel explained. "No human can read it."

"I suspect we aren't meant to." Jack reluctantly released him and settled onto the sofa. He slipped a biscuit into his mouth and lifted the first book from the pile.

It was a tragedy. Jack was only ten pages in before the lovers were separated by war, and he knew that by the end of the book, they wouldn't be who they were at the start, and therefore would not end up together.

He didn't like that ending.

The second was lighter. A widower falls in love with a shopkeeper and they move to the country with their dog, from what he could piece together by the sections he read.

In the third, two men fall in love but then marry women. No, wait. One becomes a priest when the other marries. A bit boring.

Raziel's pen stopped moving.

The fourth was a romance about two girls who had been best friends until one kissed the other. Then she fled into the arms of a man.

"Are these all tragedies? Is the shop girl with a dog the only one to have a happy ending?"

"Do you actually read the books or just flip through them?" Raziel asked with an air of irritation.

"I'm seeing which I want to commit to. There is nothing wrong with getting a sense of each."

He slipped another biscuit defiantly into his mouth.

"Is that what you're doing?" Raziel's lips twitched. "Tasting before commitment?"

He lifted the pen and went back to his records. Jack returned to his book, but his eyes kept straying above the page. He watched Raziel work, the long curve of his jaw splendid for tracing with the eyes.

God help me, I'm half in love with him already.

Silver's mask flashed in his mind's eye. The way he'd looked when he'd scaled the balcony and stepped into Jack's bedroom.

I came for you.

Leave with me. Please.

Was he silly for chasing Silver halfway across the demon world? He supposed he was no more rash than any of the idiots in these books piled beside him.

But for what? Because of his infatuation with a man whose face he'd never even seen? He'd told himself that it was for answers. That it was to make sure the demon who'd wanted him did not come for his mother or sister. That he could be sure to confront his problems head on.

That had been but a part of it.

The rest had been plain: he wanted to save Silver. He wanted to save him, and in doing so, perhaps Silver would love him.

Then this one came along. He treated Jack so kindly, as if he mattered, but wasn't he little more than a meal? A diversion? A way to pass the night. Why did Jack have to get silly thoughts in his head for anyone who paid him half an ounce of attention?

It's not my fault. What right does he have to be so beauti-ful? Jack thought.

"I'm sure many have thought the same of you."

Raziel was leaning back in his chair, watching Jack with that unreadable expression of his again.

"What?" Jack pulled free of his thoughts, closing the book he was holding.

"I said, I'm sure many a lord and lady have looked upon your face and thought, 'What right does he have to be so beautiful?'"

Jack doubted this. Yet he had seen the way others looked at him, how their eyes lingered on his face, his body. And how often had his friends commented on some attribute or another? His curls, his lashes, his chest and hips?

"I might be beautiful, but they do not love me," Jack said.

Raziel looked deeply unhappy for some reason.

"I've ruined the day with my mood." Jack forced a smile and good cheer. "I'm being silly. Ignore me."

"*Don't*," Raziel growled.

Jack stopped talking.

"I will not ignore you," he went on. "But I will make a suggestion."

Jack's stomach turned. He didn't want Raziel to be angry with him.

"Instead of worrying whether or not Lord Silver will love you, or if I love you, or if anyone else loves you, love yourself. If you do nothing else with your life, do this."

Then he rose from his desk. "I must go."

"Forgive me," Jack said. He wasn't even sure what he was apologizing for, and he hated himself for how easily the words left his lips, how desperate he was to make whatever offense he'd committed right again. "Whatever I've said to upset you, I beg your pardon and—"

Raziel cupped his cheeks and met Jack's eyes. "Stop."

"But I—"

Raziel hushed him.

"I'm not leaving you," he said tenderly. "I will see you every night that you can bear it, and I will come when you ask me to. But I cannot be here now."

"Why?"

"She is waking, and for the sake of us both, you do not want me here when she does. She won't be happy to be here again."

Jack's shoulders sagged with relief.

I'm not the reason. Then doubt crept in. *Or is he only being kind?*

"She won't be happy to be in Hellebore? She seemed rather fond of it last time."

"Not Hellebore. In my bed," Raziel said, and kissed Jack tenderly.

Then the door clicked shut behind him.

"Wait, what?" Jack muttered into the ringing silence. "She's been in your bed before?"

His mind made a very short list of reasons why Fire would have woken in Raziel's bed before.

Then another list of everything they'd said about one another. The flirtation, the jealousy.

Of course. Why hadn't he seen it sooner?

Fire's eyes opened and she sat up in bed, one hand going to her head as her golden eyes swept the room.

She took in Jack, freshly washed and dressed. Then her gaze settled on the bed itself. The covers. The curtained posts.

Slowly, realization dawned on her.

"You idiot," she growled through clenched teeth.

"You were dying." Jack slipped the last biscuit into his mouth. "I didn't have many options."

"There are always options."

"Not when I'm stuck at the bottom of a pit with no way to make a door! I tried! I tried everything."

"Tell me what happened."

Jack recounted his terrible time in the dark with what Raziel had called the cravens. The moment she'd appeared, half dead, and how the door closed behind her. How he'd tried everything to get her out until all he had was Raziel's feather.

He did not, however, tell her about the dining and the flirting and the sex. Especially now that he was more than convinced they'd once been lovers, and for whatever reason, it had not ended well.

"What did you give him?" Fire asked.

Jack hesitated.

"*What*, Jack?"

"A kiss for the hospitality and my dreams for the rescue," Jack said. "Well, and there was the bit about my curls."

"You've agreed to let him into your dreams? I don't need to ask for what purpose."

"Good," Jack said. "The telling will only embarrass us both."

"He will know your mind," she said. "That is a tremendous power to give him over you."

"All you demons seem to know my mind, despite my efforts," Jack said. "Is this where you tell me I'm an idiot who paid too much for those medicines he gave you?"

Fire's gaze softened. "You paid a fair price. I dare say you're not unhappy with the bargain."

Jack's groin warmed just at the thought of it. He suppressed a smile. "It's not terrible."

"And he's been looking after you, keeping you fed?"

"I am well fed," Jack said. "I've had so many biscuits."

"I lost the bread rolls. I threw them at Lady Vee."

"That must have been a sight." Jack remembered Fire stuffing her pockets before they'd left Veemos's palace.

Fire tossed back the covers and stood. "Are you rested despite your...energetic nights?"

"Yes," Jack said, fighting against the heat building in his cheeks.

She grabbed her clean armor off the back of the chair. "Then let's get out of here."

CHAPTER 21

He might be so bold as to ask me, one day, how I came to love her and why it did not last. How to explain that once betrayed, some creatures no longer desire to be loved?

— FROM THE PRIVATE JOURNAL OF
HISTORIAN RAZIEL DE PLAISIR

Fire was dressed and downstairs in minutes. Jack followed silently, sensing the tension in her movements and her dark mood.

The front door loomed, and Jack began to worry he wouldn't see Raziel again, not even to thank him for his excellent care.

"Why do you always insist on leaving without saying farewell?" he asked.

"I do not waste time," was Fire's reply.

She had the door open, the roar of the street rushing in to meet them. The music, laughter, and crowds were as jubilant as Jack remembered.

"Wait," a voice called out.

Fire's shoulders tensed.

Jack turned.

Raziel held out her sword. It was the sight of it that stopped Fire in her tracks.

"That was broken in half," Jack said, stepping close to inspect it. "And burned to hell."

"I remember," Fire said, her voice low.

"You fixed it?" Jack asked.

"No, not I. I do not have the skills," Raziel said.

Fire took the blade in her hands. "Frennan?"

"The one." Raziel slipped his hands into his pockets.

"He always does good work." Fire admired the blade. Only once she'd looked to her satisfaction did she slide it into the sheath affixed to her back.

"He's in town today. He is expecting you, if you intend to prepare," Raziel said.

Fire searched Raziel's face. She looked ready to speak. The air between them felt thick with emotion. Jack tried to back away, give them some privacy, but there was nowhere to go. He bumped into a grandfather clock and it clanged loudly.

"Forgive me," he muttered, trying to steady the clock.

"It's..." she began. Then her face hardened. "I'm not paying for this."

Raziel's lips twitched. "Jack already has. On your behalf."

"I did?" Jack asked.

"You did."

"Then we should go." Fire turned away.

"He is nothing like the other, you know," Raziel called out.

Fire hesitated in the doorway, her hand on its frame. Finally, her shoulders relaxed. "I know."

Then she was gone.

Nothing like the other? Jack wondered. A new lover, perhaps? His curiosity was piqued.

Raziel turned his attention to Jack. "I have something for you as well. Two things, actually."

He opened his hand, and in his palm was a small satchel of the lemon-lavender biscuits. Beside it lay a red vial. He held this up to the light.

"If you are fatally wounded, drink this," he said, before pressing it into Jack's palm.

"May I use it on Fire?" Jack asked, accepting the biscuits next.

Raziel tilted his head. "You could try, but it won't have much effect on its own. She needs something else. This is meant for human flesh."

"I can use it on Silver then, if he's hurt."

"Will you never consider your own safety first?" Raziel asked with an air of irritation. He sighed. "Do you have your feather?"

Jack waved his hand and it appeared.

"Very good. Now, put it all somewhere safe."

Jack did as he was told and waved the items away, storing them in the in-between with his coin.

Then it was only the two of them standing by the door, with the morning sunlight cutting a line across Raziel's beautiful cheek.

"I should go. She's probably left me," Jack said.

"She's waiting outside the door."

"Oh. Then may I kiss you goodbye?" Jack asked shyly.

Raziel looked ready to devour him, his ice-blue eyes shifting to gold again. "Always kiss me goodbye."

"Very well." Jack wrapped his arms around Raziel's waist and pulled him close. It was necessary to come up on his toes to reach his mouth, given the five-centimeter difference in their heights.

And he could not work the magic as Raziel did. There was no consumption of the mind or drunken senses. It was just a very warm, very lovely brush of lips.

"Thank you," Jack said as their lips broke apart. "For all of your help."

Jack released him and turned to go.

"Wait." Raziel caught his hand. He used the fingers of his free hand to fix one of Jack's curls as he spoke. "Promise me that you will be careful. If you're hunting who I think you're hunting, be smart. Do what Fire tells you. She will keep you safe."

Keep me safe? Unlikely. But Jack didn't want to start a fight as he was leaving.

Instead, he brushed a kiss over Raziel's knuckles and said, "I promise."

WHEN JACK FOUND FIRE ON THE STREET, SHE WAS inspecting her blade with a careful eye. At the sight of him, she returned it to its sheath and started off down the road.

"Where are we going?" Jack asked, jogging to keep up.

"We need a few things."

"Battle things?" Jack asked. "We'll get them from this Frennan?"

She did not look at him. Her head was up, her eyes scanning the street. "His shop is this way."

"You seem very alert for someone who was just very unconscious," Jack remarked.

She ignored this. "Keep your eyes open for Silver. We should run into them today or tomorrow."

Jack tried to calculate the days since Lord Veemos had worked the roads. Today or tomorrow? Was that right? Fire stopped abruptly and Jack stumbled into her back, taking the hilt of her sword to his cheek.

"Ow."

"This is Frennan's place."

He peered through the shop windows over her shoulder. The inside was dim with the glow of a fire illuminating one side. Behind a counter, a round man with an orange beard laughed robustly, enjoying a spirited exchange with his customer.

"Wait here," Fire said.

"What? Why?" He wanted to see the weapons. What could be more impressive to his friends than a demon sword?

"But what if I want to buy something?" he whined.

"No," Fire said firmly. "You're getting far too comfortable making deals with demons. I'll not take you in there. You can't handle the temptation."

He pouted. "What am I to do out here?"

"Look for Silver. If you see him, call out to me. I won't bother to tell you not to leave this spot."

I wouldn't even know his face in a crowd if I saw it, he thought. *I'll only know him if he wears his mask. Why would he be here?*

Before he could protest, Fire pulled open the door and disappeared inside, leaving Jack on the street.

"On my life! What corner of hell did you crawl from, my lady?" Frennan's voice barked. "You've been scouring ten thousand worlds in search of that Judas, I hear."

The door swung shut, cutting the man's voice in half.

Jack, forlorn, leaned one shoulder against the stone front of the store and let his eyes rove the busy streets. People danced, sang, and talked as loudly as they would in any inn. Jack's mood toward it soured, feeling as he did, that Fire kept excluding him from all the truly fun parts of the demon world.

He wasn't sure how long he stood there, watching horses and carts wander by. Listening to the music and watching the ladies and gentlemen twirl.

His eyes lazily scanned the crowd, but he saw no silver mask.

But his gaze did snag on a familiar face. A woman with long blond hair spilling down her back, in riding breeches and leather gloves, a satchel thrown over one shoulder. She was scanning the signs on the shops, clearly looking for something.

Then she saw Jack and recognition sparked in her eyes.

He pushed off from the wall. "Lady Clara?"

Her eyes doubled in size. She froze.

Now Jack was sure of it. He had not seen her in trousers or with her hair down so prettily, but it was certainly her.

"Lady Clara, wait!"

She did not wait. She ran.

Jack took off after her. He dove through a flock of birds and dodged a cart pulled by a large gray creature with wings.

"God, she's fast." He leapt over a stack of crates and turned the corner. Already she was far ahead of him, knocking over barrels into his path.

Still he ran. He ran until his lungs ached with the effort.

Through the streets, through a shop with owners and patrons hissing their annoyance.

She was slowed only by a thick knot of people between the narrow buildings. Jack was able to gain ground.

"Wait! Clara!" Jack cried, barely able to speak. "I just want to talk to you. I won't tell your father you're here."

He reached out and his fingers brushed her pack. One finger hooked into the loop where she'd tied it and pulled, loosening the top. She turned, trying to seal it shut.

"Stop!" she commanded. "Let go of me!"

"Why do you run? I only want to talk."

"I can't talk to you!" She tugged hard on the pack.

"Why?" Was she angry that he'd disappeared without letting her know where they'd stood in their engagement? Jack didn't let go. He tugged back. "Why are you here? How did you find this place? How—"

The bag tipped and the contents that had been secured inside tumbled out onto the cobblestoned street. A coin purse, a scarf, food. A small blade, a pistol, a floppy hat, and a waterskin.

But the item that stopped Jack in his tracks was the silver mask.

It clattered to the cobblestones and rolled around and around on its rim, before settling to a stop.

Jack knelt down and lifted it from the dirty street.

It was the perfect replica of Lord Silver's mask. It *was* Lord Silver's mask.

"Why do you have this?" he asked.

He met Clara's eyes.

And then he knew.

He saw it in the curve of her jaw, her neck. In the soft blond of her hair and those eyes...

They were the palest blue. Silver blue.

"You're Silver," he said, dumbstruck. "*You're* Lord Silver."

Her eyes rounded. Her mouth opened and closed but no sound came out.

She isn't denying it.

Her body seized and collapsed into Fire's embrace.

The demon bore her weight in one arm as if she were little more than a doll.

"Good work, Jack," she said, golden flame dancing triumphantly in her eyes. "I knew you could do it."

CHAPTER 22

I have been running for so long, I do not know if I could stop even if I wished it. But if there was ever one worth stopping for, if there was one who filled my head with dreams that cannot be, it is him.

— FROM THE JOURNAL OF LADY
CLARA NIGHTINGALE

"Maybe she hasn't been lying," Jack said, holding the satchel in one hand and the mask in the other. "Maybe she has Silver's mask because she knows him. What if Silver is her brother?"

They were in an empty barn at the edge of town. There were piles of hay and a chair in the center. What creatures stabled here, Jack couldn't be sure. They certainly did not smell like horses.

Fire stood behind an unconscious Clara, fastening her to the chair with thick ropes.

"And why do you have to tie her up?" Jack asked.

"She's fast and likes to run. We need to talk to her. Seems simple enough, doesn't it?" Fire yanked on the rope one more time to be sure it was secure.

"Maybe—"

"Stop," Fire pleaded. "Why are you refusing to accept who she is?"

Because it means she lied to me, he thought.

"Your world is unkind to women. Of course she hid what she was."

Jack couldn't argue that point. He'd heard far too much from Selina on the subject to doubt this claim. "I still wish she'd told me. I feel like a fool."

"Because she bound her chest and disguised her voice? What of it?"

"I thought I knew him," Jack shouted, his heart racing. *I thought we knew each other. Everything but our own faces.* "I don't know her at all."

Fire stopped. "It is an unpleasant feeling when one realizes such a thing about a person."

Jack sank down into the hay. "Lord Veemos called Silver a she. Did you know too?"

"Yes," Fire said.

"Since when?"

"I saw her in your memories."

Jack fell back against the adjacent pile of hay. "I don't like being deceived."

"You wanted to know the truth. Careful what you wish for."

"I still want to know what is going on." He ran a hand down his face. "I don't understand any of it. If Silver is Clara, why did she come to my house under the pretense of marriage only to attack us? Was it a distraction? Who was that blasted demon? Surely Clara didn't make a demon pact to get out of marriage."

"Oh, ladies could do worse," Fire said.

"It doesn't account for the cubes and letters and all the rest. What is going on here?"

Fire grinned. "Let's wake her and find out."

"Wait!" Jack quickly tried to smooth his hair and straighten his vest. It was difficult to make oneself look desirable when lying on a pile of hay. Or at least, with one's clothes still on.

Fire pressed her fingers to the side of Clara's temple and the girl woke with a jolt.

"Morning," Fire said.

"Hellfire," Clara swore. The venomous look she had for Fire softened when she turned on Jack. "Jack."

"Should I call you Lady Clara or Lord Silver?" Jack said. He hated how petulant he sounded.

"Clara will do."

"Where is he?" Fire asked.

"Was it all a lie?" Jack asked in the same breath.

Fire sighed. "We should've discussed how this line of questioning would proceed beforehand."

Jack stood up. "Was I a joke to you?"

"No," Clara said.

"The dueling, the flirtation. The *letters*."

"I cherished your letters," she said softly.

He threw up his hands. "Was anything in them real? I tell you about my friends and my father and a thousand little secrets and you just, what? Made it all up?"

"No," she said firmly.

"Then as soon as you find out who I am, you come to my house and kill my father!"

She closed her eyes then, braced herself.

"What are you doing?"

"Go on," she said. "You want to hit me. Hit me."

Jack took a step back, truly horrified. "I would never hit you. Why do you think I could?"

"Because Hellsbane would," Fire said.

Hellsbane. Where had Jack heard that word before?

Clara looked at Fire for the first time. "Are you the one he runs from?" Clara asked. "The one who has been hunting him?"

"Yes," Fire said.

"I made a deal with her to get the answers to all of this," Jack said. "Like why you burned down my house and killed my father."

Clara sneered.

Jack would have been terrified of that cold glare if it wasn't directed at Fire. "You haven't told him."

"Told me what?"

"Start from the beginning. Then I will speak," Fire said.

Clara turned to Jack. She looked so tired. The bags beneath her eyes were dark. Her shoulders sagged.

"I don't know where to begin," she said.

"Start with your real name," Jack said. "Because I've already given you mine."

"Clara is the name my mother gave me when she bore me. She died when I was three. I don't remember much about her. I am told she was very patient, very kind. My father told me little about her, and none of it flattering. He picked her the way one picks a broodmare. He saw in her traits that he would have in his children."

"He wanted a son?" Jack asked.

"No, a son might overthrow him," Clara said. "He wanted an obedient servant. And I took to my lessons well. You don't understand. I can see it in your face."

"If your mother died, who was the lady who accompanied you to my house?"

"Justine was my nanny. She took charge of my lessons when I was eleven. She had her work cut out for her. By the time Justine arrived, I was practically feral."

"Why did you come to my house?"

"My father is a man of many contingences. He was not sure his original plan would work and put another in motion."

"He sounds like a terrible man, your father."

"You've met him," Clara said.

Jack scoffed. "I surely haven't."

"The night at your house."

"You're mistaken. I saw only you and then the demon who tried to rip the magic out of my mother."

"He is no demon," Clara said quietly. She looked to Fire. "He is only what the magic has made of him."

No demon. It was not a demon that came to the house and murdered his father.

There is no pact on this line, Lord Veemos had said.

Jack's mind spun. "That beast was your father?"

"From the beginning," Fire said again, from her place against the barn wall.

"It's difficult when he asks so many questions," Clara retorted.

"Jack, please contain yourself long enough for Clara to tell it properly."

Not a demon. Not a demon. True, there might have been a man's face hidden behind the mask. But Jack had felt the immense magic and the menace. How in the world could one man hold so much power?

"As soon as I start talking, he will rebel," Clara said.

"Try," Fire insisted.

Jack found his voice. "I will let you finish."

"My father found your father in an orphanage in the north of—"

"My father is the son of a baron!" Jack began.

Clara looked to Fire hopelessly.

"Jack, if you do not let her speak, I will magic your mouth shut."

Jack's anger seethed.

Clara licked her dry lips. "My father took on many children back then. He liked to use them for his experiments."

"Experiments for what?"

"For magic. He wanted to know why some worlds had a great deal and others none at all. If magical talents could be learned by a non-magical person. Or if it was an ability one must be born with. If boys held more aptitude than girls, and so on. All such knowledge was to be used for his own gain, of course. To make himself more powerful. To that end, he took the children. Some magical, some not. Some from this world, many from others. He perfected his methods in the most cruel ways. He made them compete with one another for food, water, his affection. When they succeeded, he let them rest. When they failed, he hurt them. Your father was in his care for almost ten years. Finally, he ran away, taking the Night Box with him. My father wanted to destroy him for this betrayal."

Jack saw the metallic cube clearly in his mind.

"You had the Night Box in your hand when you came through my window," Jack said. "If my father had it, it means that he was dead before you came to me."

"He was."

"Did you take it off his corpse or did your father do that?"

Clara looked ready to cry. "My father gave me the box

and told me to go fetch the other, the Day Box, which I purposely lost to you in the duel."

"Were you going to give him only the boxes or me as well?"

"I would never hand you over to him," Clara said. "I wanted to take you, both boxes, and run. I hoped the two together would be enough to protect us, but then you took the Night Box and I had no choice but to go back to him."

"I'm sure he punished you for that," Fire said quietly.

Clara said nothing.

The idea that Clara had been hurt because Jack stole the box pricked at his heart.

"How do they work?" Jack asked. "The boxes."

"My father discovered that if you open the Day Box and the Night Box side by side, it creates a field of pure potentiality. A field of magic. He could use it as a source of power. Suddenly children who could not use magic were able to. Those who could grew stronger. And the more time one spent in the field, the more powerful they became. My father spent the most time within the boxes. You saw what has become of him."

"Why didn't he strike my father down sooner?"

"Because your father used the Night Box to hide his location and evade my father for a long time. Long enough to find a wife, have children, and build a life. But he must have used the box enough to create a trail. Eventually my father found you."

"My father could do magic?" Jack asked, disbelieving.

"Not really," Clara said. "He was born without that ability. But he had the Night Box. Small magics would have been possible for him."

"When I met you at the inn, how could you know who I was?"

She stilled. "My father had heard of the duels in Lundenwick, and because his curiosity for magic is endless, he wanted to see them with his own eyes. One night he came to the inn to watch the duels and brought me with him. You'd had two duels already that night. Nothing spectacular."

Jack shifted his weight.

"Pretty little displays that were little more than flirtation. But my father saw something in you. Maybe there was something in your manner that reminded him of your father, I honestly don't know. But he told me to challenge you, and I did."

Jack remembered the first night that gold sparks struck his chest and how the crowd had parted to reveal a young man in a silver mask. How Jack had bowed and accepted so easily, thinking he was just another boy looking for a good time.

"I defeated you that night," she said. "Rather badly."

"I remember," Jack said coolly.

"I hoped it would deter his interest in you. But he told me to come back. I was to keep dueling you. I was to push you to greater and greater heights."

Jack's head spun. *The whole time.*

All of it. All of it was lies.

"Then my father caught sight of you and your father in the street one day and put it together, who you were and why your magic was so familiar. He couldn't get close to him or attack him openly. And when he tried to follow you home, the streets warped and changed around him. Somehow your father had used the Night Box to make himself unfindable."

No. It can't be.

"My father got the idea that if you took the Day Box

home, he would be able to find you at last. Because he wouldn't be looking for the house then—he'd be looking for the box. The boxes do call for each other. They are a set that long to be together. It was a risk because he wasn't sure if you understood what the boxes were and what they could do. He didn't want to risk giving you the box unless he was sure you wouldn't give it to your father. He needed to know the status of your relationship."

"That's why you started talking about fathers. Asking me questions about our relationship. You had me confessing every terrible thing he'd ever done to me just so you could find a way to destroy my life."

Clara's eyes filled with tears. "Forgive me."

"Was *none* of it real? Was anything you said in those letters real?"

"I wanted to tell you the truth every time I saw you. That night in the pit, I begged you not to take the bait, but you would not listen. You took the cube and he was watching. I couldn't even warn you or steal it back with his eyes on me. *Why* did you take it?"

"To bring you closer to me!"

Everything stopped. His voice rang off the wooden walls.

He hung his head, his jaw working. He tore off his cloak and threw it in the hay, desiring to be rid of its weight.

He tried to regain control over himself by staring, unseeing, at the dirt floor.

When he felt he'd managed some measure of composure, he said, "You didn't climb my balcony to save me. You only wanted the box. You never cared about me at all."

"That's not true," Clara said, her voice strained. "I couldn't bear the thought of him hurting you because of me."

"That's it? You helped me out of pity?"

"Not pity."

But not love either, he thought bitterly.

"I don't know what to believe." He shook his head. "Perhaps you are your father's daughter and this is only another deception."

Clara started as if slapped. "I suppose I deserve that."

His fists clenched.

No, he thought. *No, I cannot be like my father. I cannot hurt her because I am hurt.*

And yet, his anger would not abate. If festered and burned, turning his face hot and limbs heavy. His hands sweated. He wanted to hit something.

"Where were we to go?" Jack asked. "In this grand scheme to defy your father, where were we to run off to? We were just going to leave Lundenwick and never return?"

"I hadn't decided," she said. "He knows my thoughts. If I'd formed a true plan, he would have intercepted me. I knew only that I had to get you and both boxes away from him. If I could do that, it might buy us enough time."

"Time for what?"

"For her to catch up to us."

Jack frowned. "For who to catch up?"

Fire uncrossed her legs and arms then, pulling herself to her full height. "Me."

CHAPTER 23

They call him Hellsbane because he outwitted the most clever of us. He overpowered her by driving her own sword through her heart, reminding us all how treacherous one's own heart can be.

— FROM THE RECORDS OF THE
HISTORIAN RAZIEL DE PLAISIR

Jack looked at Fire as if he'd never seen her before. "Oh no."

"Yes," Fire said.

"Is this where you tell me you're in on this? You're partners with her demon father? This was all a trick to entrap me? First you get my soul. Then you hand me over to—"

"Calm down." Fire held up a hand.

"They don't work together," Clara said with certainty. "My father fears her."

This stopped Jack's fury in its tracks. The wind went out of his sails.

"Fears her?"

"She's the one we've been running from. The very reason why my father chose that night to attack your home."

"I don't understand," Jack admitted.

"He felt her closing in on us. He said we had no more time to ensnare Willard."

"Willard?"

"That was your father's name before he became Lord Talbot Siran."

"An absurd name." Jack turned on Fire. "Did you know? When I gave you the box to save Phineas's life, did you know of all this?"

"Not all of it," Fire said, her expression unreadable. "I could smell Hellsbane's magic on you. I knew you'd been in close contact. I suspected he might be the demon you spoke of. It was not so hard for me to believe that someone like your father would betray Hellsbane the way he'd betrayed me. Karma keeps the roads in order. And I knew that since you had the box, he would come for you, which is exactly what I wanted. I just had to ensure he would not run again."

"How did he betray you?"

"He stole the Night Box and Day Box from me," Fire said plainly. "He broke our contract, betrayed my trust, and stole both boxes."

They both looked to the demon, waiting for the rest of the story.

Fire crossed one leg over the other. "A power-hungry young man made a deal with a demon, in order to gain more power. Nothing new," she said. "The demon's mistake was in believing that he would abide by the terms of the contract they'd made. That he would pay his debt when the time was due. She didn't suspect that he stayed by her side only to learn her weaknesses and find ways to break and amend the contract. Then when she slept, he drove her own sword through her chest."

"Like he did my father," Jack said.

"Only it will take more than that to end me," Fire said through gritted teeth. She looked from Jack to Clara. "As I lay bleeding in my bed, subdued by the power of my own blade, he took what he believed was my ultimate source of power. The boxes. Then he kept running, knowing that the moment he stopped, I would be there. And so it was for over fifty years."

"Fifty years! You hunted him for *fifty years!*" Jack couldn't believe it. "Why did you not come to Lundenwick and take the Night Box from my father?"

"Hellsbane was not the only one your father hid himself from. He must have known about the boxes' origins and who was looking for them."

"The boxes gave him the power to do that?"

"The boxes control dimensions, including space and time," Fire said. "When used together, you'd be surprised to see what they can do."

Jack sank down on the hay, his mind spinning.

Silence hung in the barn. Finally, Clara said, "Will you kill him? My father?"

"Yes," Fire and Jack said in unison.

"Whoever can land the killing blow should," Clara said frankly. "He will not be as easy to destroy as you think."

"You don't know what I think," Fire said darkly. "He has only the Day Box now."

Jack noted the coldness. The demon didn't trust Clara. Was it because of who her father was?

Fire pulled her blade and approached Clara. Clara hung her head, as if expecting this.

"Wait!" Jack rushed forward and put one hand on Fire's hilt. "You can't just kill her."

"I will only cut her bindings," she said, and the blade sliced a line across the ropes. They fell thickly to the barn floor.

Clara shrugged out of them.

"What will we do?" Jack asked.

"She is going to take us to him." Fire's voice brooked no argument.

"He will smell you," she said.

"Then we mask ourselves."

"How?" Jack asked.

"A bath."

Jack frowned. "I don't think that's the smell she refers to. Is he in Hellebore?"

"No, he sent me to fetch the supplies," Clara said, rubbing her wrists. "He attracts too much attention, whereas I can move unseen. Usually."

"Come on. Both of you." Fire pointed the tip of her blade at Clara. "If you run, I will cut you down. I will not ask your motive before doing so."

Clara didn't even flinch. "You're mistaken. I am happy to take you to him. I want you to kill him."

"You lack the courage to do it yourself?"

"Something like that."

Fire turned away, her blade returning to her sheath.

"What did he send you to fetch?" Fire asked.

"Crow blood and everstone. He needs them to move us off world."

None of this made sense to Jack. Fire, however, seemed to understand perfectly.

"If he had both cubes, he could move without them."

"As I am constantly reminded," Clara said. "But since I

lost the second box to Jack, he must resort to more 'archaic' methods."

There was a tone when she spoke that Jack didn't like. "You really were punished because I took the box."

Clara shrugged. "Punished for losing it, punished for not losing it. It hardly mattered. My father is very good at finding reasons to punish."

Jack rubbed the back of his head. "If it is any comfort, I used it to save my friend's life. Your father killed him, as he was protecting me, so I traded the box to Fire to bring him back."

Clara's eyes rounded. "Then I am glad you took it."

Jack didn't know where they were going. Fire led them through the streets of Hellebore, her head up and eyes sharp.

Then she threw up a hand, commanding them to wait where they were.

Apothecary, the sign read.

The door to the shop slapped shut behind her.

"She's in a hurry," Jack remarked.

His eyes kept slipping to Clara to ensure she would not try to run away.

She hadn't. She'd stayed quite close to his side, her pack thrown over her shoulder.

"Why aren't you running?" he asked.

"Maybe I'm tired of running. I've been running all my life. Maybe that will end tonight."

"Do you think Fire can kill him?"

"I don't know," she said. "He runs from her, which speaks for itself. I believe he had the element of surprise before. He won't this time. He was with her for almost two hundred years, you know."

"Two hundred years!" Jack cried. "Impossible."

"The pact was for immortality," she said simply. "He did not wish to die."

"What will you do if we do kill him? Will Lord Silver go off and start a new life for himself?"

"Is that what you think I should do?" she asked, squinting against the light.

"You could pretend to be a man. You do it convincingly," he said, feeling the bitterness rising up in him.

"What kind of life is it where no one knows you and you are a stranger even to yourself?" she asked. "No, thank you. I've had that life."

Jack had nothing to say to that.

"Besides, you are bound to her, aren't you? Where she goes you must go?"

Jack touched the brand at the side of his throat self-consciously.

"What did you sell?" she asked quietly.

"My soul."

Her eyes widened. "What was worth the price?"

You, he thought. But he dared not say it now that Silver —*she*—was here.

"I thought the demon—your father—would come back for me. Only a demon can kill a demon."

"He would have come back for you. When he sets his sights on something, he is not deterred."

"Good to know I didn't sell my soul for nothing then," Jack said.

"What else did you want?" she asked.

"Pardon?" How could she know?

"You gave her the box and your soul. What else did you bargain for?"

I also wanted to find you. I wanted answers.

"That my mother, sister, and friends be safe." He

shifted his weight. "Was every bit of it truly your father's plan? Were you just doing what he told you?"

"Jack." Her shoulders slumped and her hands fisted on the strap of her satchel.

"Forget it. It's my own fault." He turned his face away. He couldn't bear to look at her.

Once Fire had what she wanted, she led them away from the city and into the foothills. Jack climbed the rocky slopes until his legs ached. He was about to beg for mercy when the path broke open and a hot spring appeared.

The slate-gray water burbled and steamed.

"The sulfur will mask our scent," Fire said, stripping out of her armor. Jack averted his gaze but not before he caught the deep star-shaped scar between her breasts.

Clara, too, was looking at the scar.

"You next," Fire said, her eyes on Clara.

"Why?" Clara frowned. "He knows my scent."

"I'll not have you on the shore with my blade and trousers," Fire said. "*Get in.*"

Clara sighed, gathering up her hair and fixing it to the top of her head so it would not get wet. Then she undid her vest and pulled her white shirt out of her riding breeches. Jack took her satchel and put it on the rocks beside Fire's blade.

Every movement, every shift of Clara's body, reminded him of Silver.

Because she isn't playing the part of lady now. This is who she is. Not quite the woman in my parlor, nor the man in the inn, but someone between.

When the shirt began to slip off Clara's shoulder, he

turned completely, relying more on his ears than his eyes to gauge her progress.

The crickets sang and the frogs croaked. His eyes roamed the dirt path and boulders, not really seeing anything.

"I'm in," Clara said, and Jack turned back. Both Fire and Clara were up to their necks in the gray water.

"Now you," Fire said. "Unless *you* want to run off with my sword and trousers?"

Clara watched him undress. She did not avert her gaze or pretend to not look at his body as young ladies often did when presented with the opportunity. She didn't steal shy glances.

She looked her fill.

Jack's face burned hotter than the water.

"How long must we soak?" he asked once the water reached his chin.

"Ten minutes should do it. Then he will not be able to detect the cloaking potion over the scent of the sulfur."

Fire moved toward the other end of the pool, where the rocks cast darker shadows. Jack stayed where he was, within arm's length of Clara. When she rose a few inches from the water, his eyes traced the dip of her shoulders and collarbone.

"Were my father here, perhaps we three could drown him," Clara said with a tired sigh. "He hates water. I don't know why he fears it so, but he does. That water trick you used in our last duel. You should try it on him if you ever have the chance."

She looked up and met Jack's eyes. "Are you disappointed that Lord Silver has a few more endowments than you thought?"

"No."

"Ah, I forgot. What did you say? You like to undress gentlemen as well as ladies? I suppose it makes no difference to you then when I should bind my chest and lower my voice."

His stomach tightened. "Lower your voice."

Clara regarded him for a moment. "Why?"

"I want to hear it."

Her lips hovered just above the water. The surface rippled as she spoke. "Good evening, my dear Peacock. I wondered if I would see you tonight."

A perfect mimicry of the shivers sliding over his own skin.

It was Silver's voice. Truly. And the voice affected him as it always did.

Her face darkened. "Do you despise me now? It's one of my many tricks."

Clara turned, and Jack thought she would swim away then. Perhaps disappear into the thick shadows with Fire.

Instead she rose, standing to her full height in the pool, exposing her back to the open air.

Along her back were countless scars. Some thick and twisted, others thin and pale.

On the surface was a fresh layer of bruises and lines of red that were just beginning to heal.

She had indeed been punished for losing the cube.

Jack recognized the older scars made by blades and also a horsewhip. Those matched his own. But there were other marks he did not recognize. Perhaps they were made by torture devices he couldn't imagine.

"Did your father do this to you?" Jack asked, his voice strained.

"He expects perfection," Clara said coolly. "I am not perfect."

"Finish up. We must leave soon," Fire called from the shore. She looked to the sky and noted the rising moon.

She'd slipped past them without Jack even noticing. Now she began to wipe the water from her skin and uncorked a vial with her teeth.

"At night?" Jack asked.

"We have the Night Box," she said. "Night is our advantage."

Clara lowered herself into the water.

"He shouldn't have done those things to you," Jack said.

"I've seen your back," she said. "It seems your father was no better."

"He never took a blade to me." He didn't know what else to say.

Her eyes were on the water when she said, "You asked me if they meant nothing. Your letters."

Her jaw clenched.

"It's true my father read every one. He thought they were part of the entrapment. Proof that his plan was working and I was doing my part to capture you. But for me..."

Her voice trailed off.

"I would lie in bed at night and read them. My body hurt, but your words...your words were a great comfort to me. Braggard though you are."

Her smile was weak, half formed.

Jack's heart kicked.

"When I was with you in that way, I wondered what my life could be like, if everything were so very different. What it would be like to be a normal boy, loved by someone."

She exited the pool, her body dripping.

"Clara," Jack called out, still waist deep in the water.

She turned, looking down at him from the edge, the

moon hanging above her. In the fresh moonlight, her profile looked more like Silver's than ever.

"I wrote those letters to you," he said. "Not just some normal boy."

Her face twisted. "No, Jack. You've never met *me*."

CHAPTER 24

*I do not trust myself with him. After all this time, I cannot
tell where my deception ends and my father's begins.*

— FROM THE JOURNAL OF LADY
CLARA NIGHTINGALE

Jack was cold. The chilly night air had been
unforgiving after leaving the lovely warmth of the
hot spring. He dressed as quickly as he could,
silently begging the heat to find him again.

"I can open the portal," Clara said, loosing her hair.
"But how do you want to enter?"

"With my blade to your throat," Fire said, her golden
eyes bright.

Clara only laughed. "You overvalue my life. To threaten
me with death will have no effect on him. You'd do better to
put a blade to Jack's throat."

Fire considered this.

"I could go first and leave the portal open, and you
could come after?" Clara adjusted her jacket across her

shoulders. Jack admitted, if only to himself, that she was quite handsome in boy's clothes. He wondered what she might look like in *his* clothes. "He might believe you followed me."

"Portals are unstable," Fire said. "It could close after you, and then we would be unable to cross."

"I'll go with her," Jack said.

They both looked at him.

"I'll cross with Clara," he said again. "She can tell him that she found me and I demanded to be brought to him. I want satisfaction for the insults against my family."

"No," Fire said.

"In truth," Clara said, "it's a good plan. He does want Jack's magic."

"He can't have it," Fire spat.

Because you want it for yourself.

"Jack could create enough of a diversion for you to cross unseen," Clara went on.

"The portal could still close," Fire said. "And there's the matter of why she found you in Hellebore?"

"I was looking for him. And you can still find me. You said yourself that because of my mark, you can find me anywhere."

"That takes *time*," Fire said. "More than fifty years in Hellsbane's case. Do you want to be at his mercy for fifty years?"

"It won't be fifty years because I will not run from you," Jack said calmly. "You will find me."

Fire scowled at him.

"It's the best plan we have. It will buy you the time you need to enter unseen and position yourself well. Clara and I will distract him. If it's my magic that interests him, I'll use it."

Fire took Jack by the arm and pulled him away. At a distance, she whispered, "It could be a trap. It's possible Clara *was* sent to bring you back and separate you from me. Did you consider that?"

Jack had. "I trust her."

Fire scoffed. "Yesterday you thought she was a man."

"I trust her." Jack stood firm. "And I trust you."

Fire's eyes widened. "Then you're more stupid than you look. And those long lashes make you look very stupid."

"You do that when you're nervous."

"What?" she hissed.

"Insult me. But I forgive you because I know you're wrong. I am very handsome." Jack smiled. "And the fact remains that this won't work unless we work together. When you faced him on your own, you lost. When I faced him, Phineas died. And you saw Clara's body. If she could have killed him, she would have done so already. None of us can defeat him alone. Our best chance is moving together as one, and that will not work unless we are in possession of some measure of trust."

Fire pinched her brow. "Hell's bells. No wonder Raziel adores you. You're as idiotically romantic as he is."

Jack pulled back. "More insults. I forgive you again."

"It's the eyes." She batted her eyelashes. "I can't stand it."

"I could call Raziel, if you think even the three of us can't defeat him."

"Don't," Fire growled. "Unless you want to get him killed too."

Jack did not. To have Raziel help him from a pit was one thing. To call him to battle another. Jack would not do that to anyone.

"I choose trust," he said. "Pooling our strengths is our best chance."

The planes of her face softened. "Then you should know something."

Jack's heart stumbled. "What?"

"I will take my payment tonight," she said.

His throat tightened.

"Before I kill him, I'll take it."

"You must?" he asked. "Now?"

"I suspect I can pin him but not finish him. Your fire will make me far more powerful than he could ever hope to be. With it, we can win."

Jack felt as if he couldn't draw enough breath.

"Are you all right?" Clara called out.

"Just a minute." Jack threw a weak wave in her direction. To Fire he whispered, "Will it kill me?"

"Possibly." Her brow pinched, her eyes slid to her feet. "I hope not."

"When will you take it?" he asked. "May I at least prepare myself for the moment?"

"I'll know when the moment is right. Jack, listen."

Jack tried despite the pounding in his throat and temples. His arms and legs were going numb. "Go on."

"Your best chance is to give it up willingly."

He laughed, a tight, strangled sound.

"If I take it by force, I will do more damage, do you understand? But if you hand it over, there will be less injury. Less...mess."

Less mess of me.

"Willingly," she said again. "Remember that."

She turned away.

"Wait," Jack called after her.

She stopped. "What?"

"You have to hide the mark. He will recognize it, won't he?"

"You're right." Fire pressed her fingers to his throat and the strange tingling returned, as when she'd tricked Raziel. Jack said nothing. He could say nothing.

Tonight. I will die tonight.

"You didn't answer me. Are you all right?" Clara wrapped a hand around his arm. "Who died?"

Me.

"We were just clarifying the details of our plan."

Fire rolled her shoulders. "You and Jack will cross under the pretense that Jack demands satisfaction for your father's insults. Focus on keeping your father's attention. Jack's life depends on it. Hopefully the three of us will reek of enough sulfur to hide the scent of the cloaking potion I wear."

"I'll hold the portal open as long as I can," Clara said. She lifted her satchel from the ground and threw it over her shoulder.

Jack was struggling to draw breath into his tight chest. A chilled sweat had broken out on the back of his neck.

"Are you ready?" she asked him.

"Yes, I'm ready when you are."

Clara raised her hand and pressed it against the face of the rock. Green light rippled and spread until the rock became like water, shimmering and fluid.

She took Jack's hand. "On three?"

All of Jack's attention went to her hand and the way it felt in his.

"One..."

Fire grabbed his opposite arm, her eyes bright. "Be careful."

As if you aren't about to kill me, he thought. But there

was something in her eyes that kept him from slinging the accusation.

"I will," he said.

"Two…"

He truly believed their best chance of destroying Hellsbane was to work together. That meant that for better or worse, Fire was his ally. For now.

Fire released him.

"Three!"

He wasn't sure what he expected to feel, passing through the portal. He'd felt nothing stepping from town into the demon world, nor when he crossed from Hellebore to Fireside or Fireside to Lord Veemos's palace.

Yet this time, there was the strange experience of suction. Of being pulled and stretched between two points in space and time, half of him moving forward while the other half tried to stay behind.

Then there was a pop, and the darkness broke open.

Jack opened his eyes and found himself in a great house. Nothing so grand as the night palace, but it was beautiful. High, polished bannisters and a chandelier of candlelight.

"Father?" Clara called out, pulling a blade from her hip sheath. "Father!"

"I am here."

A man stood at the top of the stairs. He wore no dinner jacket or cloak, no formal wear of any kind. His shirt was a simple white, the vest the same midnight blue that Jack recalled from the night at Ansley Hall. A color, it seemed, Hellsbane favored.

His hair was the same soft blond as Clara's and hung past his shoulders freely.

But he did not share his daughter's silver-blue eyes. No, this man's eyes, if he could be called a man, were as black as pitch. So dark Jack could not tell pupil from iris. And the features had none of Clara's softness. His face was gaunt, all angles and sharp lines.

It was a hungry face.

"I sent you for supplies and you bring back a young man," Hellsbane said with a lift of his brows. "You see how terrible my daughter is at following my orders. Of course, I'd hoped to see you again."

There was something hypnotic about the eyes, Jack realized. *I must not stare.*

"Did you come here of your own free will or under that ridiculous pretense that you would marry Clara?"

"I demand satisfaction," Jack said, drawing in a deep breath in hopes it would clear his mind.

Hellsbane raised both brows. "You want to challenge me?"

"You destroyed my home, killed my father, and injured my mother. If you have any honor at all, you will accept my challenge to a duel."

Hellsbane looked positively delighted. "A duel of swords or pistols?"

A pistol would be too quick, Jack thought. A sword too, considering that this man must have decades of experience on him. He recalled the rapier through his father's chest. And his father had been very skilled with a sword. He'd won a duel against the Baron Bromley when Bromley accused him of having an affair with his wife.

No. Best stick to the weapon he used best.

"Of magic," Jack said. "A simple three-round challenge to determine who is the better conjurer."

"Of magic!" The grin on Hellsbane's face didn't sit quite right. It stretched over the bones as if the face were not made for such emotion. "Of course I accept. What are the terms?"

"If I win, you die."

"Unoriginal, but succinct." A flick of the brows. "And if I win, you die?"

"You'll have my magic," Jack said.

"Of course. A man cannot live without his magic," he added.

"*If* you win," Jack said, hoping his face betrayed none of his fears.

"If," Hellsbane laughed. "I admire your pride, boy. You get it from your father. No matter how I hurt him, burned him, beat him, I could not cut the pride from him."

Jack's face warmed. "You'll find I'm nothing like him."

"I hope you're right. He was a disappointment. I should've left him in the shit-filled gutter where I found him."

Jack did not take this bait. Instead, he said, "Do you accept the terms? Your word is your bond."

"My word is my bond," Hellsbane repeated, and Jack felt the magic tighten in the air the way one might tighten the strings of a guitar. "I accept the terms you've stated."

"Where should we duel?" Jack asked. "Have you a garden or—"

Hellsbane snapped his fingers and the foyer fell away.

In its place was a ballroom, emptied of its chairs and tables. The ceiling overhead curved in a beautiful ornate arch of white carvings. The soft orange walls were unmarred.

Too much space. How is Fire to creep up on him here?

"This is more...open than I'm used to," Jack said, his eyes on a half-clothed virgin pouring water from a pitcher, her stone mouth forever fixed in a sultry pout.

"All the better to conjure with," Hellsbane said. "You'll have plenty of room to show me what you can do."

Clara's face was unreadable. If she feared what Jack feared, she was better at schooling her features than he was.

"Are you changing your mind?" Hellsbane said. "Because if you are, I should tell you I would amend the contract."

Jack's heart kicked. "What?"

"Just a simple forfeiture clause. Should you end the match early or forfeit for any reason, I win by default. Do you accept?"

You have bravado and arrogance, Clara had told him once. *If he begins to frighten you, use it.*

It had been Lord Silver's advice on how Jack should deal with his father.

"I have no intentions of forfeiting." Jack kept his head high and back straight. "Who goes first in this round?"

"I will," Hellsbane said, unbuttoning the cuffs of his shirt and rolling up the sleeves. "If you begin, you might start us out with ponies and ribbons. I want to see what you're *truly* made of."

Jack felt the air in the room change. It turned static, the hair on his arms prickling to attention.

"Let's see what you can do with this."

Twin whips of gold light cracked across the ballroom floor. One wrapped around Jack's right arm, the other around his left.

He was jerked forward onto his knees with one pull. The more he tried to wrench himself from the magic's grip, the more it tightened.

"On your knees so soon," Hellsbane said. "I'm disappointed."

The binds warmed, burning his skin.

Jack screamed, and from his pain something was born. It unfurled its wings like a great bird and shot forward.

Made of blue light, it crossed the ballroom in a breath and struck Hellsbane in the chest and throat.

Or rather, it struck the golden shield he erected at the last possible second to absorb the blow.

The vines of gold coiled round Jack's arms slackened long enough for him to shake them free and build a barrier around himself, gaining the idea from the shield Hellsbane used.

Hellsbane shook his hands free of the magic.

"You learn quickly and can conjure mimicries."

"Mimicries?" Jack asked, rubbing at his tender flesh. His sleeves were burned through, and scorch marks marred each of his forearms where the golden vines had coiled.

They were too tender to touch.

Because this isn't a game, Jack thought. This wasn't like the duels played beneath the inn by lads looking for a good time. *That* was magic meant to impress. Jack performed it to show off for a boy or gain the admiration of his friends.

This magic was meant to kill.

"You do what I do by sight alone," Hellsbane said, pacing a circle. "It's a talent. Then there is the matter of your pain."

"That you like to cause it?" Jack asked.

Hellsbane grinned. "That your magic strengthens when you're in pain. That also is a talent. A rare one. It can only be cultivated after many years of conditioning. No need to ask who conditioned you. Your father was an attentive teacher, I suspect."

"You sound pleased by that." Jack tried to catch his breath. His arms hurt. The welts from the burning vines ached.

"That he's prepared such a gift for me? Of course."

Jack paced to maintain the distance between himself and Hellsbane.

Hellsbane prattled on. "Most people, when they are physically hurt, lose strength. It is rare that I see the opposite. Your pain bore anger, and you use that anger to make yourself strong."

Jack's arms were burning. He wanted to wrap them. To tend to them.

He dared not look away from Hellsbane.

"But there are many kinds of pain, Jacinth," he said with a menacing grin. "You may have developed a tolerance to physical pain, but I am sure I can find the one that will undo you."

A chill climbed Jack's spine.

"Your turn," he said.

He fears water, Clara had told him.

Water it would be. Jack took a deep breath, and from the depths of his soul he called forth a torrent. Blue-gray water rose in front of him, rearing its head like that of a cobra until Jack couldn't hold the power with his mind any longer. He released it, squinting against the burn in his skull, and watched it snap forward and slam into the man, eclipsing his form completely.

As the wave washed away, he was no longer there. Where he had stood were only the undulating waves of a blue-gray sea, somehow held in place by an invisible moor that none of them could see.

No, he thought. It could not be so easy.

And of course it wasn't. The water began to swirl. It turned from left to right, spiraling in and out of itself before rising higher and higher until it formed a singular funnel cloud.

It was here that Jack realized his error. He'd tried this attack on Silver the night of their last duel. Hadn't Clara said her father had been watching that night?

He had only a moment to reinforce his barrier before the water came crashing back upon him.

With great effort, he absorbed it, taking the magic back into himself.

His limbs shook with the effort, leaving him feeling cold and drained. He'd never moved so much magic through his body or his mind before. The tremendous shifts in energy were depleting his strength and his will.

Better use it while you can, he thought bitterly. *If Fire plans to take it all tonight, shouldn't my last hurrah be grand?*

At the other end of the ballroom, soaked and blistered, Hellsbane scowled.

His shoes squeaked against the floor.

"Water," he said, running a hand through his wet hair.

Hellsbane's eyes cut to Clara. "I wonder who you've been talking to."

Clara coughed, her hand going to her throat as an invisible fist wrapped around it.

"Stop it," Jack screamed.

"No?" Hellsbane asked. "You give a damn if I kill her or not? Do you know that she is your precious Lord Silver? Do you know how she lied to you? Deceived you? She told you everything *I* told her to say."

Clara's face was too red. Her legs swung wildly above the floor where she was suspended.

"You dare to interrupt your duel with *me* to discipline your daughter?" Jack said in his haughtiest voice. "Where is your focus?"

Please let her go.

Hellsbane's face turned to stone.

"Don't think that this petty distraction will get you out of your duel," Jack said.

Hellsbane released her. "You question my honor?"

"I question your commitment. I came all this way to gain satisfaction. Not to witness your petty family squabbles. If this is an attempt to escape before you can give me the satisfaction I deserve—"

"I will not *escape*," Hellsbane spat, the first real irritation betrayed on his face. "You do not have to seal the room as if I'm a child."

Seal the room?

Jack hadn't done anything to the room. Given the fact that Clara's face was the color of a beet and her eyes barely open, Jack didn't think she'd done it either.

Did the portal close when Hellsbane attacked her? Was that what he felt now? Was Fire locked outside?

Think, Jack, think!

"My apologies for subjecting you to my petty family squabble, as you call it. Let us begin our third round," Hellsbane said.

There was murder in his eyes.

"No," Jack said.

He arched a brow. "No?"

"You haven't demonstrated your round-two attack. You countered my water, but you haven't taken the offense. Do so, and *that* will complete round two."

And buy me time to think. Think.

Fire? Fire, where are you? I'm here. Hurry, damn it!

Nothing. The mark on his neck didn't even itch.

Meanwhile, Hellsbane looked ready to skin him alive. Jack expected something ruthless.

Perhaps a man-eating lion or some strange and terrible

creature to rip him apart. Maybe even another natural disaster to assault the walls of the ballroom, which were now watermarked from Jack's flood.

What he did not expect was a boy.

The child was thin, no more than six years of age. He was underfed to the point that he was mostly elbows and knees, the skeleton showing beneath his pretense of a face.

"Please, sir," the little boy begged, clasping Jack's trouser leg with desperate little hands. The last of the golden light faded off his shoulders and hair. Only the barest glint remained in the eyes. "I'm so hungry."

Jack couldn't move. "What is this?"

"Your father as I found him."

"Please," the boy said again, and Jack saw himself in the blue eyes and dark hair.

They looked so much alike, this child could be Jack's own son.

"Please," he said again.

Then the boy's head snapped back, his lip blooming with red. His hold on Jack weakened and he tumbled to the floor in a heap.

Hellsbane stood over him, pulling him up by his collar.

"Worthless," he spat into the boy's face. "Pathetic little street trash. What good are you?"

He threw the boy to the ground again.

"Please, master!" the boy screamed, tears in his eyes. "Forgive me!"

"Stop it," Jack said.

A foot flew out and connected with the boy's stomach. The sound ricocheted in Jack's ears and sickened him.

"Stop it!"

"Good for nothing," Hellsbane said. "I should never have saved you."

"Forgive me!" the boy begged. Tears bloomed in his eyes. "Forgive me, master."

"Not worth the clothes I put on your back."

Hellsbane grabbed his shirt, ripped it, exposing his bare back.

"Stop, I said!" Jack grabbed Hellsbane's arm. He wrenched it back so he could not strike the boy again. He shoved, but Hellsbane did not move. He was a wall of a man.

Not a man. A monster.

"You will leave him alone!" Jack commanded.

Clara screamed, the high, shrill sound of it piercing all of Jack's senses.

He whirled to find a dagger had been driven through her left shoulder.

She stumbled away, her hand on the hilt.

For a moment, confusion burned bright in his mind. He did not understand what he was seeing.

Then Jack saw his error. The Hellsbane Jack warred was false, a mere replica of his true target. And in Jack's distraction, the true Hellsbane had crept up on him, no doubt with the intent to end Jack's life.

Clara pulled the blade from her shoulder and held it out at arm's length.

"You cheat, Father," she said, her breath ragged.

Her eyes were glassy with pain, but they were focused on Hellsbane. The blade's point remained fixed on him.

"I would not approach her if I were you, sir," Jack said. "I believe she means to kill you."

"Here I thought of my daughter as my own," Hellsbane said bitterly.

Do not look at her. Look at me. I am your target.

"More family squabbling," Jack said coldly.

"You don't care for her?"

"Why would I? She is a manipulative liar just like her father."

I care. I care too much.

But if Hellsbane had any idea that Jack cared for her, he would use that against him.

"You wrote such pretty prose to one another," Hellsbane said, his gaze intent as he swept his hair back from his face.

"Do you think she is the only one who can write empty words, pretty as they may be?"

Clara, forgive me.

"And here I thought your feelings sincere."

"She's insulted me. Made a fool of me. I would say that is enough to have extinguished all sincerity."

"Then I will kill her for you," Hellsbane said. "Would you like to see that?"

"We have one final round, sir. I beg you to remain focused on the task at hand. Must I keep reminding you?"

Fire, where the hell are you?

Jack was struggling to maintain this façade. Seeing the boy's fear and pain had shaken him. He could not get that tear-stained face out of his mind.

His father. It had been his father. He had known him by his dark hair. By the blue of his eyes. But the boy had been on the small side for his age, his face round and sweet. He was as tender as any of the boys Jack saw on streets.

You cannot let him know he has affected you.

"And I ask that you remain on your side of the room, if you please. None of your tricks."

Hellsbane took his position several paces away. Clara lowered the blade, but not her gaze. It remained fixed on her father.

Jack didn't like the look of her shoulder. Blood soaked her clothes from throat to gut. He wanted to tell her to put more pressure on it but did not dare.

There was Raziel's elixir, but that too was conspicuous. How could he give it to her without Hellsbane seeing him?

Then he remembered the letters, the way they'd send them across the dueling pit to one another with only the smallest wave and look. Jack did that now. He met her eye and touched his pocket once.

He saw the subtlest shift of her hand to the pocket.

He touched his lips. *Drink it*, he begged.

If Clara understood, he couldn't be sure. He had to divert his attention to Hellsbane.

He was watching Jack again with a cold, steady gaze.

Fire. Please hurry.

"Trying to conjure another child?" Jack asked wearily. He was shaking from cold. "I'll not be fooled again."

"Not a child," Hellsbane said. "Something you truly fear."

A pillar of gold light formed in front of Hellsbane, building and growing until it was near solid in its luminescence.

Then a man stepped forth as if from a portal into the very room.

Not just any man.

"Father," Jack whispered, and all the air left him.

CHAPTER 25

What I fear most is Jack's belief in the greatest of lies. He believes he deserves it.

— FROM THE JOURNAL OF LORD
ALBERT LOCKWOOD

The golden light disappeared, leaving only the Baron Siran, as imperious and disdainful as he'd ever been in life.

"Jacinth," he said, his nose wrinkled in distaste. "Look at you."

"You aren't real," Jack said. "I'll listen to nothing you say."

"Do not speak to your father that way." He undid his belt and removed it.

"You aren't my father," Jack said. "I saw you dead on the study floor."

"I'll teach you to speak to me that way. You don't know what pain is, what suffering is."

The belt cracked and Jack moved from its path,

feeling the air shift where he had stood the moment before.

"You don't know how good you have it."

"I suppose I *am* alive," Jack said. "Which is more than you can say."

The belt whipcracked in the air and connected with Jack's face. It stung like a slap.

He tasted blood.

"You have always been a disappointment."

"Jack!" Clara cried. "Don't fight him. He's not there!"

"The belt feels real enough," he murmured.

"That's what he wants. He wants you to lose yourself in the illusion. That is how he will win."

Jack met Hellsbane's eyes and saw the pleasure there.

He's learning my weaknesses, as he did with Fire. This is how he wins.

The belt snapped again, striking Jack in the ear. He staggered. The side of his head exploded with fresh pain.

"Eyes on me," the baron commanded.

Jack's anger rose to the surface.

Why? his mind demanded. *Why does he keep doing this to me?*

"Look at me when I'm talking to you."

"How could you?" Jack said. *No—no, it's not him.*

He shook his head.

"How could I what?" his father asked. But there was a strange quality to the voice. It was doubled somehow, as if someone else wore it like a glove.

"How could I what, Jacinth?" his father asked, trailing the belt along the ballroom floor.

"How can you speak to me as if I'm nothing."

"You are less than nothing. You're a hindrance."

"Why?" Jack spat, his magic sparking along his skin,

pushing his anger higher and brighter than ever before. "Why couldn't you treat me like a son?"

Why do you not love me? Why was I never enough?

"I wanted to love you," his father said. "But you made it so difficult."

"Me?" Jack asked, feeling as if he'd been struck. "*I* made it difficult."

A voice, a small, sad, heartbroken voice, the voice of a child, a boy nearly forgotten, rang through Jack's mind.

Yes, I made it hard. I made it so he could not love me. Because of what I am. Because I cannot be who he wants me to be. Because I am not enough. I fail him in every way. He cannot love me because there is something wrong with me.

The strength in Jack's arms weakened. The resolve in his mind softened.

The ghost descended on him, slamming him into the ballroom floor.

"Don't let him win, Jack!" Clara screamed. "Don't let him use your fear against you!"

My fear? What is my fear?

It wasn't this ghost. It wasn't even the man he imitated.

His father's hands kept him pinned against the floor, the weight of his body rendering his limbs immobile and useless.

"There *is* something wrong with you," his father said. "I felt it the moment you were born. The inadequacy. The disappointment. You aren't what I wished for."

There is something wrong with me. I'm not enough because there's something wrong with me.

Jack's heart felt cut through.

He waited for the killing blow.

When it did not come, he opened his eyes and saw a blaze of red hair.

Fire. Her sword was through Hellsbane's chest, her smile triumphant.

Hellsbane grimaced, his hands on the blade. Blood spurted from his mouth and dribbled down his chin.

"*You*," Hellsbane snarled, his teeth red.

"*Me*," Fire said, and twisted the sword.

Hellsbane cried out but could not lift himself off the blade. He struggled to take a step back, but the angle of the sword kept him on the tips of his toes.

"Pay me," she said.

"No," he cried. "I broke that contract. I nullified it. You can't make me pay it."

"The hell I can't." Fire twisted her sword again.

Hellsbane hissed through his clenched, bloody teeth.

"Jack," she said. "It's time."

Jack hesitated.

"Would you betray me?" Fire asked.

"No, but—"

"Willingly. As best you can."

"What's happening?" Clara's eyes were still glazed with pain. "What does she want you to do?"

"Pay my debt." Jack took a breath and called forth his magic.

It was tangled with his anger. All that residual fear and fury from facing his father—or what Hellsbane had made of him—had nowhere to go.

He had no choice but to offer it all together.

"Take it," he said, trying to relax his mind, his body.

"No! You can't!" Hellsbane cried. Fire twisted her sword until he screamed.

"Take it," Jack begged. "Before I lose my nerve."

When she entered his mind, it wasn't like Raziel's passionate inspection. She was a warm breeze.

Gentle, he thought. She really was trying to be gentle.

But it wasn't his magic she seized.

Nor was it his soul.

The heat was leaving him. His strength.

The more she took, the louder Hellsbane screamed.

Wait. What is that? he thought. *What—* Then he knew.

She was taking his anger. All that protective heat that shielded his broken heart. She unwrapped it slowly, and the more she took, the louder the voice inside him became.

The little boy voice. The crying voice.

He never loved me.

He never wanted me.

"Jack, stop fighting me," she said, her voice gentle.

But he couldn't stop fighting. He needed his anger. He needed to stay mad at his father because anger was stronger. Anger was safer. Anger meant not believing anything his father had ever said about him.

No, he thought. *I need this.*

Something tore, wrenching a cry from deep within him. A sadness long buried.

Where his anger had been, a new, cold emotion rushed in to fill the space it left behind.

No one can love me because I'm disgusting, despicable.

His teeth began to chatter. He was cold, so cold.

No one can love me because I'm weak, worthless.

His body seized.

Clara cried, her hot hands pressing to his face. "Jack! Stay with me, Jack!"

But Jack couldn't stay.

He was down in the dark deep now.

In that place with the cravens. With the mask wearers who couldn't bear to look at their own pain, let alone feel it.

No one can love me.

No one.

No—

The last thing he saw before his eyes closed tight was Fire.

She plunged her hand into Hellsbane's chest and opened him from the inside out. As the ravaged remains of his body fell away, a golden light coalesced in her palm, a miniature sun that she raised to her mouth and took between her fangs.

Hellsbane was no more.

CHAPTER 26

The others do not see him as I see him. Sometimes, when he looks out a window, I can see the boy. The one who first ran crying into my arms. What I wouldn't do for him, then and now. But he has not run crying into my arms for a very long time.

I wish he would.

It is better than watching him hide himself away from me.

— FROM THE JOURNAL OF LORD
ALBERT LOCKWOOD

Jack was in the dark and someone was screaming. It was a long time before he realized the terrible hurt-animal sound came from his own lips. Some distant part of him noted the torment as if it were happening to someone else.

It was someone else who twisted in the arms that tried to hold him.

Someone else who begged, "Kill me. Kill me, please."

"I will not," the demon said. Her hold on him remained firm. "The only one who can do that is you."

If it was only his father's rejection down there in the dark, in the complete and total absence of his love, perhaps Jack could live with that. He could survive it.

But that wasn't all he found in the darkest parts of himself.

In the dark was where the little boy lived. The one born of the first whipcrack across Jack's back. When he'd been born, it had nearly destroyed Jack.

He'd survived only because he'd swaddled that child in his anger.

But the anger was gone now.

The desperate, heartbroken boy was all Jack had left.

"Kill me," Jack begged, his face covered in tears. "I can't do this."

"Sleep, Jack," Fire said.

He saw her golden flames burning even with his eyes closed tight.

A wet cloth was pressed to Jack's lips.

"He won't drink."

"Keep trying."

"What do you think I'm doing? Giving him a lip bath?"

"A few drops is better than nothing."

"He's stopped screaming at least."

"He's so cold. Why is he so cold?"

"Fetch another blanket."

"He has three! And we can't make the fire any bigger."

"I preferred the screaming. This is worse. I can't stand the empty look in his eyes."

"Close them."

"I've tried."

FOR A LONG TIME, JACK FELT NOTHING BUT PAIN. THEN the pain receded, but there was only the cold. Until the cold folded into tranquil emptiness. At last empty, he wandered a darkness he could not see. There was a child calling to him, but Jack did not want to hear it. So he turned away. He chose the darkness. Twisting something in his grip, he tried again and again not to hear the crying.

This is death, he thought. *This is the end.*

He hoped it was the end.

Only the end did not come.

Dreams came.

First as only smoke and shadows, scraps of pain and darkness. Someone was calling his name.

He wasn't sure how much time passed before there was a hand in his hair. A hard, reassuring body pressed against his. Someone was holding him tight.

"Jack," a sweet voice said.

"I can't," Jack said.

"Jack, look at me."

He felt tears on his face. "I can't."

"Of course you can. Look at me."

Jack opened his eyes to find Raziel above him. He pushed his fingers through Jack's curls again. They were in Raziel's large four-poster bed, the candles burning bright around them, the gossamer curtains aglow.

"You were much harder to pull from the pit this time," Raziel said. "You made me go quite deep."

He dabbed at Jack's tears with the sleeve of his nightshirt.

"She took her payment, I see."

He pressed a hot hand to Jack's brow.

"I'm glad it was not your soul or your magic."

"It was worse." Jack folded into his grief again. Fresh tears spilled from his eyes. "There is a boy. He hounds me night and day."

"Yes, I've seen him," Raziel said. "I've heard his crying."

"You must leave. You cannot love me. You cannot because I—"

Raziel pressed his fingers to his lips. "Stop it."

"I speak truth."

"You speak *pain*. Rarely is that truth."

He did not love me. He never loved me. I tried everything, but it was never enough.

"He did not. That is true. But we do." Raziel pulled him up to sitting. "See for yourself. Jack, look around you."

The end of Raziel's bed disappeared, giving a wide view of a field at dawn.

And in the field stood dozens of people, all of them watching him with worried faces.

There were his mother and his sister. There were Albert, Silas, Baz, and Phineas. There was Nanny, and even his horse, Starlight. He also saw Phineas's parents and three younger sisters, and recognized many of the servants from Ansley Hall. There was Oxley. Lord Pickerington.

Even Fire stood off to one side, half in shadow, her flaming sword propped against one shoulder.

And there in the front, Clara. Beside her, the shadow of Lord Silver, his mask fixed to his face.

There were more faces than Jack could count.

"Your father did not love you, but you *are* loved, Jack," Raziel said, placing a kiss on his cheek. His ear. "You are *loved.*"

Jack pinched his eyes closed. When he opened them again, they were still there. They were still waiting.

Raziel wiped at the tears again with a tender hand. "Would you punish us for your father's sins?"

"N-no," he choked out.

"Then open your eyes," Raziel commanded.

CHAPTER 27

— FROM THE JOURNAL OF
HISTORIAN RAZIEL DE PLAISIR

Jack opened his eyes.

He was in an oversized bedroom he did not recognize. The bed was large enough for three bodies, though he lay in it alone.

Given the sounds from the street, he thought he was in town again, though he did not know how he'd got there. He caught the scent of orange flower and fresh bread and knew they must be in Bloomsbury House, the townhouse on Seventh Street, as it was across from the bakery that specialized in bergamot cakes.

At the right side of his bed, Silas sat in a red armchair, a book propped open on his lap, his brow furrowed in concentration.

He glanced up from the book at Jack and back down again.

Then his head snapped up for a second time. "Jack? Are you awake?"

"I don't know," Jack said. His mouth was so dry. "I thought perhaps I was dead."

"Jack!" Silas stood and threw the book into the chair. Then, louder, "Jack! Jack's awake!"

The clatter of dishes and thunderous pounding that followed were either the wrath of God or a torrent of boots on the stairs. It shook the house.

Then the bedroom door burst open and Albert, Baz, and Phineas rushed in.

They yelled his name, repeating it over and over as if it were a ward against demons.

"Jack! Jack!"

They shook the bed. They placed their hands on his face and chest and covered legs as if he were a saint.

Jack, overwhelmed by bittersweet relief to see them alive and well, began to cry again.

"Stop it!" Silas pushed the others away. "You're upsetting him!"

The boys took great pains to pull themselves back. They helped him sit up against the headboard, putting pillows behind his back and adjusting the covers over his body.

As they worked, they spoke in frantic, feverish spurts.

"How do you feel?"

"Are you in pain?"

"Are you thirsty?"

"Hungry?"

"Please slow down," Jack begged them, squeezing his eyes shut.

"Forgive us." Albert ran his hand through his hair before clasping the back of his neck. "I'm just so glad you're alive."

"*We're* bloody glad!" Baz countered. He still had the crumbs of some abandoned lunch on his mouth. Silas offered him his handkerchief, motioning to his own lips.

Baz took the cloth.

Phineas knelt by the bed, putting his forehead on Jack's hand and then kissing it.

"Phin," Jack said. He hadn't known how glad he would be to see Phineas with good color in his cheeks. "Are you well?"

The tears were bright in Phineas's eyes when he lifted his head. "Thanks to you. Jack, a *demon*? How could you? You should've never!"

"*You* should've never," Jack countered. "What were you thinking, stepping between me and that demon?"

"Only what we would all have thought," Albert said.

"How can I ever thank you?" Phineas asked, tears falling freely down his cheeks. "There aren't enough words, or money, or love in the world."

"I would say we're even. You saved my life and I saved yours. Let there be no debts between us." Jack tried to smile, but it didn't feel right on his face and faded quickly. His head ached. "Your parents? I hope they weren't—"

"Oh, no. They *adore* you," Phineas said with a little laugh. "They want to give you all three of my sisters and twice their dowry. When I told them that wouldn't suit anybody, they asked if I would marry you."

Jack laughed despite himself.

Phineas was encouraged by this and continued with increased drama. "Though I explained we are brothers, not lovers. That Albert is the only one of us you've even kissed—"

Albert blushed. "Why did you have to go and tell them that?"

"—so they settled for sending our personal physician three times a day since you arrived," Phineas finished.

"Drink this," Silas said, forcing the water glass to Jack's lips. "Or Nanny will have my head."

Jack drank until his stomach cramped.

"How did I get here?" Jack asked. "I was..." His voice trailed off. How could he finish?

In the palace of my father's murderer? In some in-between place at the edge of a demon city?

"I was far away," he ended lamely.

"That demon of yours brought you to me," Albert said.

"What?"

"Oh yes," Albert said, eyes wide. "I was in my bedroom and she appeared. You were thrown over her shoulder like a sack of potatoes, and she puts you on my bed and says, 'Care for him.' Then she was gone. You were—"

Albert's face pinched.

"You weren't well," Silas offered. "For almost a month."

Embarrassment flooded him. "You've been at my side for a month?"

"Where else do we have to be?" Baz scoffed. "We'd been searching the countryside for you for five weeks before that."

Over two months. His father died over two months ago.

"What happened to you? Where did you go? Did the demon take your soul?" Phineas asked, still holding tight to Jack's hand.

Albert slapped the back of his head. "We agreed not to ask that."

"We searched his whole body!" Phineas protested. "There's no mark on him. He paid her *something*."

"It wasn't my soul," Jack said.

"What was it?" Albert asked. "The way you screamed, it must've been terrible. It sounded as if something was eating you from the inside out."

"I will only say that I paid. Let us speak no more of it." Jack tried to shake the nightmare of a dark and endless place from his mind. "Tell me what I missed while I was away."

They took turns speaking, telling him how, in his absence, they'd fully transferred his estate from Ansley Hall to Bloomsbury House, the grandest of his father's town-houses, and put the staff to work making the property suitable for full-time inhabitance. Jack's horses were being housed at Hatfield Manor, Albert's estate, and Albert had been sure to ride and care for Starlight himself. Shifts had been spent going through the remains of the house to retrieve what could be retrieved. Then there was the matter of transferring the barony. Phineas's father had been a great source of direction in that regard, given that he too was a baron and thought of details that the young men had not yet considered. For this reason, the estate and its assets had been transferred in full to Jack's name and the title of baron conveyed to Jacinth Edmund Siran.

Despite how he felt about it, he was truly Baron Siran now.

They'd also given great care to his mother, who Jack was thrilled to hear was awake. Though her recovery had been slow, she spent her days resting in her parlor, eating lightly and walking the city's gardens on Selina's arm.

"I fetched her from that awful school myself," Silas said, with more than a bit of color in his cheeks.

"Have you married her?" Jack asked.

"She'll not have him!" Albert snorted. "She doesn't care to be a wife."

"Who can blame her," Baz said. "I'd not want to be a wife either."

"Jack, we also found these," Phineas said sullenly. He placed three black journals on the bed beside him. "No one else has seen them but us."

Jack opened the burned cover and read the soot-covered passage that someone had marked.

H.B. is close. I can sense it.

I must not let him near Jacinth. If he senses the magic in the boy, that will be the end of him. He'll devour him as he has all the others in his care. Malachi, Russell, my dear Edmund...I will accept the count's proposal and marry him off. Surely H.B. will not go so far as Terrytown. There would be no reason in it.

Jack lowered the journal.

"He was sending me away to protect me," Jack said.

"Not that it makes him any less of a bastard," Albert said coldly.

"A literal one at that," Baz said. "We also read—"

His voice broke off when Phineas, Silas, and Albert all turned on him.

"Right," Baz said, his face turning red. "Sorry. I forgot we weren't goin' t'mention it."

"I already know what my father was and where he came from," Jack said.

"How did you find out?" Silas asked.

Jack told them of his great adventure across Devil's Field. Of the forest of Thought. Of his time in Hellebore. Of meeting Tromwell. He even spoke of Raziel, and the price he'd paid to be rescued from the pit, how he visited him every night in his dreams. That it was Raziel who'd pulled him back from the brink of his despair.

To which Baz said with a snort, "Dreams more pleasurable than actual company? Does he know of any lady demons who'd like the same of me?"

"I'll ask."

"And Silver?" Albert asked. Because Silver was the only part of the story Jack had omitted. "Did you find him?"

"I did." Jack hesitated. "He was not who I thought he was."

He could not tell them more because he was embarrassed. Besides, there was no need. Clara would disappear now. Free of her father's rule, she could go anywhere she wanted. Be anyone she wanted.

She had no reason to stay in Lundenwick. Not even for him.

Albert squeezed his shoulder.

Jack said, "I will understand if you leave me."

Phineas looked alarmed, his grip on Jack's hand tightening. "Why would we leave you?"

Albert spoke up before Jack could. "Because this idiot thinks we will disown him because his father was a bastard street rat. Have you forgotten that your mother was the daughter of an earl? Do you think we care about titles because we have them?"

Jack met Albert's gaze but found it did not match the anger in his voice.

"My mother was a seamstress before she married my father," Phineas said.

"And none of my cousins are titled," Baz added. "My mother was the only one. You forget that she had to marry m'father because the family had gone broke."

Silas pushed his glasses up on his nose, frowning. "Did you honestly think we cared about that?"

"No," Albert answered for him. "He's just trying to give us a reason to be rid of him."

Jack's throat tightened.

Albert leaned forward, leveling Jack with his hazel eyes. "Try harder then, *Baron*. You'd have to murder all our families and burn down the city before we'd consider it."

"Even then I don't think you'll be rid of me. My own parents would forbid it," Phineas said, fussing with his curls.

Raziel would love those curls, Jack thought. And despite himself, he felt a pang of jealousy at the thought of Raziel taking Phineas into his arms.

Phineas continued, unaware. "If you do not dine with us every night, I think my mother will kill me."

Someone rapped at the door, and a tray was brought in and placed over Jack's lap.

"Please eat," the young servant girl said. "Nanny will kill me if she comes back from market and finds out I've not fed you first thing."

Jack thanked her as she dipped a curtsy and fled from the room.

He ate while his friends filled him in on the city gossip and bits of amusement he'd missed in his absence. Most interesting of which was the fact that Lord Pickerington was engaged to the Duchess Worthington.

"Though I think he'd crawl through your window here if you gave him the smallest of invitations," Albert teased.

"Yes, I've passed him twice in the street, and both times he's asked after you," Silas said. "I told him you went abroad."

"In a way, I did," Jack said. "Most would find the demon city Hellebore to be very foreign."

"I'd like to see it someday," Baz said. "Especially if all the girls are half dressed and dancing in the streets as you say."

"It's a dangerous place," Silas said.

"Jack will keep us safe," Phineas said. "Though my parents would not hear of me near demons ever again."

Jack had cleared half his plate before exhaustion found him. His eyes grew heavy, and he drifted off to sleep with their voices and their relieved laughter in his ears.

WHEN HE WOKE AGAIN, HE WAS IN PAIN. HE HURT because the boy was awake. He was trying to claw his way out of Jack's throat.

Jack sat up, panting.

Albert and the others were gone. His bedroom was dark. Nanny slept in the chair, upright and snoring. She did not see the demon sitting at the foot of Jack's bed.

"It hurts," Jack said.

"I told you it would." Fire held his gaze.

"I think I'd rather you had torn me apart as you did Hellsbane."

She said nothing.

"Why did you come? To see what's left of me?"

She stared at the shadows on his wall for a long time. Then she said, soft and low, "Because Hellsbane escaped me, he made your father what he was."

"You're sorry then?" Jack asked. He didn't like the bitterness in his voice.

"I would make amends."

"Then give it back."

"I cannot. It's gone," she said. "And you could not keep it. It was destroying you."

"You don't know that."

"I do. I saw it every time I was in your mind, how many barriers and blocks you had erected. Have you any idea how small you'd made yourself? You cannot live a life like that, Jack."

It took everything he had not to scream. Not to kick and cry and lash out at her.

She shifted in the chair, leaning forward so that her elbows rested on her armored knees.

"Let it go. You cannot heal yourself until you do."

"What do you know of healing, demon? All you do is devour and destroy."

He was trying to be angry with her now. Trying his best to find a new source of strength.

But it would not come.

It folded before any real heat accumulated, the fire extinguishing itself.

You've ruined me.

Jack pressed his hands to his eyes. "Please leave me be. If you cannot help me, go."

When he opened them again, she was gone.

Jack was dreaming. Raziel's lips were at his throat when his body tensed suddenly.

"What's wrong?" Jack asked reflexively.

"The only interruption I'd tolerate," Raziel said with a laugh. "Until tomorrow, darling."

Jack woke, confusion clinging to him like a mist.

Lord Veemos was in his room.

Lord Veemos, the feather in his hat as jaunty as ever, his cloak and clothes black, occupied the red armchair that Jack had come to think of as Silas's reading chair.

"I'm dreaming," Jack said.

"In a way," Lord Veemos said. "This is a world within a world. A place where we can talk undisturbed."

That explained why his friends had not awoken. Albert breathed easily beside him.

Baz and Silas reclined on opposing sofas. Only Phineas had gone home to his own bed.

"Did Fire send you?" Jack asked. And he realized the error in his question. No one could send Lord Veemos anywhere.

"She asked that I come," he said. "I wanted to. I have my own apologies to make."

Apologies.

"Forgive me," Jack said, trying to sit up and put his back against the headboard. "I did not mean to wake your sister."

"That's my fault," Veemos said, his frown deepening. "I made you a promise and I broke it."

"It's all right."

"It really isn't." Lord Veemos laced his fingers and considered Jack's room, his covered legs, his sleeping friends. He seemed willing to look everywhere but at Jack's face. "I've thought long and hard of how I might apologize adequately. I cannot undo my sister's offense, of course. But I want to offer a gift of equal or greater value."

Again his eyes slid around the room.

"I understand the price you've paid to the daimona. Fire."

"Can you give it back?"

"You don't need it, Jack," he said. "You never needed it. You only believed that you did."

But it hurts. The boy—

"Will you rid me of him?" Jack asked.

"No. You are the boy. Would you get rid of yourself?"

Yes, he thought, without hesitation.

"Is there no cure?" Jack asked with desperation.

"There is. Though it is a healing magic that takes a long time to work. You must be willing—"

"I'll pay anything."

Lord Veemos tilted his head, coming dangerously close to meeting Jack's eye then. "She was right. You would try to bargain with me. This is *free*, Jack. This is advice."

Jack's hand fisted the covers.

"You must be willing to do what your father could not," Lord Veemos said. "You must love that boy."

"You ask the impossible of me."

"Difficult, but not impossible."

"How can such a thing be done?" Jack asked.

"Tell him all that you wish your father had told you. Speak to him as you wish you'd been spoken to. Comfort him. Protect him. Love him."

"He only cries. He will not come near me!"

"He doesn't trust you, that's true," Lord Veemos said. "You've kept him locked away for a long time. You did not listen to him. You treated him like a shameful secret. It will take time to rebuild that trust, but it can be rebuilt."

"Then I will be free of him?"

"Then you will love him," Lord Veemos said. "And he will be free."

Jack wasn't sure he liked this dream. He wanted to return to Raziel's arms and the lovely distraction of his generous attention.

"For my sister's offense, I will put you on a road. A road that will be the most help to you and the boy you carry inside you. A road with more love and grace than you've ever imagined for yourself. It will not be without trouble or little sorrows, of course. All roads have their price. But when you are an old man and you lay your head down in your bed for the last time, you will not be alone. More importantly, you will not *feel* alone. Your heart will be full to bursting. That is what I offer you."

Jack couldn't even imagine it. The future Lord Veemos described seemed so foreign he must surely be joking. How could he ever feel whole after all that had been done to him?

How could he when he carried this wailing child in his chest?

But Lord Veemos did not look doubtful.

In fact, he smiled. "It will happen, Jack. Just you wait and see."

CHAPTER 28

We must never tell him he wasn't handsome—even for a moment. I have made the others vow it to secrecy. In those hours where we nearly lost him, all the light had left him, and he looked more dead than alive. If we tell him that, I know his heart will surely break.

Though Albert says it serves him right and will perhaps encourage him to never be unwell again.

— FROM THE JOURNAL OF LORD
PHINEAS GILDROY

After a week of meals, his friends' cheerful company, and nightly attention from Raziel, Jack woke one morning feeling as if he might be able to dress himself.

This was good because no one was in his room to help him with it. A first since he'd returned.

Jack rose. His legs were unsure of themselves and his hands shook as he wet the cloth in the fresh water from the basin. But he managed to wipe himself clean and scrape beneath his fingernails. He sprayed lavender water on his skin and then put on fresh clothes. Trousers and a shirt. He did not bother with socks or boots. He was sure he would not leave the house. A full vest, cloak, and jacket seemed unnecessary when all he wanted to see was his mother.

He made his way slowly down the hall, holding the bannister, and then to the stairs.

His legs were shaky, but they held.

At the foot of the stairs, Nanny was speaking to a housekeeper.

The housekeeper met Jack's gaze first, then turned back twice, her mouth coming open in surprise.

"What?" Nanny turned and saw Jack for herself. A cry escaped her. "As I live and breathe! Why are you out of bed?"

"I'm well enough to be out of it."

"If that be the case, I've words for you, Jacinth Edmund!" She gathered him up in her arms and shook his face as if she wasn't sure whether she wanted to kiss it or slap it and this was somehow the place between. "You want to put this old woman in her grave with your mischief!"

"Forgive me, Nanny."

"You escape the hospital in the dead of night. Bargain with demons and disappear with 'em!" Nanny shook him. "Then we don't see you for two months. Two months! Do you know how worried your mam has been?"

"I am sorry to have worried everyone. But I am well again."

"Are you?"

"I am," he assured her.

"An' will we be havin' any more demons burnin' the 'ouses down?" She fanned her sweating face.

"No. The debt is paid, the monsters vanquished, and we are safe again," Jack said. "Only I am worse for the wear."

"You've got a fool's luck, I say." She hugged him tight. Then stepped back and straightened her uniform. "But you're baron now. You'd best act like it."

"Never," Jack said with a weak smile. "I'll never be like him."

"Praise the Lord for that." Nanny's face softened. "The baroness will be wantin' to see you first thing. We wouldn't let her—"

She pressed her lips tight.

"We didn't want her to be seein' you like that, so we've kept her off. She fought us on that, to be sure."

"I understand," Jack said. "It would only have scared her more."

"Exactly, and she's been..." Nanny searched for a word. "She's been quite delicate since you've been gone. But you look well enough to see her."

"I will. I'll see her first thing."

"No, ye won't. You'd best breakfast first. Here now, the baron wants 'is breakfast!"

The commotion was immediate. The dining room was slung open, a fresh cloth thrown over the table. A string of servants brought eggs and sausage and tea and toast on little white plates. The paper was put on the plate beside him.

The paper, more than anything else, made Jack accept the grim fact that he was truly baron now. Why else would they think he wanted to read the town paper?

He was halfway through his plate of eggs and toast when the door blew open again.

Selina marched into the room with her usual air of command. "What's all this?"

Then she saw him. The lines on her face evened out immediately.

"You're up. Took you long enough. Leave it to you to take a holiday when there's so much to be done."

Her voice was stern, but she threw her arms around him all the same. He kissed her cheeks.

"I'm sorry I was not here to bury him."

Selina scoffed. "That was the best part. Throwing dirt on his coffin."

"You haven't been up to my room," Jack said.

"Well, someone had to look after Mother and run this house," she said. Jack saw the color in her cheeks.

She didn't want to see me like that either.

He was certain of it.

She grabbed a slice of toast and poured herself a cup of tea. "Please let me know when you're well enough to take over. I'd like to return to my studies as soon as possible."

"How is she?" Jack asked.

Selina sank into the chair. "Weak. But she improves. I dare say, a visit from you will speed it along. She was sick over your absence. She thought the demon killed you."

Jack rose. "I'll see her now."

"Good. I've just left her in her drawing room."

He took his tea with him but left the rest.

A maid with soot on her cheeks told Jack that his mother could be found in the suite at the east end of the townhouse. He thanked her and ordered fresh tea.

The door to her drawing room was open. Jack still knocked on its frame.

"Hello?"

"Come in."

She was sitting at a little table by the window with her

back to him, bent over a scrap of embroidery spread across the table in the sunlight.

"You can put the tea—" Then she saw him.

"Jack!" she cried, and was on her feet in an instant. "Oh, dear God, Jack. I heard them whispering that you were awake, but Nanny would not let me see you."

I must've looked truly terrible, he thought.

"But you're here. You're really here." She placed her hands on his face, on his throat and chest, as if to see if he was real. "Oh, Jack. Are you home now? Truly? You will not leave again?"

He gathered her hands and kissed the knuckles. "I am home."

"Praise the Lord," she said. "I am so glad you are all right. You don't know how worried I was for you. I've missed you so."

I have a good idea. He ran a thumb over her dark circles, brushing the tears away.

"The missing is over," Jack said. "Now tell me how you've been."

He seated her at the table and the tea arrived.

He poured them each a cup, asking her all sorts of questions, but she was more interested in his stories. Where had he been? What did he see?

"A mother tries not to pry, but I must ask," she said. "Is it true about the demon? Did you sell your soul to save Phineas?"

"No, I sold something else. My soul is my own." He was too tired to tell it all again so soon. "You have no need to worry about demons. The one who hurt you is dead."

She touched her throat, no doubt recalling the memory of Hellsbane's hand wrapped around it.

Shame filled him. "Forgive me. I was the one who led that demon to us."

"No," his mother said, placing her hand over his fist. "Your father's choices brought that man to our door, and I made the choice to marry your father. Some choices have steeper consequences than others. It's as simple as that."

He relaxed his fist.

"I regret nothing," she said, rubbing his knuckles. I have a comfortable life and two beautiful children. And now that you are home safe, my prayers answered, I want for nothing."

She released him and took up her teacup again.

A rough knock came at the door.

"Yes?" his mother called.

"She's here to see you, ma'am," the maid said.

"Oh, I'm sorry," his mother said, placing her teacup in its saucer. "Tell her I cannot see her today. Jack is awake."

"Very well, ma'am." The maid closed the door.

His mother said, "Perhaps we can dine together tomorrow. The three of us."

"Who?" Jack asked.

"Us and Lady Clara."

"Clara?" he repeated.

"She's been so worried for you. In that we are united."

"*Clara?*" Jack sat up straighter. "Clara came here?"

He pointed at the door.

"That was Clara calling?"

His mother laughed. "Yes, Jack. *Lady Clara.* Is it so difficult to believe she cares for you? She's visited every day since Albert found you. We haven't let her see you like that, of course. But she's come all the same."

Clara. Clara is here.

"I sense steel in her," his mother added, thoughtfully sipping her tea.

He pushed back his chair. "You've no idea."

"Where are you going? We've just settled in," his mother protested.

"I'm sorry, but I have to catch her."

His mother's concern transformed into delight. "Oh. Will you propose?"

"Mother."

"You could do worse for a wife!" she called out as the door swung shut behind him.

Jack tore through the house barefoot, his shirt open and the cool air striking his chest. He made his apologies to the house staff as he passed, all of whom must have thought him mad.

"What do you think you're doing?" an imperious voice called from the stairs.

Albert stood there. A line was etched across his cheek from sleep, his eyes still bleary.

"You shouldn't even be up."

Jack dashed for the front door. "I have to catch her."

"Who?"

"Clara."

"Lady Clara?" Albert asked. "Jack, no. This is no time to be chasing skirts. You need rest. Stop it."

Albert fought to close the front door. Jack fought to open it.

"Damn you, move!"

"No!" Albert said. "You need to lie down before you fall down."

"She's Silver!" Jack yelled. "All right? She's Silver."

Albert stilled.

"Lord Silver and Lady Clara are one and the same. I must stop her before she leaves. Possibly forever."

Albert arched his brows. "Lady Clara *is* Lord Silver. You're serious."

"Yes!" Jack said, and hauled the door open.

Albert made it outside before him to find that the side street by the park was quiet. There was only one carriage pulling away. Albert ran after it.

"Wait!" he cried. "Stop that carriage, I say!"

"What's going on?" Baz asked, coming to stand beside Jack outside the front door.

Silas was with him, trying to clean the smudges off his glasses. Phineas was rubbing the sleep from his eyes.

"Does that horse owe him money or something?" Baz asked with a yawn. Then to Jack, "Shouldn't you be in bed, mate?"

Instead, Jack ran after the carriage, which Albert had managed to pull to a stop despite the protesting driver.

"What is the matter?" The carriage door swung open and Lady Clara swept out in a fury of skirts. "Who dares delay me?"

Then she saw Jack.

"Jack," she breathed. "Dear God."

Albert released his hold on the horses.

"Are you mad?" She observed his open shirt, bare chest and feet. "Where are your shoes?"

"I had to catch you," he said, panting. Even that short sprint had nearly undone him. His ribs ached and his lungs were on fire.

"Good evening, Lord Silver," Albert said with a mischievous smile.

Clara glared at him.

Albert's smile only widened. "I see it now. In that imperial lift of your chin. Though your eyes are more gray than silver in this light. How did we miss it?"

Jack said nothing. He was still struggling to breathe.

"Will you give us a moment?" Jack finally begged through gritted teeth.

"I need to hold the horses in place, lest she run away," Albert said.

"My driver will not leave until I say so, will you, Mr. Rodger?" Clara said.

"No, m'lady," the man said. "Though perhaps we can move the carriage to the side so as to not be in the middle of the road."

"Smart you are."

Jack and Clara too moved over to the pebbled walk beneath the slope of trees.

Albert excused himself. "I'll be watching."

"Will you?" Clara asked with a tilt of her head. "How lovely for you."

He bowed to her and strode away, back toward the others, who still stood outside the townhouse entrance, naked confusion on their faces.

When Albert was out of range, she asked, "Can you breathe?"

"Yes," Jack lied.

"You need not have run all the way here."

"I wanted to speak to you before you disappeared without a trace. Tell me you won't leave Lundenwick."

Lady Clara looked up the path, back toward the townhouses overlooking the park.

"I've no reason to stay," she said.

"What about the duels? My mother's company? And you could meet my friends. You'll like them. Truly."

"You told them I was Silver?"

"I told Albert. By now he will have told the rest."

"That explains their idiotic grins," she said. She turned back to Jack. "Surely you do not want me to stay?"

Why was she being so formal? Was she playing the part of Lady Clara here on the street?

"I do." *More than anything.*

"I lied to you. I deceived you. I manipulated you."

"And you saved my life." His eyes went to her shoulder. "How do you fare?"

"That elixir you gave me did its work. Though I hesitated to drink it, since you did not explain its abilities."

"At least you understood that I meant for you to drink it," he said, laughing.

"Where did you get it?" she asked. "I'd like to have more on hand the next time I must rescue a man."

Jealousy nipped at his neck.

"From a demon. For the price of a kiss."

Her lips twitched. Again, her eyes raked over his poor excuse for a shirt and his bare feet. "You look like a man who has kissed a few demons."

"Do I?" Jack laughed. "Where will you go?"

"Somewhere on my own two feet. Your accomplice took both cubes. Is she the one you kissed?"

"No, it was another. Well, yes, I kissed her as well."

Her brow arched. "You truly are a hopeless flirt."

"You could stay," Jack said again. "I would love it if you stayed."

"And be the Baroness Siran? The lady of your great house?"

"As long as you are in my bed each night, I don't care if you're my wife or not."

"Scandalous."

"Have you not heard? The Baron Jack consorts with demons and his sister attends university. I court scandal."

"Jack."

"My mother already adores you. She would not care what our arrangement was."

"*Jack.*"

"I would make any allowance for your happiness."

She put a gloved hand over his mouth. "Stop. What did you tell me? No begging outside the bedroom?"

She removed her hand. He did his best to recover himself.

"It remains that you do not know me. You know only what my father allowed you to see of me."

"That's not true," Jack said. "I know you."

Color rose in her cheeks. Her chest heaved.

"I know you," he said again, trying to catch her eye. She would not look at him. "I do."

"How can you when I do not know myself? What could you possibly know?"

"You're the one I wrote nightly letters to for nearly two years."

"Letters." She laughed bitterly. "I told you—"

"You are the one who climbed my balcony in the dead of night, facing her father's wrath just to save me."

"Just because I did not want you to die—"

"You took a blade for me! He could have slit my throat and you stepped between us."

"I would have done that for anyone. Anyone my father threatened."

"You are brave and kind. I've seen your cleverness in every duel. Do not tell me I don't know you. You are all I've known for two years. In every moment I've had, you were there."

She squeezed her eyes shut. "Please do not make this harder for me than it already is."

He took her gloved hands. "Tell me that you feel nothing for me. Tell me that you do not love me and I will let you go."

"Silver isn't—" she began.

"I don't care what Silver feels or Clara feels," he said. "Tell me that *you*"—he pressed a finger to her chest—"do not love me. *You.* Whoever, whatever, you might be."

Her face was full of such tormented sorrow. It hurt him to see it.

He already knew he'd lost her before she pulled her gloved hands free.

"Jack." She pinched her eyes closed again. "*I* do not know if I love you."

Her words were a horse-kick to his heart.

She lifted her head and looked out across the park, at the couples walking arm and arm.

"I don't know if I love you or if I feel what my father wanted me to feel. And no matter which is true, I cannot be what you need me to be."

"I don't need you to be anything. I only want to be with you. However you are."

She hesitated.

"Look at them." She gestured at the couples. "I am not as they are. There is something broken in me—"

"And me," he was quick to say. "But maybe together we can be whole."

She tilted her head. It made him think of demons.

"That isn't how it works," she said. "One must make oneself whole."

He hung his head.

"Do you understand? Tell me you do," she said.

He understood only that she did not want him. That no matter what he said now, she would not stay.

"I must know for myself who I am and what I feel," she said. "And I cannot answer those questions here."

He lifted his gaze to meet hers. "Where will you go?"

She forced a smile. "There are many worlds out there. More than you can imagine. It is true that I do not have the cubes, but I do have my father's tricks."

"I will be here," Jack said with great effort. "My bedroom is on the second floor, the one overlooking the park. Perhaps some night you—be you Clara or Silver or someone else—perhaps you will climb that tree, come through that window, and into my arms. If I could be so lucky, let it be so."

She cupped his face with her gloved hand, her eyes bright.

She leaned in and placed one velvet kiss on his cheek. It took everything in his control not to turn his head and take more.

She pulled back, her eyes shimmering, and released him. "Goodbye, Jack."

She did allow him to help her into the carriage before shutting the door tight.

Then he watched her go, feeling the outline of her lips on his skin for a very long time.

EPILOGUE

TWO YEARS LATER

If only wishing made the waiting easier. It does not. For the longer one wishes for a thing, the more he grows to doubt he will ever receive it.

— FROM THE JOURNAL OF THE
BARON JACK SIRAN

Jack was up late again. A single candle burned on the table beside him as he spread the papers across his bed. He wanted to be certain of these numbers before he slept. If he didn't, they would only dance before his closed eyes, taunting him.

As he worked, he felt Raziel's impatience like a whisper in the mind.

A gentle, *Would you keep me waiting?*

"Not much longer," Jack said to himself with a small chuckle. *A little patience, darling.*

He did not want to torment the demon.

Raziel had been a great comfort to him in the last two

years. What a blessing it was that he wanted Jack's company no matter if Jack was happy or sad. Well or lovesick.

He was constant no matter the swing of Jack's moods.

And they had swung considerably since Lady Clara had "gone abroad."

At first, she wrote to Jack's mother of her adventures, and when Jack had the strength to spare, his mother read the letters to him.

"A woman likes to know her own heart before she gives it to another," his mother assured him. "It's good for young ladies to travel before they're wed."

But one year had turned into two. Fewer letters came. Then his mother stopped sharing them altogether. In Jack's heart, he'd begun to accept he would not see Silver again.

Jack pretended to understand. Perhaps she had a wounded child of her own. Perhaps running was the only way to make its crying stop.

Were there not plenty of bad days for himself? Mornings when Jack woke to find his own wounded boy wailing, and no matter what he did to comfort him, the crying would not stop.

In those hours, all he could do was lie on the sofa in his study with the curtains drawn and a pillow over his face. Nanny served him quiet cups of tea in a dark room until his friends were summoned to cheer him.

Yet more and more often the good days came. Days when contentment settled upon his shoulders like a warm blanket in winter. Sometimes it found him as he rode Starlight through the park on a sunny afternoon or had a drink at the inn with a reassuring arm thrown across his shoulder. Sometimes his friends still watched the duels, though Jack himself did not fight anymore, not even when someone challenged him.

Without Lord Silver, there was no one worth the trouble—or the temptation.

He might have thought the whole adventure was a dream, if not for the subtle reminders.

His delicious, endless nights with Raziel.

The time he'd seen a boy and a girl in the street. The boy with hair as black as crow feathers, the girl with hair the shade of fox fur. He'd caught them pickpocketing the viscount outside Everdeen's.

When he'd called out to them, named them Mischief and Mayhem, the boy had stuck his tongue out and blown, his fingers twisting in his ears. The girl had bared her teeth.

But he'd seen the playful glint in their eyes and knew he'd not been wrong.

More than once he'd seen a lady in the street with hair so bright he'd called out, "Fire!" before he could stop himself.

It was never her. Only a woman, deeply confused, turning toward him with a troubled, "Sir?"

Fire had both cubes now, he'd remind himself. *She could be anywhere.*

The tree outside his window rustled.

A storm, he thought.

He gathered the papers together in a neat stack and put them on the table. No point in trying to work any more tonight. He was too tired. If he closed his eyes now, sleep would find him in an instant.

He undressed for bed, noting distantly that there was no wind. No roll of thunder.

Perhaps not a storm.

He turned toward the window again just as it swung open and a lithe form slid into the room.

The figure turned, its shape familiar. As familiar as the silver mask fixed over its face.

"Hello, my dear Peacock," Silver said, standing in his bedroom as if he had any right to be there. "It's been a long time."

Jack sank to the bed, his shirt open, chest bare.

"You're an apparition," he said. "A marvelous dream."

Silver came to the bed. He took Jack's hand and placed it over his beating heart. It was racing as fast as Jack's was. "I'm no dream."

Jack reached up and grabbed him, pulling him down onto the bed beside him.

Silver's gloved hands went up to undo the mask.

"Don't," Jack said, seizing them.

"I'm not a dream," he laughed from the flat of his back. "I will not disappear."

"It's not that." Jack pressed the gloved hands to his chest. "It's only that I've dreamt of removing that mask and seeing your face for as long as I can remember. I want to do it."

The gloved hands fell limply to the coverlet. "Then do it, sir."

Jack's fingers went to the back of his head, found the ribbon in the tangle of blond waves, and pulled.

It loosened and slid free.

Slowly he lifted the mask.

First the chin, the cheeks, then those bright gray eyes he'd missed so much.

"Lord Silver, at last," he whispered. "*Are* you Lord Silver? Or Lady Clara?"

"Neither. Both. Something between." They shrugged, their cheeks red.

"What shall I call you?"

"Silver will do at present," they said. "I'm rather fond of it."

"Silver," Jack breathed. He wrapped his arms around them, squeezing them tight. He inhaled the scent of their neck, their shoulder where the shirt had slipped.

"I missed you," they said, their arms tight around him.

"You really came back. Why on earth? You had the world."

"Funny thing, that. I *did* search the world over and found nothing so interesting as a magical boy who consorted with demons." Silver brushed the curls back from Jack's face. "He even ran after my carriage on bare feet."

Jack kissed their exposed wrist. "You found none so handsome either, I dare say."

"I *find* him as vain as ever," they said, but their smile was kind. "I'll admit only that there was no face I longed to see more."

"Will you stay?" he asked.

Perhaps Silver would stay only the night or a mere hour. Jack dared not get his hopes up too high.

They shrugged. "Why not? I just got to town and have no place to sleep."

They patted his bed.

"This will do nicely. What is the price for lodging here, sir?"

"A kiss." Jack had learned more than a few things from Raziel. "May I kiss you?"

"Oh, there will be a great deal of kissing, I suspect, but you will not make a lady out of me," they said earnestly, holding his gaze.

"I wouldn't dream of it," he said. "Though I should

warn you that you will grow tired of me. I fear that as baron I'm not half as entertaining as I used to be."

"Is that a challenge, my dear Peacock?" Silver said, pulling him into the kiss. The words were hot on Jack's lips. "I accept."

Did you enjoy this book? You can make a BIG difference.

I don't have the same power as big New York publishers who can buy full-spread ads in magazines, and you won't see my covers on the side of a bus anytime soon, but what I *do* have are wonderful readers like you.

And honest reviews from readers garner more attention for my books and help my career more than anything else I could possibly do—and I can't get a review without you! So if you would be so kind, I'd be very grateful if you would post a review for this book.

It only takes a minute or so of your time, and yet you can't imagine how much it helps me. It can be as short as you like, and whether positive or negative, it really does help. I appreciate it so much and so do the readers looking for their next favorite read.

If you would be so kind, please find your preferred retailer at ➡ https://korymshrum.com/jack and leave a review for this book today.

With gratitude,

Kory

GET YOUR THREE FREE STORIES TODAY

Thank you so much for reading *Jack and the Fire Eater*. I hope you've enjoyed Jack's story. And if you *did* like this book, let's make a little pact, shall we? You sign up for my free newsletter, and I will send you stories from my others series. What do you have to lose? You might just find another character (or ten) that you love.

If exclusive bonuses sound like your jam, you can sign up here ➜ https://www.korymshrum.com/free-starter-library

As to the newsletter itself, I send out 2-3 a month and host a monthly giveaway exclusive to my subscribers. The prizes are usually signed books or other freebies that I think you'll enjoy. I also share information about my current projects, and personal anecdotes (like pictures of my dog). And of course, you can unsubscribe at any time.

If this is not your cup of tea (I love tea), you can follow me on Facebook, Instagram, or Bookbub in order to be notified of my new releases.

ACKNOWLEDGMENTS

Lucky nineteen. We did it again! And now I have the usual suspects to thank for this undertaking.

First and foremost, of course, is my wife Kimberly, who tolerates my stares and heavy breathing over her shoulder when she's trying to beta/proofread for me. Thanks babe!

Then we have, in no particular order: Kathrine Pendleton, Angela Roquet, and Monica La Porta. They're always my first line of defense for all grammar and story issues. I appreciate your kind words and keen eyes as always.

Professional assistance came from editor extraordinaire Toby Selwyn, who will be very sad if this remains a stand-alone novel. So I will assure him (and the readers) that should another demon come calling with promises of adventure, I promise to make the pact. Just for you guys.

This gorgeous cover was done by the amazing Christian Bentulan. You've really outdone yourself this time, Christian! Thank you so much for always giving me exactly what I ask for. As for all the inner bits and the art of making a book look like a book, we have Alexandra Amor, my sweetheart assistant, to thank. You're always a big help, A!

Then we have my amazing street team. You guys are always spotting those last minute typos and leaving the first reviews—two critical tasks required for each book's launch and subsequent success. You continue to show your love, support, and infectious enthusiasm for all that I do. To top it

off, you tell your family and friends about my work and send
loads of encouraging emails. All of this means more than
you know.

Thank you!

The City / 2603 novels

The City Below

The City Within

The City Outside

POETRY (AS K.B. MARIE)

Birds and Other Dreamers

Questions for the Dead

You Can't Keep It

NON-FICTION

Who Killed My Mother?

You can also support her on Patreon or visit her website to learn more about her work.

ABOUT THE AUTHOR

Kory M. Shrum is author of the bestselling Shadows in the Water and Dying for a Living series, as well as several other novels. She has loved books and words all her life. She reads almost every genre you can think of, but when she writes, she writes science fiction, fantasy, and thrillers, or often something that's all of the above.

In 2020, she launched a true crime podcast "Who Killed My Mother?", sharing the true story of her mother's tragic death. You can listen for free on YouTube or your favorite podcast app. She also publishes poetry under the name K.B. Marie.

When not writing, eating, reading, or indulging in her true calling as a stay-at-home dog mom, she can usually be found under thick blankets with snacks. The kettle is almost always on.

She lives in Michigan with her equally bookish wife, Kim, and their rescue pug, Charley.

She'd love to hear from you!
www.korymshrum.com

9 781949 577563